SEBASTIAN

THE VAN DER BILTS

Nicole Adair

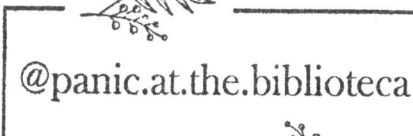

Copyright © 2021 by Nicole Adair
All rights reserved.

ISBN: 978-1-0683126-0-1

This book is a complete work of fiction. The characters, events and places are completely fictitious and any similarity to real persons, living or dead, events or locales is purely coincidental and not intended by the author.

No part of this book may be reproduced in any form without written permission from the author, except for the use of small quotations used in book reviews.

As always,
My Insignificant Other,
G x

Table of Contents

CHAPTER 1	1
CHAPTER 2	13
CHAPTER 3	26
CHAPTER 4	35
CHAPTER 5	42
CHAPTER 6	54
CHAPTER 7	66
CHAPTER 8	77
CHAPTER 9	88
CHAPTER 10	101
CHAPTER 11	114
CHAPTER 12	122
CHAPTER 13	133
CHAPTER 14	145
CHAPTER 15	159
CHAPTER 16	169
CHAPTER 17	184
CHAPTER 18	195
CHAPTER 19	206
CHAPTER 20	217
CHAPTER 21	228
CHAPTER 22	238
CHAPTER 23	253
CHAPTER 24	261
CHAPTER 25	273
CHAPTER 26	286
EPILOGUE	300
AUTHORS NOTE	311
ABOUT THE AUTHOR	312
ACKNOWLEDGMENTS	313

CHAPTER 1

As I walk into the dimly lit bar and head towards my table near the back of the room, I let out an exhausted sigh, ignoring the eyes lingering a little too long. Some colleagues I have worked with over the years at the company, some simply recognizable faces from the building. My firms bar restaurant isn't a place I frequented much before my whole world collapsed and it's still not somewhere I come very often. The bar staff kindly keep me a quiet secluded table once a month, when I pop in for a nice meal and large drink before heading home for a weekend of loneliness. Patiently waiting for Monday morning to come back around with the knowledge I will be leaving early and my boys will finally be back home when I get there. A pile of dirty laundry, sink full of dishes and stories of the weekend's events will await me but still, I miss them so much when they're away.

The last Friday of every month, the boys load up in the back of their grandparent's old station wagon to spend the weekend fishing, camping and god knows what else teenage boys get up to doing 'manly things' with their Grandpa Jack, whilst poor Grandma tries her best to keep them fed and watered over the course of their stay. I swear they eat more than their whole football squad combined! My in-laws love spending time with the boys so much that they don't seem to mind. I'm just glad they still go along with no complaints and enjoy spending the time together, even though they miss hanging out with their friends. I do however hate how much I've grown to loathe returning home when they're not there.

I stop myself from sinking into the melancholy coming over me and lower into my seat as I look up to see a man whose face, I sort of recognize but can't quite place step up to my table. Putting his hands on the chair in front of me, he smiles leerily and I dread what's coming and already feel bone tired of dealing with this kind of nonsense.

"What an unfortunate sight it is to see a woman as beautiful as you stuck in this dark secluded corner ready to drink all by herself," he frowns as if he actually feels sorry for me, "Why don't you pick your lovely self-right back up and head over with me to enjoy a proper drink in my booth." He looks so sure of himself I find it hard to gather enough energy to be offended.

"I'm fine thank you; I prefer to sit alone." I say softly giving him a brief smile.

"Aw come on now, no need to play coy, you already have mine and well, most of the men in the bars attention, let's not waste time pretending you're not going to come with me and just cut straight to it." He grins as if he's being alluring. God this stuff gets on my nerves.

"Look, I'm sure that style of persuasion may work on someone who actually wants companionship for the night however I simply wish to have quiet drink in peace, so if you wouldn't mind, head on over to your own table and have a good night." I say as I look around him and give Brad the barman the nod that he can bring my drink over and tell chef I'm ready to eat.

The guy stands in front of me, face glowing redder by the second and I fear it's not going to be pretty.

"Why walk into a bar all silky as shit, making every guy watch you sass past them if you're not out on the prowl?" He genuinely asks, "I mean what women comes and sits in a work bar alone?"

"Well considering I'm one of the people who decided *our* firm could use a nice place for colleagues to have a meal or drink without having to head out somewhere else, I think I am the kind of women who makes her own god damn decisions, like if she wants to enjoy a drink alone in a bar, she designed, without being harassed! Now please leave."

I level him a stare and he stammer's to apologies whilst hot footing it across the room, I don't miss the '*stuck up bitch*' he mutters under his breath but as Brad places my drink down in front of me and asks if I want him to call security, I just smile gently,

"No, I don't think he will stay very long." I say and sure enough he's gulping down his drink on the way out the door.

"I'm awfully sorry I wasn't quick enough to intercept him Ms. Chalmers." he says with a frown.

"It's ok Brad, that's not in your job description" I shrug, "However telling Chef Romero I'm famished may be." I smile as he nods and wanders off to get my food.

As I take a sip of my drink and briefly glance around the room, I notice an older gentleman smiling softly in my direction, he's sitting in one of the private VIP areas that are reserved for the firm's managing directors, partners and their guests. The poor guy who has his back to me and is currently engaging in a very one-sided debate, has no clue that his companion hasn't been listening to a word he says and is very much watching me with close intent.

I smile back, roll my eyes and lean over and pull some paper work from my briefcase to work on whilst

I wait for my meal.

It only takes a few moments when I think Brad has returned with my food and I start to clear away the work on my table when I look up and see another man's face who I certainly don't recognize smiling down at me,

"I have to give that guy props for having the balls to come over when you obviously didn't look like you wanted company however, *he* clearly had no tact." He smirks.

I am slowly beginning to regret my decision to come in tonight, the place seems full of more than the usual number of leaches.

"And yet here you are doing the exact same thing?" I say clearly unamused.

"Ah but there is a difference you see, I am not going to interrupt you whilst you enjoy your solitary drink or meal even," he smirks even though that is what he is currently doing.

"I'm pretty sure that's exactly what you're doing right now" I tell him.

"Nope, I'm just leaving you this for... after." He says as he slides a silver keycard across the table towards me with a grin splitting his face, like he's a real catch.

"Oh, for Christ's sake!" I snap. "Take your crappy hotel card and grinning face out my sight and preferably this bar before I have you permanently removed from the building, you creepy jerk!" I fume.

Before he gets a chance to say another word Brad appears at my table with my meal and a loud,

"I've called security Mrs. Chalmers; Butch is on his way to deal with this." He glares at the man as he places my meal on the table.

The guy has the cheek to look offended as he grabs his card from the table and strolls out of the bar. Brad asks me if I am ok, as I hear a slight grumble from across the room. I refuse to look, smiling warmly at Brad and ask him what the heck is in tonight's cocktails.

After I assure him, I'm fine and he brings me a refill and heads back to his post I notice the older gentleman is now alone, staring this way with a strange expression on his face. When he sees my frown, he simply nods his head gently and goes back to his drink.

I eventually get some peace to enjoy my meal but I am a little sick of the same old crap, I come here to avoid going to a bar or restaurant where I would stand out as some single woman on the hunt, this is my place of work.

To be clear, I am not some strikingly stunning beauty by any means. I am attractive enough, the long blonde hair and bright blue eyes, added with the drop in my weight lately, does make me look a little bimbo-ish hence why my hair is always tied back in a neat chignon and I dress slightly more conservative than I would probably prefer but in such a male orientated industry it pays to play my femininity down rather than up.

The problem stems from the fact that the firm of Van Der Bilt and Sons doesn't have that many single women workers. I wasn't even one until recently. Single, I mean not a worker. I've been at this firm working my ass off to be taken seriously for the last fifteen years. I started as the lowest junior you could possibly imagine and have worked my way through coffee runs and late-night errands, all whilst having twin boys who could've easily been spawns of Satan himself. I was one of the few women who managed to navigate through the office politics and land an internship under Miss Valerie Van Der Bilt, one of the only female partners in the firm.

She has been a revelation for someone like me, who never truly thought I could reach my full potential as an Architect after falling pregnant half way through my first year at University. Now don't get me wrong we are not friends, she is as harsh a ball buster as they come but her work ethic and business acumen are second to none. Well, maybe to her brother Mr. Anderson Van Der Bilt the second and his grandson Sebastian. Their work is truly remarkable and although they are very rarely here at the office or anywhere in public really, unless they absolutely have to be, their work speaks for itself.

"What on earth did that steak ever do to you I wonder?" I look up to see the older gentleman from before now standing near my table but far enough away he's giving me much needed space, whilst I realize I am carving my meal up brutally.

Since he bore witness to the earlier disturbances I quip,

"I'm fairly sure that although this fillet steak is delicious, I'm also certain it was of the male species and I feel a little vengeful to their kind at the moment." Whilst giving him a humorous glare.

He throws his head back and laughs the most heartfelt chuckle I've heard in a while.

"Oh, I knew you weren't going to disappoint my dear." he says mischievously.

I just smile and ask if there's anything I can help him with.

He gets his chuckles under control and asks if I could try not to take it the wrong way if he asks me to join an old man for a drink. All the while, he has this glowing grin and devilish look in his eyes.

I take a minute to really look at him whilst he stands there letting me assess the fact that there is absolutely no way this man is hitting on me, not only is he old enough to be my grandfather maybe even great-grandfather, he is sporting a lovely shiny well-kept wedding band on his finger and the whitest mop of bushy hair on his head.

I think he sees my thoughts so clearly that he winks and says,

"Third time lucky, eh? Let's go sit at my table and avoid any more delinquents harassing you tonight, hmm?"

I laugh and as I've managed all I'm going to eat I signal Brad and tell him I'm moving seats; he gives me a wave and I grab my bag, whilst my new friend pops his arm out for me to take like a true gentleman.

I take it with a chuckle,

"Wow, chivalry *isn't* dead!"

He laughs that full hearty laugh again and we head over to his lovely private dining area.

What I wouldn't give to be able to come here. The VIP section is a cornered off area that has its own private staff and although you can still see and hear the other patrons slightly (obviously) and observe the room, it's sort of an unspoken rule that people in these booths are not to be disturbed for any reason which leads me to think, who is this guy?

"So, you're probably wondering who I am and why I am asking you to come sit with me?" he guesses, echoing my exact thoughts.

"Oh, I thought we were here for a secret rendezvous?" I banter.

He barks out a delighted laugh which shakes his whole body and you can tell from the crinkles in his eyes he does it a lot.

"Oh, I hate for you to be the one on the receiving end of rejection tonight but I'm actually a happily married man, much the shame, as I'm sure you could keep me laughing for the rest of my days." he smiles and it's so sweet I feign pouting.

"Just my luck!"

"You, young lady have made my night, giving an old man like me a right chuckle on a day that's been really quite poor!" he says kindly.

"Well, I'm glad to have helped." I smile.

"Ok, so I'm going to make you a proposition…"

"Now, now, what would your wife say?" I place my hand on my chest faking offence.

"Ha-ha smart Alec." he says, "No this is a perfectly innocent offer from an old man to a very bright young woman… But I have to ask you two serious questions. What is your name and how often does that kind of thing happen?" he gives me a very pointed stare.

I laugh aloud, "My god of course… I'm Leona." I say shaking his hand.

"My friends call me Andy." he says, "Now you look like you could use a little peace every now and then from the vultures."

I blush slightly at his wording, and he pats my hand kindly.

"It's not what it looks like." I start to say when he frowns, "Ok it is kind of what it looks like but probably not nearly as bad as you think, I only come in once at the end of the month before I head home for the weekend. I take a little 'me' time in the spa and then come here for a nice meal and glass of wine."

"Not rushing home to the husband or family?" he asks gently whilst looking at my now bare finger that still holds an indent from my ring, which unfortunately kept sliding off due to the little bit of weight lost and I was scared to keep it on incase I lost it.

"My boys visit their grandparents at the end of every month and my husband passed away, so no rushing home for me I'm afraid."

I try to make it a-lot less depressing than it sounds but it's hard to inflict the right level of tone when I don't really feel it, so I just casually shrug my shoulders and take a deep drink of my wine.

He pats my hand and I feel the urge to spill all my secrets to him. God it's time to cut back on the wine but still my mouth keeps moving.

"I didn't remove my rings; I don't think I was ready if I'm honest but they've gotten a little loose and I was afraid I would lose them, so they're at the jewelers being resized. Probably should have grabbed a fake replacement to scare off the vultures, eh?" I laugh.

He smiles softly,

"I am genuinely sorry for your loss Leona, Losing someone is never easy under any circumstances but to be made a widow at such a young age is a very hard task to be charged with and you have my utmost respect for how you handled yourself earlier."

"Thank you."

"Now about my offer." he wiggles his brows, lightening the mood.

"I am almost never in the city, in fact I'm only here for a few hours tonight and I really hate to come if I can avoid it." He chuckles, "However, I do have these wonderful VIP perks and I would like to offer you the use of them whenever you wish."

I stare at him like he's lost his mind,

"It's very kind of you to offer and I appreciate the gesture but I couldn't possibly accept."

"Now, I knew that's what you were going to say but think about it, I very rarely come here, it goes utterly unused and from what I've observed tonight, you could really use it more than me."

I'm about to refuse again when he holds his hands up and goes on, "I'm not doing this completely out of the goodness of my heart, Leona, I have a favor to ask in return."

Hmm of course you do I think and he can see my thoughts clearly.

"I do! I will give you my VIP card to use at your discretion, if when I do have the unfortunate task of having to come here you would do me the honor of joining me for dinner. My wife simply isn't fit enough to travel back and forth and I'm not ashamed to say I miss her greatly when were apart and you my dear remind me so much of her. I would love to catch up with you whilst I'm here. What do you say?"

I laugh out loud and he grins back.

"You really are one smooth talker Andy, and I hope your wife keeps you on your toes!" I chuckle.

"You bet she does and has for the last 59 years of marriage!"

We carry on talking and I learn so much more about his family and wife who honestly must be a saint to put up with this scoundrel. It's such an easy conversation and we chat for so long I almost forget we've only just met! I think it's the first time in long time where I felt completely at ease and he seems to have felt the same.

His phone chimes again for about the fourth time in the last three minutes and I smile,

"You know it's really rather rude to ignore someone when you've already checked to see who it is." I smirk.

"I know, I know but he is a right stick in the mud and I am having such an entertaining night I didn't want him to spoil it but I suppose duty calls." he sighs.

"Yes, yes, I hear you, keep your undies on I'll be right up." He says into the phone whilst I book myself a car.

"Well, my lovely Leona, Are we agreed that this deal is concluded, my proposal has been accepted or do we have to schedule another meeting to re-negotiate terms?"

I laugh out loud, I can't help it, he is honestly the most charming and witty man I've had the pleasure of meeting in a long time and frankly I would happily meet up with him again anytime, no VIP offer needed. When I tell him this, he smiles so brightly I can't help but smile back and feel a lightness in my chest I don't often get when I'm not with my boys.

"Ok then I better go before…" the phone starts to ring again right at that moment and we both laugh. "I will walk you out." he says and holds his arm out and this time I take it easily.

As I step outside, I see my car pull up at the curb and turn to give him a quick squeeze and gentle kiss on the cheek,

"You my dear sir have made me laugh so much tonight that I don't hate heading in this car back home to an empty house. I can't tell you how much I enjoyed your company and I'm looking forward to meeting up with you whenever your back in town."

"The pleasure was all mine Leona, really my dear,

now off you go before my grandson comes out here and thinks I'm stepping out on my wife." He croons.

I chuckle for what seems like the hundredth time tonight and get into my car and head home, feeling less depressed at the thought.

I arrive back home and am rummaging through my bag for keys when I clasp my fingers around a small hard card and pulling it out, I laugh out loud like a looney, standing alone on my front porch. The sneaky old devil has not only entertained me all night long, he has also very subtly placed a shiny black VIP card into my bag with a little post it note attached.

THANK YOU FOR SUCH AN ENTERTAINING NIGHT, PLEASE MAKE USE OF THIS, IF ONLY TO KEEP AWAY FROM THE VULTURES AND MAKE AN OLD MAN HAPPY, ANDY X

He must have written this when I went to the bathroom. Yeah, sneaky old devil, I truly feel for his poor wife.

CHAPTER 2

The next few weeks pass by in a blur and it's almost time for the boys to head out again, oddly this time I'm not so saddened at the thought. How pathetic my life has become that the highlight of my month is that I may get to have a nice conversation with an eighty-year-old man about how much he loves his wife and family. And if I don't, well at least I know I can have a nice meal in the VIP area without being badgered by '*the vultures*' as they've now been dubbed.

When I arrive at the bar, I have no companion awaiting me, only a very unwelcome shock. A young lady, who introduces herself as Mindy, states that had I shown up she was to inform me Mr. Van Der Bilt is sorry he's not in the city this month but he is extremely glad I took him up on his offer and he really hopes to catch up with me soon, then she kindly asks to escort me, Mrs. Chalmers, to my booth!

What the heck! The old goat either knew who I was all along or found out after but he most certainly new I had no idea that he, 'Andy' is in fact Mr. Anderson Van Der Bilt, the man in charge of the firm that I currently work for alongside, ok under, way under his sister! Wow, he really is a sneaky old devil, I stifle a laugh.

On a serious note, he is my boss and the thought of him seeing what transpired when we met is a little embarrassing. He obviously wasn't too offended to have asked me to keep him company, so small mercy's and all that.

I have what can only be described as a lovely quiet

meal and drink, no creepy pervs or annoying disturbances, it was simply a lovely peaceful evening, even if it was a little lonely but hey that's my life now so I dig deep and order a car to take me home.

As I signal Mindy to let her know I'm ready to leave and settle my bill she tells me it's all paid for on Mr. Van Der Bilt's account. I groan wondering how I'm going to pay him back when she hands me a business card with instructions on how to contact the man in question and heads away to carry on her shift with a smile.

When I return home, I immediately fish out the card and go about calling 'Andy' and giving him a gentle piece of my mind but when I see the time, I decide to leave it and call him at a more reasonable hour.

I end up waiting until Monday afternoon to make the call whilst taking my lunch as I didn't wish to disturb him over his weekend. He mentioned how much he loves spending time with his grandchildren and great-grandchildren on the weekends.

I expect to get his assistant or receptionist when I call, so I am a little taken aback when he answers directly with a chuckle and speaks.

"I can't believe it! My damn wife, who hasn't even met you in person, called it that you would wait until after the weekend to tear me a new one!" he laughs.

"Yes, well sounds like your wife is the brains of the operation and you are just a mischievous playboy." I don't want to be too harsh; he is still my boss.

I hear a warm laugh come through the phone line and a deep chuckle, sounds like these two are just as bad as each other.

They must put me on speaker, as the next thing I hear is a lovely soothing voice.

"Well, I am glad you don't sound like you're the type of women who is going to pander to this old scoundrel, so I can rest a little easier knowing he will have more than one chaperone when he's away galivanting in the city." She laughs.

"Well, as entertaining as this is…" he starts, "I'm sure you are a busy lady, so how can I help you my dear?"

"You know fine well what you can help me with," I start, "Firstly you neglected to tell me you are my boss!"

"Hmm doesn't sound like you remember that at this moment." I hear him grumble and I choose to ignore him and carry on.

"Secondly you very sneakily placed an elusive VIP card in my handbag, you paid my bill without my permission and you either knew who I was when we met or you again 'sneakily' found out after, which feels very weird and your only saving grace is the fact that you are as charming as you are conniving, which I'm sure your good lady will attest too."

I do realize I have just shouted at not only my boss but maybe one of the most respected men in our business but if his loud guffaw is anything to go by, he hasn't taken offence just yet.

I hear his wife chuckle gently in the background,

"Oh, Andy, I like her," she says, "I cannot wait to meet her."

These people, they sound as mad and as happy as each other.

"Ok dear," he starts, "I truly am sorry if you feel I have betrayed you in any way but I was acting with honest intentions. Now I did know a lot about you before we met, my dear sister may not seem like she pays any attention to me however she does keep me informed on my company from time to time." He laughs. "I wasn't completely sure who you were, however there isn't another Leona in our building so when you told me your name it did confirm my suspicions."

"Well, that's slightly less creepy, I suppose." I grouch.

They both laugh again.

"Now I know you're a little mad at me but can I ask, Was the card useful? Did you have a nice night?" he asks.

"Yes," I grumble, "It was a pleasant undisturbed evening however I do not like being indebted to anyone, let alone my boss." I say sternly.

"My dear, If I had told you before that payments are not accepted in the VIP area you would never have contemplated going, ever!"

"You've got that right." I say.

They both simply laugh again.

"Ok, now that we've got all that out the way and we agree that it actually makes a large amount of sense that you use my account, can we discuss how much I or should I say we, have enjoyed this conversation and would love if we can keep in touch Leona."

How can I stay mad at this old fox when he's so charming?

"I'm not so sure I actually agreed to that at any point in this conversation." I say huffily.

"Okay dear, we will agree to disagree."

I really can't help but laugh.

"How on earth have you managed to put up with him for 59 years Mrs. Van Der Bilt?" I wonder.

"Its May dear, just May, but honestly I have no idea

some days, other days he can be quite the charmer."

"I'm pretty sure most days he's a charmer." I quip.

They both laugh and the conversation goes on a little bit longer in the same vein. I'm trying to sound stern and their just laughing at me sweetly but honestly, it's the nicest conversation I've had in such a long time.

After hanging up I am bewildered with how on earth I've managed to form a friendship with my eighty-year-old boss and his wife.

The next few months fly by in the blink of a 'groundhog' eye. It's all the same work, running around after the boys, moan so much about said boy's general boy-ness (cue smelly rooms, piles of washing, eating me out of house and home, you get the point) cry myself to sleep missing said boys when they are gone on the weekends. Ok, so I don't actually cry myself to sleep much anymore but I do generally feel low at the thought and they're out so often. It's hard to not miss them even when they're not away. But they need the freedom, they've had a hard few years and I'm just happy to see them back out laughing with their friends.

I really wish I had kept better contact with female friends but being a married pregnant teenage University drop out really doesn't give for a lot of time making gal pals. The female co-workers who I do know or socialize with are all part of the married couple's scene that I used to be part of and it feels awkward to try and force a friendship with any of them now.

Its times like this I wish I had a sister or even any family. But nope no siblings, no parents, no kooky grandma or crazy uncle. Just all lonesome me and of course Matts parents but they live so far away and are quite old, ironically close to the Van Der Bilt's age but it's just not the same, they're my in-laws.

Anyway, with the weekend fast approaching I know Andy's not visiting this month as per his email, yeah, he emails me now as well, with all sorts of craziness, so I have the booth all to myself and as much as I'm not overly looking forward to the solitude, I have found Mindy incredibly entertaining with each passing visit. She has waited on me almost every time I've been in, she says she likes to take the end of month weekend shifts because the VIP-er's tip extremely well and she gets to swoon over the rich men, whilst fantasizing about how one day she will wait on some rich gorgeous man who will come in and sweep her off her feet, pay off her student debt and whisk her out of her two bed three people apartment and they'll live a jet-setting life.

I laugh at her wild fantasies on the regular now, especially when she then sinks to the reality of the patrons. It is quite amusing and she really is a sweet girl.

Unfortunately, when I head for my meal this time Mindy is MIA but it's quiet enough in the bar and I have a ton of work to get through for Monday so I decide to get a bit of a head start and order a large glass of wine and pick at my meal on and off whilst going back and forth through work.

I didn't realize how late it's actually got and when I glance around the place is a whole lot busier. I start to gather the items that are now haphazardly spread all over the table when I hear a rough,

"Oh, for Christ's sake… Miguel, what the hell is this?"

When I look up, I stare straight up and up, into the

darkest brown, almost black, stormy eyes which are literally rolling in disgust, right at me.

What the heck! I know I've made a bit of a mess and sure, I probably look a riot, what with hunching over all the paperwork but it's really not that bad.

Poor Miguel is in such of a panic it's like he's completely forgotten that he's been waiting on me for the best part of... shoot almost 3 hours! How did so much time pass?

"Would you care to explain how on earth someone, who is not me, is sitting in my god damn seat?"

I start to rise and attempt to figure out the situation when he carries on, "What have we said about you feeling sorry for some floozy and letting them sit in an empty booth? If they're here alone, that is their problem, not bloody mine." He's not took those damn eyes off me and is glaring at me like he could make me disappear.

Well, hold on a damn minute! Who the hell is this jerk?

Poor Miguel looks frozen and I am pissed because seriously this guy is hot, want to start fantasizing like Mindy hot, but still, what a jerk!

"Excuse me, there is no need to be so rude or to harass the poor staff in such a manor." I start when I swear, I hear a god damn growl.

"I do not have time for this nonsense... Listen lady get your stuff together, your free ride is over for the night; I hope you enjoyed the high life but it's time to go back to the other side of the bar or anywhere quite frankly, as long as it's as far away from my table as possible. Do not worry about the bill, it will come out of Miguel's wage."

He says sharply, whilst glaring at Miguel for a

fraction of a second before swinging those deep orbs back over to me with what can only be described as severe impatience.

I think for a second, I'm as flabbergasted as Miguel!

"Oh, come on, enough with the deer in headlights look, you had a nice free meal but it's time to get your shit together and go, I have had a very long day and am about to have a longer night, so if you could just get a move on, I'd appreciate it."

He states it so simply that I can't help it, I burst out laughing. Not a quiet delicate trickle, nope a full-on guffaw. Poor Miguel looks ready to flee and the brute, yeah, he looks ready to blow.

"I'm sorry but who the hell talks to people like that? You think I'm just going to scurry away and do your bidding; poor Miguel has to just stand there and take abuse because what… you *know* someone who has nice VIP connections and you think you can just charge in here and make a scene." I realize as soon as I say this that I am indeed the one most probably making a scene but what the heck?

He leans right over towards me in a smooth controlled manner and in a low deeply throbbing voice says, "*You* lady are the one making a scene, I can talk to Miguel however I wish and I can tell you to get yourself the hell out of this booth, not because I *know* someone, as you so nicely put it but because I fucking own it!" he seethes staring straight into my widening eyes.

Unfortunately for me, maybe it's the wine or the way he speaks to me so roughly or it could be the fact that when he does this and I am ashamed to admit it, I feel a little flushed at the huskiness in his voice and the flames in those god damn eyes, that I glare right back and spout.

"That still gives you no right to be a class A prick!"

Oh shoot, I can see it, he's fast past boiling point but the heat in his eyes is a little thrilling, maybe not for Miguel though, as I hear his deep intake of breath, like he's been starved of oxygen for too long when he mutters,

"Un… eh, Mr Van Der Bilt Sir, please, it's not what you think."

Oh, dear god no!

He sees it clearly, that little flash of awareness that I now know exactly who he is, Sebastian Fucking Van Der Bilt, Andy's grandson, partner and yup you guessed it, another one of my god damn bosses. He sees it so quickly because his eyes are burning right through me and I know I'm going to have to dig deep into my big girl panties to extract myself out of this.

When, he smirks!

One of those rich, judgmental, holier than thou smirks that tells the world, '*Yeah, I know I've got you by the balls*' rips through me. Nope, not happening, I'm not taking it, not a chance.

I look away and he thinks he's won, like I'm about to scarper off like a little door mouse, well not today buddy.

I turn my back on him and lean over the table to grab my bag. I can hear Miguel muttering and the jerk clearing his throat, when I finally clasp my hands around the little lifeline I was looking for and turn sharply to catch him completely ignoring Miguel and his eyes planted firmly on my ass!

I clear my throat right back at him, wait till his eyes slowly trail up my body to eventually meet mine, he doesn't even look disturbed that he's been caught ogling my ass, so I wave my lovely little black VIP card straight in is now furious face.

"Yeah, unfortunately you're not the only god damn *Mr. Van Der Bilt* who owns a booth, so if you don't mind, I'm not entirely finished just yet. Miguel if it wouldn't be too much bother, I would like another glass of wine whilst I clear the rest of this table away and if you could tell chef the meal was exceptional as always that would be great… oh, and don't worry I will leave a tip big enough to cover any expenses you might incur tonight." I say glaring toward the prick.

With that I begin to put the rest of the large paperwork away, acutely aware that both men are staring at me with completely different expressions. Miguel looks half terrified, half amused but I can see he is on the fence with who's orders to follow. As the jerk is still slightly in, I don't know shock maybe, I take advantage and say,

"Don't worry Miguel I will let *Andy* know just how helpful you've been tonight."

And with that snippy little statement, I see him grin a huge slightly mischievous smile, which may be weird but us commoners have to stick together I think, when he stuns me.

He turns to the brute, pats him gently on the back and sniggers,

"Sorry Unc, but Gramps overrules you in my book… I will go get your wine Mrs. Chalmers." he chuckles clearing the table and scurrying away.

What?

Did he just say gramps? How can it keep getting worse? How much trouble am I going to be in when Mr. Van Der Bilt Senior finds out about this? I can't help but wing it though.

In for a penny and all that.

I keep my body positioned facing away from him but I can feel his hard stare on me, so when I sit back down, slide my ledger over in-front of me and eventually look up, I am met with the most hateful glare full on.

He stands well over 6 feet tall, broad shouldered, with a hard lean body, that's looking harder by the minute from how tensed he's became. His coffee brown eyes look like black coal, matching the inky dark hair cut close on his head and the neatly trimmed stubble covering the lower half of his face.

In any other circumstance, I would be taken aback by how hot he is, you can tell he obsessively works out and will have the body of an Adonis hiding under that impeccable black tailored suit which is fitted to absolute perfection. Not a stray item out of place.

He glares, his arms tightly crossed in front of his chest, looking down at me in disgust, like I am a piece of trash. Unfortunately, It's making me a little uncomfortable, what with how attracted my body is to his, not me to him mind, just my stupid body.

He may be sexy as hell but he's still a grade 'A' jerk.

"What the fuck is your angle honey? Trying to squeeze an old man out of his money? You think you can play on his weak mind and limp dick and what? He'll leave you something nice in his will or are you just along for the ride? Whatever little perks you can pick up along the way?" he grills.

"Wow! You really are a total and utter prick!" I snap.

"Just calling it like I see it sweetheart, I've seen enough women like you to last me a lifetime, don't get me wrong…" he starts, as he scans my body again from head to toe.

My traitorous form heats at his perusal and my god darn panties start to feel a little damp. Ass!

"You have put in the work, I'll give you that, made yourself look sexy but classy enough that he won't see past the veneer but it won't work darling," he sneers, "You see my dear old grandfather is happily fucking married and although he obviously fell for some line of bullshit you've fed him, I can assure you this will be the last time you use that little black card, or step foot near him or this building!" he threatens.

"Well, that's really going to be mighty inconvenient for me…" I say.

"Tough shit…" he starts as I carry on.

"Since I work here and have no real intentions of changing that because of a prick like you!" I fume.

He takes a minute to process what I've said and though I can't get a read on him, which is pissing me off further, I'm normally quite good at that, I can see he is still furious but is starting to maybe think there may be more to the situation than he first thought.

Just as he opens that gorgeous mouth to speak, Miguel re appears with my wine and a large crystal glass full of ice and whiskey.

"There you go Mrs. Chalmers, and here, Unc, thought you could use this."

He chuckles and scurries off after a stern glare from his 'Unc?'

I didn't miss the way he tensed either when Miguel called me 'Mrs. Chalmers' either or the way his eyebrows lower in confusion and I think maybe it's time for me to make a retreat.

"Well, as entertaining and delightful as this

conversation has been, I think I will skip the wine, I've already got a sour taste in my mouth, no need to add to it!"

I get up and start to gather my things, all the while I feel his hot gaze burn through me. I am almost out of his way when I hear him chuckle darkly,

"Yeah, you do that, *Mrs. Chalmers*," he sneers, "I'm sure your husband wouldn't be too happy to know you've spent your evening wining and dining on another man's wallet, old man or not."

I really shouldn't engage, it's not even like me, but I just can't help it, something about this guy riles my blood.

"Oh, don't you worry about my husband, Mr. Van Der Bilt," I sneer right back, as I slowly look him over in the same manor, he did me earlier, "If I were you, I would be more concerned with how Andy and May are going to feel about the fact you think he's not only old, weak minded and limp dick-ed but gullible enough to get taken in by some… conniving gold digger? I'm pretty sure he will not find that just as amusing, as he does most things."

And with that little bombshell, I take my time strolling out of the bar, proceeding to notify Brad to leave Miguel a very large tip and head on home for the weekend.

CHAPTER 3

What the heck have I done now? Not only have I offended another one of my bosses who I don't think is going to be nearly as forgiving as his grandfather. I have only gone and pissed off Andy and May's grandson, who they treat more like a son.

Through all the conversations we've had, they speak about Sebastian more than any other member of their family. He's Andy's protégée, they work through almost everything together, although he's confessed on more than one occasion that Sebastian has been doing a bigger share lately as Andy's been ready to retire for quite a while. Sebastian though, doesn't think it's the right time, which has been causing a little strain on their relationship. Hence why they have both been back and forth to the city more recently.

What on earth is he going to say when he finds out I spoke to his grandson in such a way, although he won't be too fond of Sebastian's description of him as an old gullible fool either. So that's a bonus however what won't be is if Andy does retire and Sebastian takes over as planned. Will he hold that little spat against me? Surely, he wouldn't, My work and behavior has always been impeccable.

No, I'm over-reacting, I think. We both were maybe just a little over worked, it was getting quite late, maybe it just seems a lot worse in my head. I'm sure Andy will explain it all to him and he will see what an absolute idiot he behaved and really, it's not like I'm ever going to have to deal with him personally. It will all be forgotten about like yesterday's news but I still have to apologize to Andy for disrespecting his family. It's the right thing to do, even if it sucks.

I normally don't speak with Andy or May over the weekends as they try to spend as much time with their family and I don't like to intrude on that time, I know how precious it is to them to have everyone around.

However, when I come out of the shower on Saturday morning, I have a missed call from non-other than Mr. Anderson Van Der Bilt Snr and automatically my hands sweat. Shoot! Just what did Sebastian say?

I make myself a cup of coffee, trying to calm my nerves, then decide to stop being a chicken shit and make the call. No point dragging it out, if I'm fired, I'm as well knowing sooner rather than later.

"Good morning, dear, I hope I never interrupted your morning calling so early?" he says cheerily.

"Er no… I was in the shower and missed your call, Andy. How are you?" I hedge.

"Oh, we're all good here Leona, just getting ready for the rabble to arrive but I just wanted to check you received the invitation before the weekend passes?"

Shoot! Does he not know? Why would Sebastian not say anything? What invitation and what the heck do I say now? I panic.

"Are you there dear?" he asks.

"Oh yeah, sorry, eh what invitation is that?" I stammer.

"For our Anniversary party, remember May was telling you last week that the invites went out and there was an issue with the postal service. We are just checking to make sure everybody received theirs." he chuckles.

"Well, yes, I remember her mentioning it but well I didn't think…"

He lets out a loud laugh,

"Please tell me you did not think you were not invited? You know fine well May is desperate to have you come out and visit and she can't wait to meet the boys and introduce you to the whole family."

Oh, dear god no. This can't possibly get any worse.

He must hear my audible gulp because he laughs again, "Do not worry I have already warned her about playing matchmaker, there is no need to fret on that part."

Yup as usual I should know better; it always gets worse. I have no idea how I am going to get myself out of this shit show.

"Well, now Andy, you know how much I appreciate the gesture and I can't wait to meet May but I wouldn't feel right intruding on your family party. I will happily come for a visit when it's just you both and…"

"Nonsense, there's going to be about 200 bloody people at this thing, and you sweetheart are part of the family to me and May now. She will be crushed if you don't come along."

Shoot!

"Listen we can talk about this later in the week, just let me know when you've received the invite anyway so May can stop worrying about it." He says lightly.

"Sure, Ok Andy. I just wouldn't know anyone and would hate to make you guys feel obligated to have to babysit me on your big night you know, you should spend it with all your friends and family." I try to soften my tone so he knows it's nothing personal.

"I know sweetheart but what you seem to be missing is you are friends and family! We both want you there to celebrate with us. There really is nothing to be worried about, we don't bite and I know you don't scare easy, otherwise would we even be friends?" he laughs. "Now you go try and enjoy the rest of your weekend, I hope you had a pleasant night last night without the boys?" he hedges.

"Hmm, yes it was something, eh pleasant, yes." I say.

He laughs,

"Are you sure I didn't wake you Leona? You sound a little… off?"

"Nope, I'm fine." I say quickly then, "Maybe not enough sleep last night."

He bursts out laughing down the phone as I immediately cringe.

"Oh my god! Not like that! You really are an old coot, Andy." I chide.

"I know, I know but it's good to hear you back to your normal self." I can almost hear his grin over the phone, then, a deep male rumbling voice. Oh no.

"Okay, okay, Sebastian, I'm on the phone, you will just have to wait. Sorry sweetheart damn impatient kids, they have no idea how to have a little patience these young-ins." he chuckles.

He's right there, about to tell him and I need to get off this call. "Oh, sorry Andy, I need to go, someone's trying to get through on the other line, I think it may be the boys, I will catch up with you later, have a great weekend." I say before slamming the phone down and clattering my head onto the kitchen counter.

SHIT! SHIT! SHIT!

How on earth have I got myself into this situation! And more importantly how the hell Am I going to get out of it?

I worried over the situation the whole weekend and now Monday morning as I sit in my office guzzling my third coffee already, I am no further forward with a resolution. I hate the thought of upsetting May she really is the sweetest lady. She has taken to calling me up recently, telling me all the details about the upcoming party and what new and hilarious drama her grandchildren have been getting themselves into. She's only mentioned *'he who bloody shall not be named or thought about'* in brief passing, but for some damn irritating reason I can't seem to get the infuriating man out of my head. I blame lack of sleep and the unease that I may have acted a little irrationally and I was definitely rude. Something I am not proud of regardless of the fact he was a jerk first.

I am just thinking it's time to give the Van Der Bilt's a call and beg off the party, I've thought about telling them a lie, saying the boys have some type of engagement that I can't avoid and that will be that however I deplore lying in any form and the thought of doing so to people I have come to admire makes me feel physically sick, so the alternative is to come clean and tell the truth. As much as I hate to admit it, it seems like the only option.

However as soon as I make the decision my office phone rings and Valerie's assistant Ben comes on the line asking if I can pop in and see Ms. Van Der Bilt before the staff meeting.

Lord! What now? It's very rare Valerie takes personal meetings; I normally get all my correspondence from Ben.

Please god tell me *he* didn't go snitch to my boss? It sure seems like the kind of dick move he'd make!

Pompous prick. Oh man I really need to get myself together. This is my place of work and I'm calling my boss's grandson names, The same grandson who is also sort of my boss. Well fuck my life!

I take a deep breath to compose myself, check my appearance in the mirror and head on over to Valerie's office, back straight, head held high. If he has snitched then I will apologize for my actions but I will not grovel.

I pass Ben's desk and he gives me a huge smile,

"Hi Leona, How have you been? Boys all good?" he asks.

"Same old, same old Ben, teenagers you know." I say and roll me eyes.

"Oh yeah, Mary-Ellen is only thirteen and she is already a handful." He sighs.

I sympathize with him and he tells me to head on in.

I give a light knock and walk into Valerie's office. She has one of the largest spaces in the building and the views from the floor to sky windows that encompass the whole right side of the room are breathtaking, it always takes me a minute to tear my eyes away.

"Stunning, isn't it?" She says as she gets up from behind her desk and walks towards me.

Valerie Van Der Bilt is every bit the ball busting female architect renowned for her magnificent design creations which encompass all the modern-day requirements whilst having a classical feel throughout and her image is crafted in the same style.

She is a stunningly beautiful woman who does not hide her elegant beauty but also doesn't flaunt it. She holds herself with an air of such simple confidence and class that can only come with age and experience. She must be in her early seventies but doesn't look a day older than sixty. She's known for having her gorgeous silver blonde hair pinned back in a classic French roll, a tailored pant suit which is of course fitted to perfection and 6-inch heels with an enviable red sole everywhere she goes, office meetings or building site. Yeah, she's kind of my idol.

"So, Leona I wanted to congratulate you personally for the fine work you did on the Briar Croft building. The attention to detail was exceptional and the changes you highlighted to Bryce's original design were quite flawless. Well done." She smiles.

Bryce was not at all happy with my 'suggestions' and had it not been for me raising the points during the last collective meeting, he would have ignored them completely.

However, Mr. Briar Croft had been incredibly clear in his brief that he wished to keep as many of the original features as possible and quite frankly it would have been a travesty not to. But again, the ageing designer was not happy to have any extra input. I was slightly mollified that it wasn't personal, he just wasn't keen on any input, he shot poor Simon's requests down immediately.

"Why thank you Miss Van Der Bilt, the Briar Croft is an outstanding piece of history and I was glad to be involved in any way on the project."

"That's part of the reason I asked you up here Leona. Firstly, though I think we have to clear a few personal situations up first hmm?" she muses.

That god damn snake, rat bastard of a man. He snitched. What type of grown ass adult goes running to their aunt to tattle on a simple misunderstanding?

"You seem to have developed a keen relationship

with my brother and his wife and I hear they have welcomed you along to their anniversary weekend." She goes on unaware of my inner ranting.

"Oh well yes… It was actually quite an unlikely friendship."

"No need to regale me Leona, Andy and May have spoken about you nonstop since you're meeting and the whole family cannot wait to meet the lady who called Andy out on all his mischief. However, I feel it would be amiss if you show up as a friend and guest at the coming party and continue to call me Ms. Van Der Bilt." She smiles again.

"Well, yes I guess that makes sense however I would hate to disrespect you either Miss Van…"

"Valerie, dear just Valerie. And you are going to have to get more used to it as I have a little project coming up and quite simply, I would like you to take the lead design spot." She says as I stand there stunned.

I mean this is it. What I have worked and slaved for the last god knows how many years.

"Oh, Miss… Valerie, I don't know what to say. Thank you." I say gratitude clear in my voice.

"You earned it fair and square dear, and I think it's just the right project for you." She says with a glimmer in her eye that I can't quite work out. "But before we get into any more of the details, I will have to fill you in at the meeting as we really do need to get going now. Do you have everything you need with you?" She enquires and I nod,

"Yes, I left my briefcase outside with Ben."

"Ok, if you could head on along, I will be there shortly," she says and walks back towards her desk. "Leona," she calls when I'm almost out the door, "I really do have great confidence in your ability to make this project spectacular. No taking *anyone's* bullshit, ok?" she glares.

And there is the ball buster from the boardroom.

"No Ma'am, you can count on me." I say as I turn and walk out of the room, on my way to my first meeting where I will be the lead designer. I have no idea what the project will be but I know I am going to rock it.

CHAPTER 4

As I walk into the conference room, there is an audible buzz vibrating throughout. As I make my way towards my usual seat, I ask Shelby one of the newer interns who has been sitting in on a-lot of the meetings if she knows what's going on.

Shelby is technically a little old to be classed as an intern. She is Mr. Davies, one of the partners, daughters who just got out of a bad marriage and moved half way across the world to get away from her ex. She has little to no experience in architecture but needed a place to work were she felt safe and to be fair to her she is an extremely hard worker. She also keep's very much to herself, doesn't engage much with the rest of the staff, in hindsight she was probably not the best person to ask.

"Oh, I'm not sure Leona, apparently one of the big bosses landed a pretty huge project on some old building that has heaps of history and Van Der Bilt and Sons managed to scoop the contract." She says letting me know that she is definitely paying attention to what's going on around the office and I scold myself for judging a book and all that.

"Wow," I say, "Wonder what building it is?"

At that moment my whole world comes to a screeching halt!

I hear the soft murmurs and chatter all but stop abruptly, as non-other than the man of my god damn nightmares strolls in the door as if he owns not just the office or the building but the bloody world.

He does not glance my way, but continues talking to

Valerie as they take their seat at the head of the table and Valerie utters the words, I pray are not about to leave her mouth but as per the shit show that my life has become, she states loud and clear for all to bloody hear,

"Today we have received confirmation that Van Der Bilt and Sons has won the proposal bid for The Montgomery."

She leaves a pause, simply because The Montgomery is one of the most famous abandoned buildings on the outskirts of Manhattan that has faded into despair and is a legend in the architectural world. There has been rumors about investors buying and remodeling the building for the last three decades, so for it to actually be a fully-fledged reality is astounding and as I begin to get that bubble of excitement swirl, her next words are like swallowing lead,

"Sebastian has convinced the board that we are indeed the only firm who can bring The Montgomery back to its original splendor, and the Briar Croft project showed just how competent we are at this period of work." She pauses, "And that is why I am delighted to announce that Leona Chalmers will be heading up the design alongside Sebastian himself. I'm sure that everyone will agree this is going to be monumental for the company's move diversifying into restoration."

And that's when I feel it. The heated stare of the man glaring at me from the end of the table. I decide to face him full on and not cower, but when I look up into two black pittless souls I know, what I would have declared an hour ago to be my dream job, the pinnacle of all the hard work, blood, sweat and tears over the last fifteen years, has now suddenly become my worst nightmare. Because no matter how hard I try to blame the fire coursing through me on the obvious disgust he has in me and the mutual feelings I return right back at him, I know I can no longer kid myself about the obvious attraction that I unfortunately feel towards him.

This man, who makes my blood boil with an unnatural ease, is the man I am going to have to work with in such close contact over goodness knows how long, add in the fact that there is really no way to avoid him. We are going to have to clear the air and dismiss the first meeting entirely.

I look away and try to stay focused on the rest of the meeting. In any other situation I would be ecstatically listening to every tiny detail, but after the emotional rollercoaster I've been on since I first clapped eyes on Sebastian Van Der Bilt, I just feel unease.

As with everything in life, I'm good at putting on a brave face and rallying through. As the meeting comes to a close, I accept the offers of congratulations and make a note of who I would like to help me moving forward.

I edge towards Shelby, asking if she can send me a copy of her notes from the meeting just in-case I missed anything and ask her if she would like to be more involved. She immediately confirms what I thought, she is desperate to do well and learn. She is also another female perspective I would like to add into the mix.

As everyone starts to filter out of the conference room, I decide there's no time like the present to get this mess cleared up and I start to put my laptop and notes away, whilst observing the last remaining people leave. I head over towards both Van Der Bilt's who look to be in a rather heated debate. I clear my throat and start,

"Valerie, I would like to thank you again for this opportunity. I am thrilled to have any part in contributing to the restoration of such a magnificent piece of history." I say as I shake her hand.

"Well, as I was just remarking to Sebastian here, the Briar Croft design was the deciding factor in the restoration board coming to us and it only seems right that you've *earned* your spot on this project."

I do not miss the emphasis she puts on the word '*earned*' which immediately raises my hackles. Does this jerk really think I got this spot through anything other than merit?

"I really am sorry I can't stay any longer, I would have loved to get your immediate thoughts on the development however Ben has once again beeped me to say I am running late." To me she says, "I will be in touch over the next few days and remember what I said earlier." to him she simply says,

"Sebastian, I know your feelings loud and clear and they are duly noted however at this point you are simply wrong and overruled." She smiles at him as she sees the tightly contained fury lurking behind the cool facade. "Play nice." she mutters as he leans down to kiss her cheek goodbye.

And with that she turns on her heels and strolls out of the room leaving both our gazes lingering after her.

Mine it would seem a little longer, as when I take a deep clearing breath and turn to face him, he is glaring directly at me as if he can simply make me vanish from his existence through the power of thought. No such luck buddy, if that shit worked, you'd have been long gone by now.

As we stand there in the silent conference room, I am acutely aware, that at this point in time, he has no desire to talk a single word to me, so I square my shoulder and follow Valerie's word to take no bullshit. I speak first,

"Well, this is awkward." I say with a small smile as he continues to glare. "We obviously have never been properly introduced so let me…" I start.

"Oh, I am more than aware of you *Mrs. Chalmers*." he scoffs.

"I'm not sure what you are aware of Mr. Van Der Bilt other than the facts."

"*The facts*?" He goads, "And what facts are these *Mrs. Chalmers*?"

Again, the way he sneers my name has me wanting to punch this guy in the balls but I try not to falter.

"The facts, Sir," Yeah, I can't help a little snark right back, "Are that I have worked for this company for almost fifteen years. I have earned every little step on the ladder to where I am now through hard work, determination and my work quite simply speaks for itself. My friendship with your grandparents has absolutely no reflection on the decision of me being selected to be part of this project and to put it plainly, It is ridiculous that anyone would even insinuate such a thing."

"Oh, you really are that good, so believable." He murmurs.

"Look let's just get it all out in the open, I have no romantic or financial interest in your grandfather for goodness sake, he is a lovely kind man who I enjoy the pleasure of immensely," when he growls, I ignore him and carry on, "However, it's when your grandmother participates, I enjoy them best. They are remarkable people who I call friends, nothing more, nothing less. The situation the other night was just a misunderstanding and if you would stop being so pig headed about it, you would see that you were quite simply being a rude self-righteous…"

Well shoot! He did it again, he got me riled up so much I lost my temper which is infuriating, as I pride myself on my control. What makes it worse is he can see it; he knows I was trying so hard to keep my temper in check and he knows he goaded me into it. A smug smirk spreads over his face as he leans back on the desk behind him, arms folding, as he looks down that superior nose at me.

"Look," I say sharply, "How about we just start over? This project is going to be long and exhausting enough without any added pressure. I'm willing to wipe the slate clean and move on from here." I say and extend my hand out to shake his.

He stares so intently into my eyes, I fear I'm about to go cross-eyed, when he lowers them to my outstretched hand. He glares at it, as if it's a viper waiting to strike, but when I start to pull back and except his refusal, he reaches out and grasps it tightly, jerking me closer.

My whole body burns with fire coursing up my arm and he gives a slightly uncomfortable twitch, as if he felt it too but his next words turn me to ice.

"Not a chance sweetheart," he sneers, "I do not take kindly to people using my family to further their career but even less will I tolerate leeches trying to worm their way into my family, and you *Mrs. Chalmers*," he says as he very pointedly turns my hand around to show my missing wedding ring, "You, have crossed the line on both."

"Wow, you really are a total prick." I say, turn on my heel and stride toward the door but as I reach my hand out to push it open, his words are a stark reminder that I have to get myself in check.

"Yeah, that may be the case," he says calmly, "But I am also your boss and you will answer to me on this project. Until I can have you removed, you will stay far out of my sight."

My shoulders tense at his words but as my hand clasps around the door handle, his next words infuriate me, "That includes my family home, *Mrs. Chalmers*, I do not want to see you anywhere near that party or I will make it my own personal mission to see you never work in this industry again, do you understand me?"

I swear, I am normally known for my restraint, a cool hand under pressure, however there is something brewing inside and I have no justifiable reason for my actions, other than I saw red.

I turn to look him square in the eye and smile widely,

"With all due respect Mr. Van Der Bilt, Sir, FUCK YOU!" I say, as I turn and walk out of the room.

CHAPTER 5

Oh dear! What the heck have I done? I think all the way back to my office. Right now, the fact that I have to work with this man up close and personal for god only knows how long, is pushing me to breaking point but the fact that he thinks he can tell me who I can or can't speak to is plainly pissing me off.

How dare he? And what the hell is his problem? Surely, he can't seriously think I'm trying to take advantage of his family? What would I even gain? It makes no sense this level of aggression towards me.

Yet the fact that I still feel hot all over and can feel the rage burning through me gives away just how strongly my own feelings are, I've never experienced such a strong and immediate dislike to someone.

It has nothing to do with the fact that when he leaned into me and I got an up-close view of those god damn eyes that flashed with what looked a lot like desire, I felt myself shiver all over. Truth being told though; it may just have been my own attraction reflected and that only serves to piss me off further.

I decide there's nothing that can be done about the situation at this moment, We will simply have to work out a way of working together without actually being in the same room as each other and everything will be fine.

I need to turn my attention to the most important outcome of today, I am going to not only be working on The Montgomery, but am going to be a lead designer! EEK! I just love the old building. I have already visited it about a million times, just soaking up all the history and imagining it in its heyday, so I take a moment to let the achievement soak in, then pull out my laptop and get to work.

As it nears lunch Shelby pops past to give me a copy of all her notes from earlier and I can see she has a little extra spring in her step.

"I want to thank you so much Mrs. Chalmers for asking me to help out on this project, anything you need me to do, I'm on it. I just looked up a load of information on the original building and just Wow! It's beautiful. I obviously don't know a-lot about the architecture and what not but the entertainment side of it is fascinating, Sorry I'm babbling." she laughs.

I smile at her gently, "Firstly, call me Leona," I laugh, "It really is, isn't it? I'm so glad you've had a look and you're interested as I was thinking, maybe you would like to work with me on this Shelby?" I ask gently, "That is if Dan can manage without you, I know you've been helping mainly in his office but if you like I can have you transferred over here to help me?"

"Seriously? Mrs. Chalmers, Leona, that would be amazing, I think Dan is just making up jobs to give me at this point to be honest." She sighs.

I laugh as that's quite simply been the case but she seems eager to be helpful and I find her enthusiasm encouraging. I'm going to need a-lot of help on this project and it would be great to have someone I can lean on and there's just something relatable in her. Maybe it's the whole single women with kids' thing but I like her and I can clearly see she feels a little useless around the office.

"Great! I've got to be honest Shelby; this is a bit of a big deal for me as well and I really could use your help. Any chance after lunch you would want to come talk over what you got out of the meeting and I will sort things with Dan to have you relocated to me?"

She looks ecstatic.

"That sounds great, is there anything you need me to do just now?" she asks.

"Maybe just gather all your belongings and I will have Tom clear a desk for you."

She makes a squeaky noise and gives me a huge grin and I know I've done the right thing.

As soon as Shelby leaves, I phone Dan and ask him how he feels about her transferring to my office and he lets out a sigh of relief and confesses the girl is a delight but his own assistant is giving him grief about her having to find extra work for her to do.

If he didn't have Mary, he would have hired Shelby himself but Mary's 58 years old and has been with him for over 30 years, so he thanks me immensely for saving him and assures me I am not going to know how I managed before her.

When I step outside my office to go fetch myself a coffee and some lunch Shelby is already sat behind her fully kitted out desk. There is a stack of paperwork printed and labeled and I can see blueprints all laid out neatly at the side of what looks like a very large coffee and a food bag from Sal's deli. Sal's is where I regularly grab my lunch if I remember to eat and I can smell it already, making my mouth water.

Shelby hops up when she sees me and holds out the bag and the coffee,

"I figured since you haven't left your office yet you probably didn't have time to grab anything, so I phoned Sal's and got them to send you up your usual. I hope that's ok?" she says.

"Thank you, Shelby, that's really thoughtful, but please don't think that I brought you over to my department to make coffee runs." I look her in the eye and say, "I want you to help me on this project."

"I am so glad you said that because I also went ahead and got you a copy of the existing blueprints for the Montgomery and I have one of the couriers on his way back from the public library with copies of the original building before the fire that burnt down the Atrium on the East wing." She is obviously excited about this and I know I have made a great decision.

Over the next few days Shelby continues to show me just how amazing an assistant she is and I feel like there isn't a time when she hasn't been by my side.

She's also been very good at working as a go between for me and a certain man who I am avoiding as much as possible. He has decided to work from his own office next to Valerie's for the duration of the Montgomery project, so is in fact in the building most days. I choose to avoid him at all cost and his assistant and Shelby are now becoming fast friends due to our avoidance.

Unfortunately, that avoidance is all about to come to an end. As of next week, we have to begin the site visits and meet up to start looking over the physical aspects of the restorations.

With the week coming to a close, I ponder whether it would be worth trying to clear the air again however I'm simply not sure if I will only go and make things worse. As I am mulling it over, I get a call from Valerie's assistant asking if I can pop up and see her when I'm free. I figure I may kill two birds with one stone and all that when I'm there, that way we can all go into the new work week afresh.

As I head towards Valerie's, I pause near his office wondering if I should just get it over with now but when I see through the glass that he already looks pissed, I begin to pity whoever is on the other end of that phone call, I decide to just march on by and knock on Valerie's instead.

When I enter, she's on the phone so I motion to wait outside but she waves it away telling me to take a seat.

"Yes, yes, I know what you said, but as we have already discussed, the decision has already been made… I really don't care what you think Sebastian! Yes, you are as much of a partner as I am, but myself, Andy and the other partners all agree, you are the only one who has a problem so god damn suck it up and get on with the job."

She mouths an apology and rolls her eyes but she knows I know who is on that call and who exactly he is bitching about. ME!

"I know, I know but I can assure you it is not nearly the same. I will see you at the house tomorrow, Bye."

I am practically sitting on the edge of my seat, back ramrod straight and I fear I don't blink as she turns that steely gaze on me,

"I'm sorry you had to hear that Leona but now that it's out in the open I'm just going to spit it right out. My nephew is an ass." She smiles, "Unfortunately, he's family and I won't divulge any of his hare brain reasoning but it's fair to say he has a problem with you being on this project. I had already decided to ask you up here to discuss this but as you can see, I have told him in no uncertain terms, tough luck."

"I mean I don't even know what to say."

"Look Leona, Sebastian has always been pigheaded but for all his posturing he is not a spoilt little boy. He has worked his way through this company the same as you and I, however he seems to feel you have had some sort of benefit or you've taken advantage of me or Andy somewhere along the line and I have no idea why. He's not normally this unreasonable. I'm am not sure just why you rub him up the wrong way so immensely but it is there just the same."

"Yeah, it's definitely there." I murmur.

"My question Leona is can you continue to work with him on this? The Montgomery is a massive deal and I need you two on the same page."

"I was actually on my way to go and speak with him myself a moment ago but I could see he was having a heated phone call so I came here instead." I laugh.

I can't believe I am even having this discussion; this is a place of work not high school so yeah; I can deal with him I decide.

"Valerie, I have been waiting to be involved in a project like this all my life and I am not walking away from it because of one… well because of a silly misunderstanding. I will leave Mr. Van Der Bilt to cool off for a little bit, but I will speak to him before the end of day and by Monday morning we will be ready to work together as a team on this." I say with a confidence I don't fully feel.

"I knew you were the right person for this job Leona, I'm sure it will all work out in the end. Now I wanted to ask you something else, although given the situation now may not be the correct time." She chuckles. "May and Andy are hounding me to make sure that you are going to be attending their party next weekend, they are already aware of the tension between you and Sebastian and are worried that this situation is going to put you off and as you can imagine…"

I laugh, "Yes, I can already imagine they two are trying to coerce you into wearing me down but you can tell them not to worry, I will most certainly be attending. I wouldn't miss it for the world." I say as I take in her shrewd stare that does not miss a thing.

She now knows I won't back down simply because *someone* doesn't want me there.

"Excellent my dear, well if you need anything just let me know and remember what I told you." She grins "He may be my nephew but do not take any of his bullshit."

"Oh, I won't." I assure her and escape back to my office.

I managed to make it without seeing the black-eyed devil but now as the office slowly empties for the night, I know I have to make my way back upstairs to face him.

There is still has a few people lingering around but as I make my way towards the partners floor its eerily quiet. I pass Valerie's assistant on the way and he tells me most of the partners and their assistants have already left but Mr. Van Der Bilt is still in his office on a call, so just head on along and give him a few minutes, then knock.

I thank him and force my feet not to flee and try my hardest not to fidget or panic. I can do this; I can keep my cool and I will not lose my temper. This is the mantra I repeat as I wait a good seven, eight minutes outside his office. I'm too agitated to sit so I just sort of pace back and forth when I hear a loud curse.

"For Christs sake, will you stop pacing back and forth out there!"

Well so much for not losing my temper he's already

raising my hackles.

I knock on the door and just to be sarcastic I add, "Are you available for a moment Mr. Van Der Bilt, Sir or should I come back at a better time?"

"Took you long enough," he grumbles, "Come in."

I take a deep breath and enter.

Of course, he is leaning against his desk fully facing me with those arms crossed, he glares at me and I just can't help it, there is something about him that just makes me want to punch him in his too handsome face. I try to hold my composure and not let him goad me but as he stands there and slowly rakes his gaze over me from the tip of my toes to top of my head, I refuse to blink and simply stare right back.

I watch as he takes in my low black kitten heeled shoes, simple but fitted, knee length black pencil skirt and cream silk blouse. My heavy blonde hair, as always, is pinned to the back of my head, although a few loose tendrils have gone astray throughout the day.

It's such a shame he is a massive prick because he is quite probably the hottest man, I have ever saw in my life up close. I mean no disrespect; my husband was a catch. Like those wholesome American 'heart-throbs', all blonde hair, blue eyes, with a smile plastered all over his face almost every minute of the day.

But the man in front of me is the complete opposite in every single way. Dark watchful ebony eyes, inky black hair, neat and trimmed with a slight shadowed growth of beard gracing the lower half of his strikingly handsome face. A dark tailored suit, over a sharp black shirt and tie, molds to his lean but solid frame. A blanket aura of darkness surrounds him right down to the deeply setting scowl that is currently covering his face.

"Did you just come up here for an ogle *Mrs. Chalmers*? As if so, some of us actually have work to do." he sneers.

"Oh, I'm so sorry Sir, I figured I was giving you enough time for you to go ahead and point out all the obvious flaws that you've found, since your facial expression clearly finds me lacking in whatever you were judging."

The corner of his mouth lifts ever so slightly, as if he could almost crack a grin but if I'd blinked, I would have missed it, so maybe I just imagined it.

"We need to talk I think, don't you?" I say.

"No *Mrs. Chalmers,* what we need, is for you to stay away from me and my family and then we can all go on with our lives."

"Look I get it; you're used to people trying to worm their way into your family or whatever but surely you can see that you where way off base when we first met?"

"Was I?" He returns.

"You can't be serious?" I ask almost exasperated.

He simply raises a damn eyebrow.

"What exactly is this crime I am being accused of?" I cross my arms, "Why don't you just spit out what your actual problem with me is, we can talk it out and try to find some sort of common ground here because I am not going anywhere Sir and you and me are going to have to work together on this. Surely you know this?" I huff.

"There are quite simply not enough hours in the day for me to list all my problems with you *Mrs. Chalmers*," again he looks at my left hand. Why is he so concerned about my missing wedding band?

"Ok, So is your plan for us to simply keep avoiding

each other? How on earth is that going to work out for anyone?"

"I do not avoid *Mrs. Chalmers*." At my laugh he looks at me pointedly.

"Come on, you have avoided me all week." I laugh mildly.

"Have I? Or have you avoided me and I've simply responded back?" he muses.

Shoot! He's right.

"I do not think we need to '*work together*', I have no interest in being another member in your fan club *Mrs. Chalmers*."

"Oh, for Christ's sake can we drop the snide *Mrs. Chalmers*." I huff, "I have no idea why you sneer every time you say my god damn name, But maybe call me Leona and you won't have to growl so much."

God darn it, every damn button he manages to bloody push.

"I will not call you anything other than *Mrs. Chalmers* because I will not be bought in by whatever it is you have sold to the rest of my gullible family and apparently all the supposed sane men left in this building."

I look at him closely, so closely I can see the twitch in his right eye that looks like he's about to blow a fuse.

"Wow, You really believe it. You actually think I am out to con your family and that I have somehow convinced two of the most business savvy, intelligent ball busting people I have ever met, to what, give me favors by putting me on this job?" I question, "Are you really so arrogant that you think everyone is out to get something from you or is it you just can't believe that I've been asked to help on this project for my experience?"

"You have nowhere near enough experience for this job." He growls.

"Have you even taken a second to look at my resume? Did you review the Briar Croft results?" he cuts me off,

"The Briar Croft is one project, half the size of this one, you think that gives you enough experience?" He glares.

"No but my influence on the last fourteen maybe fifteen designs over the last six years… they might give you an idea of what I am capable of. Look, I get that you think your grandfather has pushed this because we have become friends lately but I can assure you I have worked my damn ass off for this company, probably more than you and for you to say it's been handed to me is quite hypocritical really since you're the one with the same job as me but also the same surname that is on the bloody building, you don't hear me questioning if your experienced enough?"

I've ranted again but for Christ sake.

"I should hope you are not questioning me?" He raises that damn eyebrow, "I am still your boss and I don't have to prove myself capable to anyone here, let alone you."

"So, as my boss, You do realize then how much sense it makes for us both to figure out a way to get over whatever issues we have now because come Monday there is no way we can behave like this. We are going to have to work together Sebastian…"

He just flinched! When I said his name, he fucking flinched, what the hell is that?"

"I'm sorry Mr. Van Der Bilt, Sir but we really do have to try and come up with a resolution for this. It seems neither of us is going anywhere." I sigh.

He just glares at me, then runs his hand through his hair and walks around to sit at his desk.

"Drop the sarcasm with the *Sir* shit, it's not cute." I smirk to myself but of course he's staring so intently at me he doesn't miss it. "Monday's a new week, let's try and keep out of each other's way as much as possible." He says, "Now if you don't mind some of us still have work to do."

He turns to his computer and I know I've been dismissed.

I turn and head out of the room when he calls out,

"Oh and *Mrs. Chalmers*, If you so much as cause a single inch of trouble for any member of my family, I will not hesitate to sack you effective immediately and I will make sure you never work in this industry again, Are we clear?" He glares intensely at me.

I pause and look him over for a whole minute,

"Why that seems to be the second time you have threatened to 'sack and destroy' me Sir, yet I haven't thought once about paying a visit to HR over your in-proper conduct," I pause and give him time to take that in, "However luckily for you, I have absolutely no intentions of causing any problems for your family. You see *they* are genuinely good, honest and kind people who I care for very deeply, so you have no reason to worry." I turn and stalk out of the office with a, "See you Monday, Sir."

And a screw you, you shit grinning prick! Screaming in my head.

Monday can go take a hundred-mile hike! It's going to be too damn soon for me to see that piece of shit again. Argh, sometimes I hate my life.

CHAPTER 6

And sometimes I just love it. Normally when I come home from work, the boys are heading back out the door. I really wish I got to spend more time with them but they're teenagers who don't want to hang out with their mom on a Friday night so I get it but when I get home, they're both hanging around the house like they've nowhere to be.

"Hey guys, I thought you were going out tonight?" I ask.

"Nope, Bobby's party got cancelled, he's got mono and so has half the team so we're just going to hang out this weekend." Says Jacob.

"What bout you Mom? Any big plans? Hot date?" Noah laughs.

"Oh me, yeah I've got a hot date, tonight," I tease and they both look up, "With two of the yummiest guys on the block," I say and they roll their eyes.

"We don't count." they chuckle.

"Not you two" I laugh, "Ben and Jerry for me all weekend long." I smirk.

"Haha, very funny." Jacob says.

Noah spins around on the sofa putting his phone down. "You know you could date if you wanted to though mom, right?" he says startling me.

"Well, I mean that's not really something I'm interested in…" I stammer.

"You're not even old, Dad wouldn't want you to be lonely." he says and it's been too long of an emotional day already that I feel myself starting to tear up.

"Aw mom, we didn't say anything to upset you, I

told you it was too soon Noah!" Jacob says glaring at his brother.

"I'm sorry mom, we just hate how alone you always are and we wanted you to know we don't mind if you wanted date or even go out with friends. You don't always have to be waiting around on us, we know we're busy a lot but we still want to spend time with you and see you happy again." Oh lord, these boys!

"You know what would make me happy, us three having pizza and movie night and me whooping Jacobs butt at that racing car game again." I smirk, hiding my mini emotional breakdown.

"Mom it was one time and it was because my batteries were running out, the buttons were sticking, you can't keep claiming that as a win." he whines.

Noah ever the wind-up man just laughs so hard,

"She did beat you dude. Sticky buttons or not, suck it up." He laughs at his brother and off they go ragging on each other. I just lean down and give them both a squeeze and tell them I will head up, get changed and order some food.

This is exactly what I need, a night with my boys to re-group before Monday.

I curse myself internally though, when Noah mentioned dating, the first person who's image flashed instantly through my mind was that damn dickhead boss. Why the heck did it have to be the devil himself.

As I think this, I type out a quick email and attach the brief I had been working on during the commute home. I take one last look and click send.

I head downstairs ready to spend the weekend relaxing knowing come Monday morning the dick in the dark suit will at least have a better idea how capable I actually am, well that is if he even reads it.

Yup, I sent him my resume along with samples of where I helped out in projects over the last few years.

The weekend was exactly what I needed. Just time with my boys, laughing and relaxing trying not to think too much about Mondays site visit. I did take a little time to think over some of the things they both mentioned though.

They obviously see me as a lonely single mom which is so not the image I want to portray, whether it's true or not. I don't have very many friends or even acquaintances to socialize with but I make a decision to try and rectify that. I decide I'm going to make more of an effort to put myself out there. I just need to figure out how.

Unfortunately, the weekend is over far too quickly and Monday morning rolls right around. I never dread coming to work, it's my one constant in my life that I truly love, out with my kids and I hate that when I should be feeling a surge of excitement this morning it's also accompanied by a massive bout of nerves which are not attributed to the job.

The only relief I have is that when I arrive at the entrance to The Montgomery building Shelby is already there and waiting and has what looks like two extra-large thermoses of steaming hot coffee in her hands and I pray one is for me.

"Morning Shelby, I really hope that extra thermos is for me?" I ask with a pleading look.

"Of course, it is," she laughs, "I figure you're going to need it today since we will be dealing with the dishy devil himself." She grins.

I laugh out loud,

"Please don't get caught calling him that or we're

both gona be in trouble." I laugh right back taking the mug from her.

"Ok, so where are we this morning?" I ask, "Has anyone else arrived yet?"

I'd told Shelby I like to get to sites before everyone else so I can take a walk around and get a feel for it before everyone else arrives and like the excellent assistant she is, she show's up with coffee.

"No one's here as far as I can tell, just a few building contractors wandering around waiting on the all clear from us to go ahead. I am going to head over to the site cabin and allocate us a working space whilst you go ahead and do your walkthrough." She says, and offers to hang back out of the way to let me wander.

"Thanks Shelby." I say as I start to make my way closer to the building and take out my notebook and pen and begin jotting random thoughts down as I take in the magnificent old building.

The outside facade still looks in great condition and shouldn't need a massive amount of repairs but the side Atrium is going to need a total overall from all the fire damage. The bones look excellent though and as I start to work my way throughout the building, I feel that familiar excitement buzz through me at what this place could potentially become.

The grand staircase will need to be removed and replaced completely but will remain the centerpiece of the building. I fantasize about all of the past and future ladies and gentlemen dressed in all their finery descending the stairs where everyone turns to watch as they travel forward into the grand ballroom. It truly is an exceptional space and with the right amount of work it will once again be brought back to all its former glory.

And with that added spring in my step I swivel on my feet ready to tackle all the work that lays ahead and spin right into a brick wall. Well, what feels like a brick wall, what I wish was a brick wall but is in fact the solid chest of my glaring boss.

As I gasp and try to move away too quickly my shoe catches and I stumble slightly off balance and he huffs as he reaches out and grabs hold of my waist pulling me upright.

Unfortunately, he either anticipated me to be slightly heavier, jerk, or my motion to quickly right myself has me crashing again flush up against him and as he stares down at me, I feel myself pause as I get a very up-close look at those dark penetrating orbs which are staring down at me so intently. I think I may be frozen because I simply can't move and he seems the same as we stand there both tight against each other, his hands firmly on my waist, staring unblinkingly.

A loud cough from behind him breaks the spell and he not so gently pushes me away although he does maneuver me so that I don't crash on my face so I suppose that's an improvement.

"Mr. Van Der Bilt, Sir, I managed to get a hold of Aleksey, the contractor but he says he will be another few hours as he is on route to the hospital with his wife. She's pregnant and they had a last-minute appointment this morning. He arranged for another interpreter to be on site this morning but no-one can locate him at the moment, he's assured me he himself he will be here as quick as he can." The man states, "I know it's only a small crew for this side of the building but I could go talk to the workers, see if any of them may be able to translate enough that they can get started on the area you requested?" he asks hesitantly.

All the while I haven't moved a muscle and he has yet to look away from me. I see a smirk start to creep over his face as he replies, "No, that won't be necessary Don, go ahead and ask the men to converge outside in thirty minutes." He says with a wicked gleam in his eyes. "*Mrs. Chalmers*, are you quite ready to join the rest of us in the main hall to go over today's schedule?"

As I look around, I can see the rest of the team just on the outside of the doors leading towards the main hall, they do indeed look like they are waiting around and I automatically feel awful as I must've lost track of time wandering around reminiscing.

"Yes, of course, I'm sorry I must have got distracted on my walk around." I say humbly.

He just glares and I begin to maneuver around him and head towards the others when he warns,

"I really hope you will try avoid getting distracted in future, this is a massive contract and we don't have time to waste, and dear god try and wear something more practical the next time we do a site visit. We do not have time for trips to the ER because you fail to show up in the proper attire." He fumes.

What the hell! Is he serious? His god darn aunt wears 6-inch heels on site visits. My shoes are heeled but hardly a danger! It was him that unbalanced me, not my god damn shoes but I can't exactly say that so I just smile sedately.

"Duly noted." I turn on my heel and start to walk towards the group, "Sir." I add and smirk to myself as I can almost feel the fury from him from here.

I join the group around a large table that has been set up in the middle of the room and feel Shelby move to my side.

He takes less than a minute and heads straight to the top of the table and begins outlaying the days plan. He explains that Aleksey, the West sides building specialist has been delayed, which means the grounds workers are converging outside awaiting instruction.

He rhymes of all the tasks that needs to be put in motion and I should probably be offended that he hasn't asked for a single piece of input from me however his work is of course thorough and detailed enough that there is really no need and it's far too early for me to be trying to stamp any authority, so I stay quiet and let him dish out orders.

He remarkably has a very easy manner with the rest of the staff and no-one else looks like they want to stab him in the eye, so I suck it up and resign myself to the fact that although he has a bee in his bonnet against me, he is dealing with it professionally.

That is until I hear him smirk my name.

Shoot. What did I miss?

He is looking at me for the first time since we began the meeting and he looks almost amused.

"I'm sorry could you repeat that?" I ask.

"I was saying, if you wouldn't mind, could you go and relay that information to Aleksey's ground staff? You know the workers who are waiting outside, since no-one else here speaks fluent Polish, I thought we could put your skills to use and you could help get the project moving along in that area, instead of us all having to wait around for him to arrive."

He says it so simply and with not a hint of sarcasm that everyone else simply looks relived that they don't have to attempt to try and explain instructions to the team.

"Why of course," I hear myself say, "Would you

like to come along and I can interpret your instructions?"

"I'm sure you can manage, thank you." He says surprisingly sounding almost normal.

And with that everyone starts to set off to complete their assigned tasks.

Now, it is not like I can't speak Polish; however, it has been a while and of all the bloody things that are down on my resume how is this the one thing he sees that he can pick apart. Although it does means that he read my email or has at least looked at it, maybe that's the reason for the fractional decline in hostility. I smile, I will take it as progress and continue to erase that moment in the ballroom when I felt his hard body press against mine from my mind.

I shake it off and head over to the group of men clustered around the entrance way.

"Dzien dobry" I say as they turn to look, "Kto tu rzadzi?"

An older man steps forward with a gently smile on his face, he looks to be around his fifties.

"To bylbym ja." He says warmly.

I explain the situation, apologize for my rusty translations and future mispronunciations. He laughs so loud I almost get a fright and he smile's some more.

"Do not worry about that." he replies in Polish, as we shake hands, "It is just a joy to hear the old language spoken from a lovely female and not barked at from Aleksey."

I smile back and thank him for his kindness and then go about giving him his orders to relay to the rest of the men.

We agree he will come to me if he has any problems before Aleksey returns and he and the team go on their way.

As I smile to myself that at least I didn't offend or embarrass myself. I look up and catch Sebastian standing on the entrance steps, arms crossed over that strong chest watching me with those hawk eyes. He simply stares for a solid minute then slightly nods his head, turns his back and walks back into the building.

He really is such a confusing man but as I said earlier… progress.

The day flies by and before long its lunch, I send Shelby off with the rest of the crew to go eat as I take a refill on my coffee and head over to the Atrium to get a better look at what we are up against.

I pause just at the entrance of the door and sigh as I take in the massive loss. This room was a magnificent addition to The Montgomery back in the day. They held a masked ball for the opening. The room was gracefully decorated and the glass paneled ceiling that allowed guests to view the starry nights sky must have been truly spectacular.

I note down a few things to mention to the board about the future of the building, with the idea of an opening night masked ball to replicate the original night. It's not really part of our job however I think it always helps to give the people who are paying for such an elaborate rebuild the idea that the people who are working on their building can also see the vision for the future.

As I make a move to step further into the room a firm hand grasps around my wrist and I yelp as I am pulled back.

"This room has not been cleared yet *Mrs. Chalmers*, you shouldn't be in here." He grumbles, as he releases me and takes a few steps back.

"I was trying to get an idea of what we are dealing with." I say closing my notebook.

"What is that?" he asks as he stares at my book.

"Oh... I like to jot down some things as I work, helps keep me focused on the task and stops me forgetting things when I'm back home." I say.

"Do you normally forget things?" he asks simply.

It's so weird because he seems to be talking normally yet there is that ever-present edge to his words when he speaks to me directly.

"No not normally, but sometimes I get a feeling of an idea and I can't quite grasp it in the moment then I may be on the subway or at home and I look at my notes and it comes to me." I notice I'm rambling and he is staring very intently at me.

He looks as if he is going to say something but catches himself and changes direction.

"You didn't have much to say at this morning's meeting? Didn't feel the need to prove any points?" he questions.

"No why would I?" I ask.

"Well, every-time we've spoken you have been very clear to point out your inclusion on this project. I would have though you may feel the need to point that out again?" he says with a genuine curiosity.

"There was no need." I say simply, "Everyone here knows my position, *they* respect me." I highly emphasize the 'they'. "And honestly, there were no points to make, your targets and instructions were exactly what I would have advised myself so why try and make a contest out of who put them across, it wouldn't serve any purpose except to cause a delay."

He looks at me closely, so closely I feel myself beginning to squirm, when I hear Shelby charge down the path.

"Leona, you will never guess who has offered to send you a dress for the Van Der Bilt ball…"

She screams with excitement until she turns the corner and sees the frown beginning to take over Sebastian's face.

"Oh, sorry Seb, Mr. Van Der Bilt, I was just a little excited for Mrs. Chalmers, only Emanuel Drake has emailed and asked if she would like to come over to his Atelier to try out some dresses for your grandparents upcoming party and I got a little carried away, hope that's ok? You look a little…"

"Enough Shelby, you know how much I hate that type of nonsense and I would prefer if you kept that type of thing to your own time and not on the company's." He barks at her.

She looks a little shocked at his tone and I feel a little stunned at how she seemed to be very relaxed in her chattiness towards him, almost as if they were quite comfortable around one another and she was about to use his given name or is Seb a nickname?

Shit, have I been bitching to her and they are more than work colleague's?

"Oh yeah sorry about that, It won't happen again." she smiles and he softens his tone,

"It's ok Shell, just remember to be aware of who's around when you're talking about private or family matters in future, okay." He says and smiles warmly at her. Like actually smiles! I am about to freak the heck out.

"Now back to work, and Mrs. Chalmers please don't come back down here until it has been cleared. I'm sure I've been very specific about accidents." He pointedly looks down at my shoes and turns and storms off.

I look up from my shoes and into the very guilty looking eyes of my assistant.

FUCK!

CHAPTER 7

"Ok, so please don't freak out... it's not what you think." she starts, "I mean it's a little like what you think but definitely not totally what you think... Ok this isn't how I wanted this to go, I had it all planned out how I would tell you and now it's like... Leona are you alright?" she hurries.

"Alright? I am about the furthest thing there is from ok at this point Shelby, what in the actual hell?"

I can't help it I'm freaking out. How could she listen to me bitch and moan about someone when they obviously have some sort of relationship or whatever, I just can't even think straight.

"Look I have not betrayed your trust at all, I would never do that. Everything *we've* ever bitched about has stayed completely between us and yes, I do have, well I would not call it a relationship or even friendship really with Seb... Mr. Van Der Bilt, it's just it's complicated." She says as I look at her stunned. I don't even think I can form coherent words right now.

"Look Leona I'm gona be really honest here, you are the closest thing I've come to having any sort of friendship since I moved back here and I really don't want to screw that up, well any more than I already have, I know that probably sounds pathetic to someone like you," she frowns, "What women my age hardly has any friends right? Sad, I know but it is what it is at this point and I honestly would like to be your friend and still keep my job, if you give me the chance, I can assure you it's nowhere near as bad as you think."

She hurries it all out and I look at her, really look at

her. She is genuinely a good kind person and Jesus who am I to judge anyone, and of course her words ring a little too close to my own truth. I sigh and she smiles softly at me.

"Here's what I propose… you and I get through the rest of this day and since we are already close to the city how about we head out for some dinner or maybe a drink and I tell you all my sordid past and what the deal is with Bosman, you can listen, judge, whatever and if you still think I've let you down then I will say thanks anyway and I will ask to be moved to another department." She smirks and I have to laugh.

This quiet timid mouse of a woman has come so much out of her shell over the small time I've known her. I can see she isn't completely quiet or timid she just has a lot of baggage and likes to keep her head down, until she feels comfortable around you.

"Shelby, trust me regardless of whether you are secretly spying for the boss and feeding him all the bitchy things I say about him, or are sleeping with him and it just all comes out as some sort of twisted pillow talk let's get one thing straight, You work with me!" I say sternly, "Christ, I don't even know how I managed before you and I'm going to be honest, I don't think I've much chance of replacing you, so your stuck with me for as long as you continue to want to work with me." I smile sadly and she burst out laughing.

"Well thank the lord for that cause I really don't want to swap departments again." she grins.

"Ok, well I'm going to go sort out the temporary office as bloody Alan is literally the most unorganized person, I think I've ever seen and I'm about ready to smack him round the head with a set of blueprints if he messes up my system again." she sighs, "Just let me know at the end of the day if you fancy that drink," She holds up her hand to stop me interrupting,

"Leona it's fine if you don't, just at least think about it, I won't hold a grudge if you want to keep it strictly business, just think about it the rest of the day and know that I would never break girl code! No matter how dashing the devil is." She winks and marches off towards the cabins.

I stand there for a few moments longer to gather my wits. I think over all my bitching and snipes I've made and really there not that bad. Shelby didn't seem offended or insulted so I don't think I have too much to worry about and she did seem to care if I believed her.

I think about the promise I made to myself over the weekend that I was going to make every effort to become more sociable and Shelby has unknowingly handed me the opportunity gift wrapped.

With a nod of my head, I decide to take it, I will hear her out and then take it from there. With the decision made, I head back to work and don't have another minute to think about it again.

The rest of the day goes by in a blur, and before I know it, everyone's packing up and getting set to leave. As I head out towards the cabins I slow as I see Shelby laughing at someone out of sight but as I get closer and begin to see around the bend I take in his slightly grumpy looking demeanor as Shelby just continues to laugh him off. He must hear me approach as his head jerks sharply in my direction and he glares directly at me. As I make my way closer, I hear him mutter,

"I mean it Shell, be careful, and keep me out of your nonsense." He says gruffly as he starts to walk towards me.

I pause as he gets closer thinking maybe he has something to say about how the day went or to ask how I got on with Aleksey when he eventually arrived four hours later but nope,

"You really do have this little miss innocent deal down don't you *Mrs. Chalmers*?" he glares, "I thought it was mostly only the male or elderly population you could wrap around your little finger but it seems your conniving has no limits but let me assure you, I won't fall for it! Do not test me *Mrs. Chalmers* and do not hurt or manipulate Shelby… that girl has been through enough and she doesn't need someone like you making her think you are her friend. Taking advantage of her, Do you understand me?" He growls at me.

Wow, I mean what the heck do you say to that?

"Aw, and it was going so well, you really seemed less of an ass today but I suppose your mask had to slip at some point huh," I snipe right back, "You understand me though, I have no intention of manipulating or hurting Shelby, She's a big girl who I'm sure is capable of making her own decisions and whether you want to believe it or not I don't really give a damn, So, piss off!" I almost shout. God this guy really winds me up. I don't look back and just march over to Shelby as she is gathering her bags.

"Ready to go? I could really use a drink right now how about you?" I ask and she bursts out laughing and latches my arm with hers.

"Oh, Leona, I knew you and I were gona be friends. Drinks it is."

As we head together towards the car park, I can feel his eyes burning into the back of my head but I am so fuming I don't care.

I messaged the boys earlier today to see what their

plans were after school and practice, they both sounded far too happy when I said I was thinking of going out for a meal with a colleague after work.

I unfortunately hadn't anticipated the level of sass though, asking if it was a date and should I not come home and get changed. Little shits but when I explained it was a female colleague on a platonic dinner, they seemed fine and it made me realize just how serious they both were about thinking I was lonely. So, I tried to make an effort to convince them I wasn't a complete loser.

As we get closer to our cars Shelby spins towards me suddenly.

"Look this going to be a really awkward conversation and it's going to need a lot of alcohol. I'm talking major large glasses, how'd you feel about coming to my place, ordering takeaway and raiding my fully stocked bar?" she blurts a little nervously.

"That actually sounds great! I think I may just leave my car here and take the car service, means I don't have to worry about how much I drink. After today I think I'm inclined to join you in drowning myself in wine." I chuckle, "That sound, ok?"

"I knew I liked you." she grins.

It's not long before we are pulling into an underground parking space, below an extremely fancy and secluded tower block just on the edge of the city. The place screams money and I realize I never gave much thought that Shelby is Mr. Davies daughter. The Davies are as blue blooded as the Van Der Bilt's.

"I know it's kinda snobby but the views are spectacular and to be honest when I moved back, I needed somewhere private and my dad was a little paranoid, so here I am." she shrugs modestly.

I follow her into the elevator and watch as she types in an access code and we begin to travel upwards, Very upwards. Not quite the penthouse but damn near close.

As we step off the elevator and head into her apartment, I notice there is no other doors on this floor, Private indeed.

When I enter the apartment, I have to agree with her, the views are spectacular and I would sell a kidney to wake up to that view every day. Floor to ceiling windows surround almost two sides of the room. It's all open plan living with neutral tones allowing the view to be the main attraction. It actually reminds me of Valerie's office in the simplistic design.

"I haven't really added anything to the place yet, I'm still not sure about how long I will stay and it is really depressing shopping on your own with no-one to ask for opinions from." She says a little sadly as she walks into a door off to the side of the kitchen returning with two bottles of wine and two very large glasses.

"Yeah, I hear you," I say, "We had a flood a few months back and needed to totally redo the ensuite in my bedroom, I think I stood in the tile store for about an hour looking at samples and had a mini meltdown right there on the shop floor. I ended up with an exact replica of what I had before even though I always hated how dark the room was. Figures huh." I say and we both laugh gently.

"Red or White?" she asks.

"White for me thanks." I reply and we move into the lounge area which has a sunken floor with large cream couches facing the view and an open fire place sitting off to the side.

She pops off her shoes and motions that I should do

the same and slides her feet up onto the sofa. She undoes her hair and I breathe out a sigh as I let the weight of mine fall gently down my back. It feels great to let it loose. We sit like that for a comfortable silence just sipping our wine. I feel the need to let her know that she doesn't have to tell me anything about her past.

"Shelby, look I think I sort of understand why you and… I will use your less aggressive nickname, 'the Bosman' have a relationship and I really do not need you to tell me anything about your past that you're not comfortable with… I don't expect full disclosure before we can be friends, I think it's fairly obvious I've got my own issues and I would hate for you to judge me on them." I say.

"We do not have a relationship." She chuckles. "And I'm going to need a lot more alcohol when I tell you about why." she rolls her eyes as if she's almost embarrassed, "But I think you should know a little about why I came here which is not based on office gossip." She sighs.

She goes on to fill me in on how she was young and in love, Daddy didn't like her choice in man, they eloped, got pregnant and then he took control of every aspect of her life. They moved abroad away from her parents and friends so he could easily control her money, her movements and before long she was so beaten, broken and embarrassed that she refused to ask anyone for help.

She didn't want to risk any harm coming to her daughter so she waited until she was all set to head off to college back in the states before she started planning an escape. She convinced her ex that they would only travel back home to make sure Libby was settled in her dorms then return straight home. She swore she wouldn't contact any of her family and she didn't. She kept her word.

However, what she did do was make sure that when they settled her daughter into her dorm, they did it at the same time Sebastian was helping settle Miguel, his nephew, in at his own dorm on campus. Hoping that they would 'accidentally' bump into each other and she could pass on a message to him for her family.

As luck would have it, she did indeed bump into Sebastian, quite literally and of course him being a gentleman, I know gentleman my ass, he offered to take them all out for a meal to celebrate and Neil being cornered had no option but to accept.

I can see the details are all a little too much for her and she simply says how after that night her family and the Van Der Bilt's both helped her get away from her ex and Sebastian personally arranged her the best lawyer possible to dissolve her marriage without her losing her money and helped get a restraining order against her ex for her and her daughter.

By this point we've almost finished both bottles of wine and snacked on cheese and crackers that she pulled from somewhere. We decide to order Thai food and she goes on to tell me her embarrassing story.

"So of course, here's me, like some damaged damsel in distress thinking Seb, is my knight in shining armor." She hangs her head and when she looks back up her cheeks are bright red, "I was lonely and he kept popping by to make sure I was doing Ok, I really thought… well anyway I hit on him." She says bluntly and I almost choke on my wine.

"Yup, exactly." She grins a little more lightheartedly. "He was so nice you know? Well, obviously *you* don't know but to most people he's normally quite nice." she giggles. Bitch.

"Yeah, I don't see it." I smirk into my wine.

"Well, he really is and he was so embarrassed, he thought he'd given me the wrong impression, even said he could set me up with some nice guys who would be interested in a relationship when I was truly ready."

We both burst out laughing at that.

"I know, so embarrassing but he doesn't hold it against me and our families are really close, I kind of have to just forget how humiliating it was. We get on pretty well now to be honest. I like him but definitely not in that way and I think he sees me as another little cousin that he has to look out for." She sighs.

"Yeah, he warned me about hurting you." I say gently.

"I accept I made bad choices and my family don't completely trust my judgment too much but I am stronger now and I will make my own decisions. I think Seb's problem is more with you than it is with me to be honest."

"Yeah, I think that's a fair assessment. We didn't get off to the best of starts and he's convinced I'm out to hoodwink his family into god only knows what." I say exasperated with the man all over again.

"He has major trust issues Leona; I would never betray his confidence either however it would be remiss if I didn't give you something." She sighs.

I sit up a little further in my seat.

"Sebastian's family have been targeted by so many people setting out to take advantage of them… His father fell for a woman who almost destroyed him and Sebastian has always seen it as a massive weakness. His own dating life is absurd but I won't get into that, unfortunately he thinks you're out to exploit them all, his grandparents, his aunt, lord even the company and me at this point. He becomes completely irrational when he speaks of you and I am sorry to say I may have possibly made it worse." She frowns.

Oh dear. What does that mean?

"What do you mean, worse?" I ask.

"I sort of implied that maybe Sebastian felt something other than a blood thirsting hatred for you…" she starts grimly, "I asked him if maybe you got under his skin because he was attracted to you." She grimaces. "He became furious, how could I insinuate he would have feelings for a married woman? What the hell did I think of him? He seems to have no idea you're a widow Leona," she frowns, "How is that even possible?" she asks.

Oh my god is that why he frowns every time he says my name? Why he glares at my ring finger? It sort of makes sense in some twisted way.

"I tried to tell him but he just flew off on one. I'm not sure what he's thinking but my suggestion had the opposite effect I think and I'm sorry if it's made things worse." She groans.

"It's ok Shelby, I don't think we're ever going to see eye to eye to be honest." I say truthfully.

We continue eating and drinking for a long while after and I have to admit I missed this. I never knew just how much. Like she read my thoughts Shelby says, "Leona, I can't tell you how happy I am you asked me to work with you. I actually feel like I am contributing now and not just some spoilt brat getting in everyone's way," she grimaces, "But this right here, I missed. I always had a million friends, though I suppose, now I look back on it, they weren't really friends you know. Just people who ran in familiar circles."

I tell her how I never really had time for close girlfriends and am quietly pleased when she seems shocked. She says all the staff talk like I'm fairly popular, which does make me feel a lot more at ease.

"At least it's just my boys who think I'm a lonely loser then." I laugh.

"Oh god, please don't get me started! Libby keeps trying to download dating apps for me and telling me I really need to 'get back on the horse'. It's so disturbing." She grins.

"Well, I for one am thankful to have you as a friend and I think we can agree to making this a re-occurring date, what do you think?" I laugh.

"As long as we make it a weekend thing because honestly, I don't know how my heads going to be in the morning."

We clear up and call a car to take me home before it gets any later and I give her a big hug at the door.

"I needed this just as much as you Shelby, honestly you've been a breath of fresh air and I'm so glad we met but I agree no more work night overindulging, I'm going to have to get up an hour early to work all those extra calories off." I sigh and roll my eyes.

"Maybe we need to join a gym." She laughs.

"Oh, you were almost perfect, so close." I laugh as I head to the elevator.

"See you at the site tomorrow, Shell." I say with my shoes still in my hands and my hair hanging carelessly down and head into the elevator with a big goofy smile on my face.

CHAPTER 8

I'm still laughing as I move inside the spacious lift only to find it's not completely empty, like I first assumed.

Nope. Not only is the man of the hour standing there in an immaculately tailored dark grey suit, his hair slightly damp, as if he's just stepped from a shower looking well, quite frankly looking good enough to eat, he is not alone.

Attached to his hip and clinging on for dear life, babbling away about lord knows what, whilst looking like she wants to devour him is a woman who looks vaguely familiar. She looks like a god damn supermodel. All hollow cheekbones and puffy lips. She almost matches Sebastian in height yet somehow still manages to looks petite beside him, while her stark white hair pours sleekly down her back. He stares at me whilst paying absolutely no attention to her.

I think I'm frozen in place; I can't seem to get my feet to move as I simply stare back at him.

"Are you coming in or not? Some of us have places to go sweetie." She snips at me.

"Oh right, yes, sorry." I say as I step further inside.

I feel my face flush and am aware my hair probably looks a riot. I move to the absolute furthest away point from them and lean down to put my shoes back on as gracefully as possible and straighten up. I attempt to push my hair back from my face but I know it's no use as my clips are in my bag and I accept there is no fixing it.

I can feel his stare burning into me as I watch the

numbers slowly descend floor by floor. It feels like a lifetime between each level as I pray to just get the hell out of here as quickly as possible.

"I could have come in upstairs for a little bit Sebastian," she practically purrs and it sounds like she has a slight European accent. "I would like to be invited in just once you know." she pouts. Actually pouts.

I can see them in the reflection of the mirror and I find it hard not to smirk a little at her petulant tone. Unfortunately, just as I can see them, he can see me and my smirk does not go un-noticed. Shoot!

"Did you have a pleasant evening *Mrs. Chalmers*?" he glares, completely ignoring his date, as she begins to look back and forth between us.

I refuse to even turn around as I say, "Why yes Mr. Van Der Bilt Sir, I had a lovely evening thank you. I think me and Shelby are going to become the very best of friends." I smirk.

He actually growls, but before he gets to comment pouty perks up.

"Oh, Are you another one of Sebastian's little damsels?" she chuckle's and her beauty starts to fade.

"Excuse me?" I ask, as I turn to face her fully.

I can feel my rage start to bubble as I think of all Shelby confided tonight and to have this bimbo be so blasé about it immediately raises my hackles.

"Oh, you know," She says as she snuggles into his side with a fake giggle, "My Sebastian can't help but come to the rescue of any wronged female, he's a regular knight in shining armor. Just ask little Shelby." She sneers and I wonder to myself how I even thought she was stunning; this woman is wretched.

"Well, I don't know about you Miss…?"

"Kournikova, Melania Kournikova." she says smugly, like I should know who she is, I mean I do now but I won't show her that.

"Well Miss Kournikova, I don't know about you, but personally I admire someone like Sebastian offering his help unselfishly to someone in a difficult position and I would never disrespect another female for any circumstances she unfortunately finds herself in."

I glare at her and ignore his sharp intake of breath at my mention of his name. "And I most certainly wouldn't insult her to the man who helped, the same man that I was obviously trying to get into's pants. Seems like the wrong way to go about things if you ask me." I turn on my heel at her shocked gasp and pray we are almost at my floor before I blow my cool anymore.

Thankfully I have a little luck on my side as the doors slowly start to open on what I hope is my floor and I'm about to march straight out when I hear her exclaim,

"Are you going to let this, this *woman* speak to me like this Sebastian, seriously?" she pouts again.

I can't help it. I wish I could but it's not in my make up to just walk away, so I turn slowly on my heel and pierce her with a disgusted glare,

"You Miss Kournikova, are a disgrace to females everywhere and let me assure you… I don't give a damn who you think you are, if you ever speak disrespectfully about my friend in front of me again, I will not be so nice next time." I stare directly at her for long enough to see I'm deadly serious.

I turn my gaze towards Sebastian quite simply not caring what reaction I'm going to see there but amusement was the last emotion I would have expected.

"And you, Sir, have terrible taste in women." I snap at him. "I hope you both have an awful evening."

As I walk away, I almost freeze again when I hear what can only be described as the sexiest blunt laugh, I have ever heard. I feel it vibrate all the way through me but I force myself to keep walking straight out the building and do not stop to look back. Thankfully my car is idling by the side of the road and the driver rushes around to open the door quickly.

I am just getting settled in the car when I glance outside to see Sebastian receiving an earful of his 'date', he's still completely ignoring her and is staring directly at me.

He smirks as the car begins to pull away and I feel the heat of his stare on me.

Shit! That stare is going to haunt my dreams because unfortunately I can feel it warm me all over and I won't ever admit it but I think my panties just got a little damp. I blame the wine. Totally and completely the wine.

When I return home, I expect the boys to be in their rooms already but nope they are both sitting squarely in the living room, both angled just the right amount that they can play their games on the tv but also just enough that they can see me come in the door.

"There she is the dirty stop out!" Noah laughs.

"Hey mom how was your girls night?" Jacob smiles.

They both look at me so expectantly I almost laugh. They must truly have been worried about me and I'm not ashamed to admit I love it. It's so hard with teenagers, you feel them pulling away and becoming their own person and you just never know if you're ever going to get that closeness back. God, I hope I keep it and they don't abandon me completely. How sad is that.

"You know what guys it was actually pretty great." I say and smile.

They both grin right back at me.

"That's great mom, It's good to see you smile." Jacob says.

"Yeah, mom but I gotta be honest me and Noah, both discussed it and we think you have to pay the pot. You were out drinking on a work night and we're not sure if that's a good example. What you think… say twenty bucks?" he grins.

The pot.

They used to make me and Matt pay the pot anytime they wanted to come places that were adult only or private functions they couldn't attend. They were saving up for some new computer at the time and thought it was a good way to guilt us into adding some extra bucks to their jar. The jar hasn't been touched the last few years or so and I'm sure the boys already have that computer but I see it as progress for our family.

"You know what…" I say as I grab my purse, "You are totally right guys, and just to be on the safe side I'm gona slide a few more twenties in there just in case I start to make a habit out of this galivanting about town." I laugh.

"Wow, mom you're going wild!" Noah laughs hysterically as I grab him and give him a big squishy squeeze.

"Yeah, you guys don't know what you've unleashed now." I say as I reach over and pull Jacob into our squish-fest.

"Aw mom," he cries but secretly I think they still love it. That's what I tell myself anyway.

As I head up to bed, I stop on the stairs to look down at my two boys who are turning into mature adults in front of my eyes. I love them so much and I'm glad they don't feel just as sorry for me anymore but when I start to move on, I hear them murmur.

"God it's good to see mom smile again Jake." Noah says.

"I know man but don't push her. I know you think she needs to start dating again but I'm not so sure she's ready, not sure any of us are to be honest." He says quietly.

What the hell?

"Yeah, I hear ya man, I just want her to be happy again. It sucks seeing her just constantly working, it's like that's all she's ever done you know." he sighs.

"I know one step at a time, she's getting there. And who knows maybe her new friend will help her get back out there." Jacob says.

"Yeah, or like I said before dude, there's always an app." he laughs so loud I scramble upstairs before I get caught eavesdropping. I hear a grunt from Noah from what sounds like a pillow being thrown as I turn into my room and close the door.

What on earth was that. My boys think I'm an unhappy workaholic. And that I need to date! Or use an app. God Damn, interfering teenagers. Christ, I can't even imagine dating.

But the moment I think it, I slump down on the edge of my bed. Well, yeah actually I can. Unfortunately, the guy who stirs any form of longing in me is the same guy who can't even bear to hear me say his name.

I keep trying to convince myself that all I feel is burning rage and hatred towards the man, yet he is a barrel of contradictions that bewilders me. He protects his family fiercely, helps out people who need it, with no strings attached and seems to be a genuinely decent human being too everyone but me, sure his taste in women is severely lacking.

I mean granted, on first glance Miss Kournikova is stunning, all long limbs and waif like, but her beauty is outdone by her sheer ugliness as a person. What type of woman thinks it's ok to discuss another person's private business in front of strangers?

But what type of man dates a bitch like that? He confuses me to ne end, if only I didn't see that amused smile when I close my eyes or here that husky laugh. I can still feel how much it aroused me even now. I blame the wine and vow no more crazy drinking on a work night.

I now have to get up and go to work tomorrow and probably find some way of apologizing, without actually apologizing, to him for calling his date a bitch. I mean I'm not sure if I actually said it out loud but it was heavily implied. Maybe I can take a sickie.

I hate hangovers.

They are a cruel reminder as to why I am not a very big drinker and stick to only two glasses max. Shelby's friendship may test me in more ways in one but I really can't help but smile about it.

I'm not smiling half an hour later when I come back from my morning jog ready to puke. But as the boys said last night, I can't set a bad example, so I'm up showered and dressed when they come downstairs already on my second cup of coffee.

"Aw man, I for sure thought I'd win that." I hear Noah say as he heads over and pops a dollar in the jar.

I raise my eyebrows at them both when Jacob chuckles.

"Seriously? No way mom was gona take a sickie over one night of drinking." He laughs.

Me, I almost choke on my drink.

"Did you guys make a bet on me?" I shriek!

As they both just laugh and I realize this jar is quite literally going to stir the pot in our little home. Lord help me.

I decide to leave it be and work up the nerve to ask the boys the question I've been putting off but after our last few discussions maybe they will be up for it.

"Ok, so I have to ask you guys how you would feel about coming out of town with me for a few days to a sort of work but not work gathering?" I hedge.

I had an email from Andy and May last night asking if I thought the boys would prefer to stay close to me during the ball or if they would want to stay over in the cabins with their grandkids.

"What exactly does that mean?" Jacob asks.

I explain about the Van Der Bilt's Anniversary weekend and how they have invited us all for the weekend. I explain they have a load of teens who will be staying out on the cabins and swimming and boating on their lake and honestly the boy's couldn't look any more excited.

I also explain that although this is not technically a work function these people are still my employers so best behavior will be required at all times and they will be expected to attend the formal dinner with me. This is where the groans come. They both hate being dressed up in suit and tie but they reason with each other in front of me that it would probably be worth it to spend a weekend at the lake and stay in a mansion.

Oh god I hope these two can actually behave.

So, with that discussion out of the way I realize I've procrastinated enough and I really need to get myself to work. The car service is obscenely quick and I find myself arriving at the site perfectly on time.

Just as I arrive, I spot Shelby looking just as rough as me and almost laugh out loud at the state of us both. She is glaring furiously at her electronic device and I would hate to be the person who put that look on her face.

"Morning Shelby, I see your fairing just as well as me this morning." I chuckle and she grimaces.

"Yeah, I think I must've somehow forgot just how bad hangovers were, it's like bloody morning sickness all over again but there's no bundle of joy at the end." She groans. "And unfortunately, it looks like the day isn't going to get any better, I'm afraid." She sighs and hands me a coffee.

I thank her and ask what's going on.

"Oh, just Sebastian apparently deciding that he doesn't have to come into work this morning, 'Due to unforeseeable circumstances' I mean what the fuck does that even mean? And have you seen his list of tasks!"

I frown, has he really sent all the info directly to Shelby and bypassed me completely, Is it because of last night? Surely not, I know he was probably pissed but this is too far. I pull out my phone and check for any missed emails and yup nothing.

I sigh and look at Shelby.

"Can I see that," I ask, "Seems like I was missed in the communications." I say,

"Wait? Are you serious? He didn't copy this to you?" She asks.

"Nope, must've been an oversight." I say.

"Oversight my ass Leona, that's just a dick move!" she frowns.

"Ok can you just forward it to me and we will get started." I say as we head towards the office. I am silently fuming but hope that I hide it well enough.

I call the meeting and gather everyone around to give out the days tasks and to be fair Sebastian has detailed every item so precisely that I really don't have anything to add to it, so we just all get on with the task at hand.

The day flies by and before I know it it's time to shut down for the day. We have made great progress and even though Aleksey had been called away early in the day I managed to keep everything on track with the outdoor crew. Jakub has been a god send for following my broken Polish but it seems to be doing the job well enough and we have managed to avoid any translation mishaps. I shut everything down for the day as Shelby comes into the office.

"What a day huh." she grins.

"Yup something like that, I don't know about you but I can't wait to get home and relax in a nice hot bath." I laugh.

"Aw I thought we were going to paint the town red?" she mock frowns. "Any word from Bossman?"

"Nope, not a word." I sigh.

"You know I will back you up if you feel like you need to take this lack of co-operation to the board. I mean I like Sebastian a lot, but this is very unprofessional, and you really deserve so much more respect that this Leona." She fumes.

I love that she has my back but I'm just not ready to go snitching just yct.

"I appreciate the support, Shelby; I'm going to email him directly myself first and I will take it from there. But you're right and if it gets any worse, I will be left with no option I just hope it doesn't come to that." I say.

"Well, you're a bigger person than me, I want to kick him in the nuts the next time I see him." She laughs.

We lock up and head out to the car lot.

"Let me know how you get on and I'm here if you need to vent." She smiles and heads off to her car as I make my own way home.

CHAPTER 9

When I get home, I decide not to put it off any longer and head straight to my office and fire up the computer. I decide to keep it strictly professional and simple.

I tell him there must have been a mix-up in the communications and that I had not been included in this morning's correspondence and if he has any other notes to pass on, he can contact me directly. Otherwise, I will see him tomorrow at the site. Plain, simple and professional. I even managed to avoid adding a sarcastic Sir in.

I sit back pleased with having got it out of the way when a reply pops up almost immediately.

Mrs. Chalmers,

I was not aware that we had moved onto corresponding directly. Other than your highly illuminating resume email of course, all other contact has been sent directly through our assistants, hence the normal procedure.

However, if you are feeling over looked or undervalued then I will seek to rectify that immediately. As per this morning's correspondence, an unforeseen circumstance has arisen and I will not be back on site this week. I will email yourself, Shelby and Marc so we are all on the same page with my instructions for the weeks

progress and I should be back in the offices next week with a basic outline of the first draft.

If you have any problems, you may contact me directly or go through, Marc whichever you prefer.

Yours,

Mr S. Van Der Bilt.

Wow, I can't believe he can still be a condescending prick over email.

Yeah, no shit Sherlock I have a problem, YOU! I think as I type out a response.

Mr Van Der Bilt,

I appreciate you responding so quickly when you obviously have more important things to be dealing with at this moment however, I am more than capable of organizing the weeks itinerary so there is no need for you to over extend yourself.

I would obviously be more than happy to accommodate an appointment, around your busy schedule, where we can both work on the first draft together as per standard procedure. Just let me or Shelby know when suits you and we will coordinate a suitable time.

I will keep you informed on the progress at the site and I have attached an update from today's work. I have included a quick draft of my plans for the week, feel free to add anything you think I may have missed, Sir.

Yours,

Leona Chalmers.

TAKE THAT YOU SMUG PRICK!

I wait patiently for his response whilst hoping I haven't over stepped. He takes a while, so I head out of the office and start to get myself organized for the night. I begin to make dinner for myself and the boys and before I know it, I've completely forgot all about the darn emails.

The boys come in like a hurricane and the night goes by in a blur. I'm heading to draw myself that bath when I pass the office and notice the light from the computer still on. Shoot, I rush over to check for a response and yup it's siting there, with another one blinking right after.

I click on the 'follow' thread and read it through.

Mrs. Chalmers,

I do not appreciate the sarcasm in your tone.

I am an extremely busy man who does not have to babysit a project site, hence the reason we only hire the most competent workers.

You Mrs. Chalmers continually claim to be one of these workers so please keep your personal opinions to yourself in future. It is unprofessional and beneath us both.

Your outline for the week is adequate and I will be in touch if I feel anything needs to be added. As for scheduling a 'drafting' session I prefer working alone, as I said I will keep you informed.

Yours,

Mr S. Van Der Bilt.

I click the next email he has attached.

Mrs. Chalmers,

It has been over two hours since your last response and I assume you have realized your level of unprofessionalism but pleased be assured I will not hold it against you. In fact, I will be happy to send you a copy of the first draft as soon as its complete and of course feel free to highlight anything you may feel necessary.

Also, I would like the situation with Aleksey to be dealt with quickly, if he cannot show up at work on time, please find someone who can. I will not tolerate unreliability. We do not know how long your translations will hold up as we progress through the development.

Yours,
Mr S. Van Der Bilt.

Oh, the god damn cheek of the man! Well, there is no way I am taking that!

I begin typing furiously at my keyboard and ranting along to myself.

I really shouldn't let him goad me and I really shouldn't press send. Not when I check the time and notice its well after 11pm or when I read through the reply but should've, would've, could've aren't really my thing and off it goes.

Mr Van Der Bilt,

With all due respect, the only person who has been unprofessional since the day I had the unpleasantness of our meeting, is you Sir. You have quite simply been rude, disrespectful, condescending and patronizing and I do not take kindly to it. I have given you every opportunity to work together on this but you are making it difficult at every turn.

So, I will be very clear with you, I am not one of your minions to order around at your beck and call. I am as much a lead designer on this project as you are and I will forward *you* a copy of *my* first draft which *you* can feel free to inspect.

I will run my site how I see fit and if you have a problem with that then you can show up in person like the god damn rest of us.

Do not waste your time replying to this email, as unlike some people, I actually have a life outside of the office and my office hours have well past. If you have anything useful to add you may contact me during working hours otherwise,
with all due respect...
PISS OFF, SIR!
Yours,
Mrs Chalmers.

ARGH! WHAT AN ARROGANT PRICK.

I should be worried about my job however I noticed earlier he responded from what looks like a personal email and not his work assigned one, even though it would be completely irrelevant if he brings it forward, I can't seem to bring myself to care. I force myself to log off and shut my computer down completely, then lock my office door. No temptation for me.

I try my hardest to unwind and run myself a bath, but I can't seem to relax, stubborn prick, I feel like I am lying here stewing in my own fury.

Who the hell does he think he even is? I refuse to back down or be walked over. He is making it harder than it has to be and of course his bloody instructions perfectly mirror my own, it's like he copied and pasted straight from my hand book.

"Unprofessional and beneath us both."

What an ass! I can't believe he is spouting that crap, What because I insulted that bimbo? Surely, he didn't think it was acceptable for her to run off at the mouth about Shelby? And how many other people has he helped? It makes no sense; he makes no sense.

But that amused look on his face, I know I saw it, there's no way I could have imagined it. Darn thing still haunts me. Was it because I insulted his taste in women? He laughed at that; he did not seem offended at all. I just don't get the man, but lord if only he wasn't such a huge prick because that damn laugh and smile plays on repeat in my damn head. It still brings out shivers. Nope that's the cold bath water. Yup I'm out of here.

I force myself to walk straight past the office and refuse point blank to check my emails. I will not engage but as I lay alone in bed, I can't help but think of him. He brings out a side of me that I'm not entirely uncomfortable with, he sparks a passion in me that I thought had long been smothered.

Maybe I should think about getting back out there, but the thought itself makes me feel ill. Sure, it would be great not to spend every night all night alone in this big bed but when I think of spending it with another man only one smirking face comes to mind and it just pisses me off. Why couldn't I feel a bit of lust for anyone else? Why does it have to be the single last man on earth that I could possibly act on, maybe it's my subconscious telling me I'm not ready.

After a fitful night's sleep, I'm up run complete, showered dressed and on my second cup of coffee before I open my laptop and scan my emails. I just know there is going to be snarky condescending reply or I could be lucky and it could just be a termination letter.

At this point I'm not sure what I'd prefer! But of course, it's neither which feels worse, so much worse. There is no reply period. No snark, no outburst of authority, not even a simple 'You're fired' nothing!

Which, if I'm completely honest, makes me very uneasy. I sit for a full twenty minutes just watching and waiting. When the boys come barreling downstairs, they look shocked to see me still sitting there starting in to space.

"Sorry mom, we know we're late." Jacob says as he hauls things out the fridge.

"Why are you still here mom?" Noah pauses as he grabs the clean sports kits from the counter.

"SHIT!" I say as I scramble about throwing my laptop in by bag, I must have been dallying for longer than I realized and if I don't move sharp, I'm going to be late.

"MOM!" they both screech. "Dollar in the jar!" they both laugh.

I spin and throw them both a death glare.

"I don't know who's idea it was to bring that damn jar back but we're gona need a new one before bloody Christmas at this rate!"

I slide a couple dollars in the jar, kiss them both on the heads and sprint out the door and put the boot down on my car desperately trying to shave a few minutes off the journey. I'm still well within the speed limit but I normally take a leisurely drive in, enjoying the scenery.

Of course, my life completely sucks, as when I look like I'm almost about to make it on time I see the reflections of blue lights behind me and I cannot believe that I am being pulled over by a god damn cop. What the hell did I do in my last life to deserve this type of shit. I better come back next time as the god damn queen or bloody billionaire heiress.

I slowly pull over to the side of the road and shut off the car. I gather my license and registration from the glovebox and wait, I would say patiently but my hand tapping repeatedly on the steering wheel would be a dead giveaway of how pissed off I'm becoming with this day already.

"Morning Ma'am, Do you know why I asked you to pull over today?" he asks and I force myself not to roll my eyes. I mean if I knew that I would have simply not done anything which would cause me to be pulled over, obviously.

I look up at him and have to keep looking up, he's extremely tall and a lot younger than I would have expected to match the gravelly voice. Wow, he's actually very handsome, all sandy blonde hair and blue eyes.

I look around to see if I am actually being Punked, this guy looks like a surfer or stripper masquerading as a police officer. I realize I am simply staring at him when he smiles showing off a perfect white smile.

"Ma'am, Are you ok?" he asks.

"Sorry, yes, yes I just, hmm, you don't look like a police officer." I mentally slap myself as he laughs loudly.

"Yeah, I get that a lot." He rubs at the back of his neck and smiles brightly, "But I can assure you I am a fully qualified member of the Sheriff's department Ma'am and I am going to need to see your license and registration."

I fumble with my documents and he laughs again, it's so pure and unfiltered, so unlike he who shan't be bloody named. Shit. Why the hell did he pop into my mind! Damn Satan!

"No rush, Ma'am, Thanks." He says as he reaches over and takes a look at them.

"So, any ideas why I pulled you over?" he asks again.

"Er you wanted to comment on my fabulous driving skills?" I muse.

He laughs again and I am amazed at how many times he's done that in the past few minutes.

"Well, that's not really part of the job description and I'm not so sure that people would appreciate being pulled over just for me to congratulate them on their driving skills." He grins.

"Well, I'm sure no-one would mind if *you* pulled them over... Aw shoot that sounded way more inappropriate out loud." I actually slap my head this time.

He barks out laughing and grins so much I feel a little less like a moron.

"Well, I appreciate the sentiment ma'am, my day would be a helluva lot more enjoyable if I got to pull over pretty ladies for compliments every day." he smiles.

Wow is he flirting? I can't tell, I don't even know anymore.

I'm so flustered I have no response. I just keep smiling like a total goon.

"I just have to run these details a minute and make sure you're not a fugitive on the run, you good to sit tight another few minutes?" he asks.

"Sure, yeah that's fine… eh can I send a quick txt to let my office know I'm running late?"

"Yeah, no problem." he smiles, "Be back in a sec."

I send a quick txt to Shelby telling her I've been held up and I will be in as soon possible.

I watch as he strolls back toward the car and note just how handsome he is, I thought he was all lanky tall but he has some muscle going on under that blue suit and that smile is devastatingly hot. Like panty soaking hot combined with the damn uniform and cuffs.

Oh my god I am not right in the head. Maybe it's like early menopause or something! My hormones are way out of whack.

"So, you have no outstanding warrants or fines Mrs. Chalmers but you do have a break light out, you also took that last turn rather quickly but I'm guessing you were pretty close to the speed limit so I'm just gona over look that one since your record is impeccably clean." he smiles, "But you need to get that light fixed immediately. Is that something you can do on your own or can you have your husband do it right away?"

he smiles easily.

"Eh no, sorry no husband, I'm a widow." I say simply.

"I'm sorry to hear that, Ma'am. My sincerest condolences. Did you lose your husband recently?" he asks.

"Oh, a few years now." I reply.

"Still, I'm sorry for you loss." He says.

"Thanks."

"So about changing that bulb, Boyfriend maybe?" he grins. "Or am I barking up the wrong tree altogether?"

Shit! He is totally flirting and he is like hot! Smoking hot! And cute and funny.

"Erm, thanks and no not the wrong tree, no boyfriend." I smile and definitely blush.

"Ok, so how about I fulfil my civic duty and I offer to switch that brake light over for you and instead of writing you an immediate ticket, I maybe write my phone number instead. Or if you prefer, you can switch it over yourself and drop by the station and I can verify it for you." He smiles.

"Wow you would do that? I'm not gona lie and pretend to be some sort of raging feminist, I mean I'm sure I could google it and work it out but I am already super late for work and I have no idea whether the garage will be able to fit me in and… and now I'm rambling." I cringe.

"So can I ask if you are totally not getting that I'm subtly trying to give you my number and ask you out or are you maybe just interested in me helping you out with your car and sending you on your way?" He says it so casually, "I promise I won't take offence if you knock me back, I mean sure I will be devastated and I will cry into my beer tonight about the one that got away but I won't hold it against you." He grins.

"Well, I have to be honest with you Officer…" I peer at his badge, "Marks, I don't date, I haven't flirted in god over maybe eighteen years and I have no idea how this all works now or if I am even ready to try dating yet and I would hate to lead you on. You seem young and carefree and I have a lot of baggage." I rush out.

"Well, here's the thing I used to work at Dallas International before I became a cop and I just so happened to be a baggage handler, so technically, I'm an expert with baggage and I'm not asking you to marry me." he grins, "Just maybe let me fix your car, swap numbers, maybe go out for a nice steak meal and get to know each other a little bit." he grins, "That sound like something that would appeal to you?" he asks.

You appeal! Like totally, I think to myself.

"Well, when you put it like that, it sounds really simple, huh." I grin.

"Ok, so where are you heading to right now?" he asks throwing me for a loop.

"I'm actually working just round the corner at old The Montgomery building." I reply.

"Are you going to be there all day?"

"Yeah, I'm probably going to be there working overtime now since I am so late." I laugh.

"Gotcha, how's this sound for a plan. I follow you to the site so you don't cause any accidents with that broken tale light, I need to take off but if you promise not to drive the car again until its sorted, I will pop round on my lunch or at the end of my shift, switch over the bulbs then switch over our numbers." He wiggles his brows, "And then you can decide whether to answer when I text you later that night to ask you out. Sound good?" he smiles.

"I mean again you make it all sounds so simple." I laugh.

"You know sometimes it really is just that simple." He laughs.

"Yeah thanks, that actually sounds good." I smile.

"Great, ok I'm gona pop back in my car and I will just follow you but no speeding or fleeing the scene of the crime, I'd hate to have to arrest you before I get your number." He grins.

"Ok, thanks." I say and he hands me my documents back and off he goes to his cop car. I watch him get inside and fire up the engine. He gives me a cheery wave and I pull away and head the whole five minutes to the site. I keep to well below the speed limit and force myself to stop staring in my rearview mirror to just keep looking at him. It's hard but I think I pull it off.

CHAPTER 10

I turn into the parking lot and pull into my space. I grab my messenger bag of the seat and get out the car. Officer Marks has pulled up beside me and I smile down at him.

"Wow, you are even more stunning in full size." He chuckles and I laugh along.

"Well, thank you very much Officer Marks, I really appreciate you letting me off with this and being so helpful." I say.

"All part of the service ma'am," he grins, "Maybe when I come back to fix the car you could just call me by my name, I mean I love the whole 'officer' thing you have got going on but since you are just venturing back into dating it may be a bit of a bold request." He grins sexily and I can't help myself, I burst out laughing.

"You are going to be trouble Officer Marks." I smile.

"Just Jackson is fine." He grins. I grin back and I've got to be honest my cheeks actually hurt from smiling as much as I have. I need to get pulled over by hunky cops more often.

"Ok, just Jackson, I do really have to get to work, I am so late." I grimace.

"Can I trust you not to flee with those keys then?" he asks.

"Impeccable record, remember." I smirk and turn on my heels and begin power walking towards the office cabin.

"So can I call you by your first name now or we

sticking to Mrs. Chalmers?" he says at a loud enough decibel I look around and laugh.

"For now, Officer Marks." I smile.

"Got it, see you soon." He smiles and drives off. I pause only for a second to watch him go and turn with a huge smile on my face that drops immediately.

"Are you fucking kidding me?"

Sebastian is blocking the path to the office door, arms crossed over his chest, looking like he just rose up from the depths of hell, rage glowering and a look of absolute disgust spread all over his face.

"Excuse me?" I say. I am shocked still that he is here, after his last reply saying he would be out all week, I did not expect to see him up close and personal so soon.

"You *MRS. Chalmers* are the biggest hypocrite I ever have had the displeasure of meeting. You cast all sorts of accusations in everyone else's direction yet you are the biggest fraud around. You call me out for my unprofessionalism, telling me to be here on site to do my job, then you have the audacity to show up yourself the very next day, hours late with a man, who is very obviously not your damn husband, unless you two are into some sort of kinky stranger role play shit, which again proves your total unprofessionalism." He spews, "Keep your sexual affairs, whether extra marital or not away from my place of business. I do not need you on this project and if it was up to me, I would have you forceable removed altogether but alas you and your bewitching skills have convinced every damn male around that you are some sort of god damn martyr. I have had enough of it, stay the hell away from me on this project *Mrs. Chalmers*, I mean it. Do your god damn job but stay as far from me as possible." He snaps, storming off, leaving me standing there, stunned in to silence.

I mean there are no words! I know he has insulted me on every level, he just insinuated that not only am I some sort of whore who would betray her marriage vows but that I am unworthy of my position in the firm. And to be honest, I don't know what pisses me off more.

Right now, I can't even think, I just need to get to work. He was right about one thing I did pull him on not being there to oversee the project then continued to do the same. I won't give him the opportunity to cast that stone again. I draw in a deep breath and head into the office, I saw the blinds twitch, so I am under no illusions the gossip spreading around the cabin, but regardless of what that dick may say, I can put on a professional face.

I step inside and apologize immediately to everyone, I explain the drama with the break light and everyone is immediately sympathetic. Bryce huffs if he got pulled over, he would never have got away so easy but Dave says that's because he has more driving offences than the whole cabin combined.

Everyone laughs and gets back to work as Shelby rushes over with a large thermos of coffee and ask me if I would be ok to pop over to get a look at the Atrium now it's been cleared. She says Aleksey's men are over there waiting their orders now they've finished out front.

"Aleksey just got a call from his wife that she had to head over to the hospital again, complications with the pregnancy, Mr. Van Der Bilt sent him away to deal with it and he came asking were you were. I would have made up an excuse for you but he asked Bryce before I could get to him." She grimaces.

Of course, that would be the case,

"It's fine Shelby, I don't want you to lie for me, people are late all the time, these things happen." I remark, "Mr. Van Der Bilt is just looking for excuses, don't worry about it."

"I don't even know why he's here today." She frowns, "May, his Grandma took a bit of a bad turn and that's why he couldn't make it in yesterday, he was over at the house, I thought for sure he would be gone all week."

"Shoot, is May, ok?" I ask.

"Oh, Leona sorry I forgot you guys are friends! Yeah, she's fine sometimes they have to switch her meds and they make her a bit week or sickly. They all get a bit worried over her, she's the patriarch you know. She holds them all together. Apparently, Sebastian threw a fit when they refused to cancel the Anniversary weekend. And The Mandarin contract is running over his own schedule which would be fine for anyone else but not the Bossman, he always sets his own timeline and works mostly alone or with Anderson so he's pulling double the work on that one. So, I guess he was already in a foul mood." She says sympathetically.

"Well, as long as May's doing ok, I will give them a little call later to check in. I agree though he probably shouldn't be here." I muse mostly to myself because unfortunately guilt is settling in and I know I'm the one who's responsible for making him feel like he had to be here. And he's the lead on the Mandarin contract. That is a huge development on its own! Now I'm going to have to suck it up and apologize.

We reach the Atrium and look around for Aleksey's

team but no-one seems to be here. Shelby shrugs and we head inside. The place is buzzing with bodies all working away and I spot one of the younger guys who always hangs around Jakub and I call him over.

"Dimitri, gdzie jest Jakub?" I ask.

He smiles and tells me Jakub left with Mr. Van Der Bilt to look at the main ballroom.

I ask him if Aleksey is back from the hospital and he replies no.

"So, who is translating for Mr. Van Der Bilt?" I frown surely, he's not wandering about making hand gestures for Jakub I sigh.

"Mr. Van Der Bilt needs no translator," he laughs, "He speaks perfect Polish… Just maybe not as nicely as you Mrs. Chalmers." he grins.

"Of course, he does." I say mostly to myself. I double check everyone knows what they are doing and head on out of their way.

I tell Shelby to head back to the cabin and get on with her own work, I'm just going to a walk around the outside and double check a few measurements and stuff but really, I just need a few minutes to compose myself.

My mind is full of a million different thoughts and feelings, colliding and collapsing around me and I know I have to pull my shit together. I am big girl and I know when I am out of line. Sure, Sebastian has crossed way too many himself but if I look at everything objectively I can kind of see why. I do not agree with his assumptions or lurid suggestions but I can see how it would look like that to him.

I start to pop my notebook away deciding I need to get this over with quickly, but as I move to head in the direction of the main ballroom, I collide directly with the man himself.

"Oh darn! Sorry." I say as I lean down and begin scooping up all the junk that's came crashing down from my bag.

I hear him lower down beside me and start snatching things up as well.

"To bedzie wszystko Jakub, dziekuje." he says in perfect Polish.

I look up and catch his eye expecting some sort of smirk or glare, instead he just looks tired.

I smile at him and give Jakub a quick wave as he wanders off.

"It's ok, I can get it all, thanks though." I say as he starts to move away. We were far too close to eye level and he turns away sharply, his hand reaches out and grabs hold of my notebook which has flipped open showing all my scribbles and doodles. He straightens up to his full height as he holds on to my book steadily staring down at it.

I stand upright shoving everything back in my bag.

He is now flicking threw my book as if he's completely forgot I'm even there. I don't normally mind showing people anything I've jotted down but somehow this feels a little different.

I hold my hand out and cough gently.

He snaps his eyes to mine and blinks.

"My notebook?" I say.

"Oh, here." He hands me it and I very carefully take it from him making sure not to touch a single part of his hand and squeeze it into my bag.

He attempts to turn on his heel and I reach out to stop him but pull my hand back sharply. He sees and he raises that damn eyebrow at me.

"Mr. Van Der Bilt Sir, I owe you an apology." I say

getting it out as quickly as possible.

He pauses and I can see his whole-body freeze. His posture is completely rigid as he turns to look at me, I can see that heat travelling back into his eyes.

"I beg your pardon?" he says staring me directly in the eyes. No flinching, just deeply penetrating as if he is looking for my god damn soul. Satan himself I tell you.

"You heard me clearly enough the first-time sir…" I say softening my tone, "I think it is completely obvious that you and I will never be able to work together amicably on any project and I will contact Valerie and the partners today and put in a request that we are never paired up on any development again in the future. I will make it clear that it's nothing personal,"

Yeah, I smirk a little. I'm not that much of a walkover, "I will inform them we are too far apart creatively and it simply wouldn't be productive for business." I pause to give him time to mull this over. He just keeps staring at me like I've grown an extra head. "But we are going to have to come to some sort of understanding for the immediate future because I am not leaving this project. I worked hard to get it and I want to be involved."

"That does not sound like an apology *Mrs. Chalmers.*" he says.

"No, you're right, it doesn't. I just want you to be aware of where we stand." I pause and take a breath. I've got this, I can do it without being snarky. "I am sorry though Mr. Van Der Bilt." I say looking him directly in the eye. "I was wrong to call you out for not showing up the other day, I should not have contacted you and bitched you out over it and I should not have made you feel anything but comfortable with leaving the site for a few days to look after your family. That was incredibly unprofessional of me and if I am honest, I should not have engaged in… excuse the language… a pissing contest with you."

He just continues to stare. I don't think he is even blinking.

"I had no idea the caseload you are working on and I certainly did not know your Grandmother was feeling poorly. Had I known I would have made sure you were well aware the site was in capable hands however I felt the need to prove myself in completely the wrong way and for that, I am sorry and I assure you it will not happen again."

He says nothing so of course I keep rambling on. "As for this morning's incident," I begin and I see him flinch. Just a fraction but it's there just the same. "I was already running late but would have made it perfectly on time had I not been pulled over for a broken tail light. Now you and I both know these things happen and had I been any other member of staff it would have been a non-issue however this…" I wave my hand back and forth between us, "Animosity, between us is creating a toxic work environment for everyone. I do not wish for anyone to be uncomfortable at their work Mr. Van Der Bilt sir and this morning you cast very inappropriate remarks about my personal life which I will not tolerate or dignify with an explanation to satisfy your opinion of me." Yeah, ok, that sounds a little snarky.

He doesn't move a muscle, all bar that slight tightening in his jaw.

"Suffice to say we need to move on from this. Our plans and schedules for this project line up the same and I see no reason why we need to keep this tension going. As far as I can tell everything you have sent me or vice versa are almost carbon copies so I see no reason why you should feel the need to stay on site if your time could be better served elsewhere. I will keep you thoroughly updated and of course you are more than welcome to come and go as you please. Just know that I am extremely competent in my job and you really will have nothing to worry about."

He says not a word for a whole minute and just when I'm getting ready to lose my patience which he can obviously tell if my tapping foot is anything to go by, he says,

"Well now, *Mrs. Chalmers* that is mighty generous of you. Allowing me too '*feel free to drop by*' my own site." He says as he tilts his head slightly, almost sarcastically.

"You know exactly what I mean." I huff. "Look I am trying really hard to be the bigger person here." I snap.

"Oh, I can see that." He goads.

I am about to lose my cool, I can feel it.

"Ah there she is…" he grins, "The real *Mrs. Chalmers*, the one who thinks It's ok to comment on other people's personal life but doesn't like it when it comes back around." He smirks.

I knew he was bloody mad about that!

"You know fine well that was a completely different circumstance." I grit out.

"Oh, how so?" he asks as he folds his arms over in front of his chest.

How so!

"Are you serious? That was completely different, firstly it was well out of working hours, nowhere near work and to be perfectly honest Sir, I meant every word. Your girlfriend is a stuck up snooty self-absorbed bitch and she deserved every last word and if that is the type of person you choose to spend your time with then my original assumption stands… Your taste in women sucks."

I heave a breath. I am actually fuming. I can feel myself becoming more infuriated by the second and when he shoots that smug smirk at me all I can think about is slapping it right off his far too handsome face.

"Well, that *Mrs. Chalmers* has to be the worst possible apology I have ever heard in my life." He says and grins.

Lord give me strength. I am trying my best to formulate the right words and am gritting my teeth so hard I think I may need a dental appointment after this but no he's not finished he carries on, that shit eating grin slightly lingering in place.

"But I guess you did extend the olive branch and it's obvious your own taste in men is just as appalling considering you are hoodwinking some poor oblivious sap into believing you're that innocent mild-mannered female you spun a little earlier."

Oh dear, I'm gona smack him, like actually punch him straight in that perfect face and smash his teeth in, who the hell does he think he is?

"You…"

"Now *Mrs. Chalmer's* let's not say anything else you may regret today; you unfortunately are right on a few things. You were completely unprofessional in your handling of the situation however we do have to come to some semblance of a working…" he pauses as if the word makes him sick, "relationship, It seems neither of us is going anywhere on this project, no matter how much I pray for it, so we have reached a stalemate." he sighs.

I quietly stare, unflinchingly. My toe is tapping furiously and I am clenching my jaw too damn tight but I am honestly afraid for his safety at the moment so I carry on.

"Could you unclench slightly *Mrs. Chalmers* and calm that toe tapping it's not helping the situation." He groans. Dick! "I actually have no choice but to defer the project over to you at this point," he says and my toe tapping stops immediately,

"Yeah, I thought that would get your attention," he gently grins and it transforms his whole face. "An unexpected issue has come up at another development and I was loathed to travel to Singapore but it looks unavoidable at this point. I am putting it off as long as I can what with May…" he catches himself. And I nod in simple recognition.

He glares slightly, as if irritated at himself,

"Anyway, I'm going to try and rectify as much as I can from here but I won't be able to 'babysit' this site and although this may come as a shock to you, I have looked over your resume and your notes do coincide incredibly similar to my own." he pauses as he says this, as if he is trying to work out if I somehow hacked his computer or bloody brain to have come up with it.

"I will only be a phone call or email away and we are both well aware you are more than capable of contacting me should the need arise."

Wow, I mean just wow. What the heck am I supposed to say to that?

"Well, that Mr. Van Der Bilt Sir, was one of the worst compliments I have ever heard." I smirk slightly at him, "But I appreciate it all the same." I carry on quickly before we descend to insults again.

"Yes, well let's just try and make it through this

development and agree to never work together again huh." He says and I sigh.

"Sure, sounds like a plan." I agree.

"Ok *Mrs. Chalmers*, I expect a report at the end of every day outlining the days progress etc. and let me know if Aleksey has any more problems. I can bring in another interpreter to cover his space." He says brusquely.

"I think we will be fine for the moment but I agree there may be occasions one of us may not be here to interpret and I would hate for there to be a delay so I will monitor it for now if that seems acceptable?" I ask.

"That is fine Mrs. Chalmers." he says plainly.

He looks so tired I want to reach up my hand and soothe the lines creasing his forehead right at that moment and I startle myself.

Shit, Where did that come from?

"If you don't mind me saying so, you look a little tired, maybe you could think about heading home now, Not that I'm trying to get rid of you but you must be exhausted." I say softly.

He just stares at me as I carry on,

"How is May doing?" I ask gently. But of course, I've pushed him too far again. Broken that tender line we had just stretched.

"My family is my concern only *Mrs. Chalmers,* not yours and I would appreciate if you keep things completely work related when you deal with me in future." He glares although even that is slightly tired. So, I lower my head slightly.

"Yes Sir, I apologize for crossing the line, It won't happen again." I say.

He looks like he wants to say more but instead he

just turns on his heel and starts to walk away.

"I want those daily reports in my inbox 7pm sharp *Mrs. Chalmers*." he says.

I am about to reply 'YES SIR' when he adds,

"Let's try to avoid any more name calling or cuss words in them, they are still on the company record you know." He grins, I can hear it in his voice even though I can't see it.

I add a little more sass and salute his back with a,

"Yes Sir." I'm about to turn away when I hear a low noise almost like a laugh when I look up, I catch my reflection in the glass windows and I groan when I see him grinning slightly back at me. Yup completely caught again. Fuck my life.

CHAPTER 11

The day flies by and I don't see the 'Bossman' anywhere so I assume he has left the site which gives me both a sigh of relief but also a slightly uncomfortable sense of loss.

He makes me feel almost every emotion in the blink of an eye and it's infuriating. I am still so pissed off at him however I think we made a good amount of progress today. I get that he doesn't want to mix work with his family and I can respect his boundaries. Hopefully this will be the beginning of a less toxic environment for everyone and whether he knows it or not, I understand how difficult it is to hand over the reins on such a big project, so I appreciate the restraint on his part and the complement to my work did not go unnoticed.

I am so preoccupied with thoughts of him and work that I completely lose track of time and totally forget that Officer Marks is due to return. I have no idea how I feel about that situation at all! It all seemed so easy at the time and I do need to get my car fixed so I reason with myself that I'm not doing anything wrong and yet it sort of feels like I am.

The office is starting to empty out and I vow to work on a little longer to make up for my lateness. I'm working through some design ideas when Shelby comes rushes into the cabin.

"Leona, there is a police officer outside asking for you and I think I need to hide in the storage cupboard for the rest of my life!" she groans.

"What? Why?" I laugh.

"Oh, I don't know what the hell is wrong with me! I saw him coming over to the cabin, I never noticed the cop car! I swear!" she sighs her face getting redder by the second.

"Oh my god, what did you do?" I ask.

"Well, I don't know about you but I have never in my life seen an actual police officer who looks like that, like he's some sort of surfing stripper! Never Leona and I lived in LA for two years." She cries.

"Oh no, you didn't?" I try my hardest not to laugh I really do.

"Oh yeah, I did. I asked him straight out if someone thought it would be funny to hire a hot stripper for you and that today probably wasn't the best day to come over but I could assure him that he would be very much appreciated any other day." She sobs her head in her hands, and I can't help it I break and burst out laughing.

"I'm sorry." I say, "Truly, I am but that's hilarious."

"No, Leona it really is not. He just smiled at me, showing a perfectly white smile and laughed this kind of deep, hot sexy laugh that made my underwear uncomfortable. My fucking underwear Leona, It's not been a smidge damp in the last god damn decade, dry as a bloody desert and one smile and laugh from that real god damn police officer and I'm soaked and so bloody embarrassed!" she wails.

Thank god the office is empty I'm thinking just as we both hear a subtle cough. She freezes and looks up at me through terror filled eyes.

"No, please tell me he is not standing right behind me? My day couldn't possibly be that kind of awful, surely?" she says pleadingly.

"Eh, Well…" I start, I have no idea what to say but.

"You know as crazy as it sounds this has happened to me before Ma'am and I can assure you this is a pleasant experience compared to most of them. Normally by now I have been felt up, hit on, asked if I offer private dances. One time, I even had a hundred-dollar bill thrust down my pants, so please don't worry about it." He smiles softly and I can see he is trying so hard to ease her discomfort.

She still looks mortified but she's trying to bluff her way through it and I've got to give her props.

"Oh well, if I had known that, I would have found my purse." She smirks.

Officer Marks lets out a full hearty laugh and I see her startle a little. Yeah, he is a lot to take in.

"Well, again Officer I apologize for the confusion and I will leave you both to get on with your business. Leona, I think I will I head out if you don't need anything else?" she pauses and I nod. "Dan and some of the boys are still outside, so just holler if you need anything."

"That's great Shell thanks, I will call you later, kay." I say.

"Yeah, ok that's great thanks." She looks at Officer Marks and he gives her a look right back.

"Again sorry." She says and smiles gently as she begins to leave.

"No apology necessary ma'am, It was a pleasure meeting you." he smiles.

Shelby stares for a second then rushes out the door. He stares after her a good minute and I give a false little cough of my own and when he turns to face me, we are both smiling huge cheesy grins.

"Well, I could've sworn you said you worked at a building site Mrs. Chalmers not some beautiful woman's secret lair." he chuckles.

"And I was worried about how to deal with you earlier, now at least I can see you are just a total player." I say with a huge grin.

"Who me?" he mocks, "No way, I was just doing my civic duty and trying to make that lovely lady feel a little less embarrassed. But if you're getting jealous already, I may need to cut and run. Sorry." He laughs.

"Yeah, yeah, I believe you." I smile. "Ok, so I have just realized you never told me to pick up a new bulb and I honestly have no clue if there is a spare in the car." I say.

"Well, luckily for you… I was also a boy scout. So, I always come prepared." He says and wiggles his eyebrows as he holds up a little bag with, I am assuming a new bulb in.

Oh man this guy is something else, I laugh.

"Ok then Officer Marks, let's go." I grin as I shut my computer down.

He leads the way outside and we head over to my car. I have no clue where to even begin but he is way ahead of me. He asks for my keys and sets about pulling some sort of tools from another bag and goes about changing the bulb over.

He comments I really should be paying more attention to what he's actually doing rather than just ogling him like he's a piece of meat and I can't help but laugh at his foolishness, even though I was doing just that. I mutter he really only has himself to blame, what man that looks like him decides to become a cop?

"Well, I really wanted to be a fireman but when they said I had to run into burning buildings, I figured a cop uniform was just as sexy and probably a lot less dangerous, so cop it is." He grins.

"Ah so it was all just for the uniform?"

"Well yeah… The strip club said I couldn't keep theirs, so I had to go get my own." He smirks and I can't help but chuckle.

He seems to have the whole package. He is kind, funny, handy, smart, super-hot, like full on panty soaking nipple tightening hot but somethings missing, some spark or heat. I'm not sure, it's just too comfortable, friendly but I push it aside maybe this is a good place to start.

"All done." He smiles as he stands up and starts putting everything away in a bag.

"Wow, that was quick." I remark and he lowers his head.

"Aw gorgeous, your killing me! You know you are never ever meant to say that to a man! Like ever, for no reason, is it ever acceptable." He places his hands on his heart like I've wounded him and I almost wet myself with laughter.

"You Officer Marks are quite frankly the biggest flirt I have ever met." I laugh. "What do I owe you?" I say as I lean over to grab my purse.

"Wow you are nuts; you can't seriously think I'm going to charge you?" he laughs.

"Well, I have to at least pay you for the new bulb." I say.

"Oh no, then you will ruin my big plan." He grins.

"Oh lord, what big plan?" I'm almost scared to ask.

"Well, Mrs. Chalmers the way I see it, you now kind of owe me one." He teases. "So, I was thinking we trade numbers and when I call you, you agree to have a drink with me and here's the masterstroke… You pay." He smirks.

"Wow, is that how the playboys do it nowadays?"

My actual face hurts from grinning.

"Well, I have no idea what you mean but I just think it's a fair trade and I'm all about equal opportunities you know." he smiles, "But if you're not so inclined, I suppose I could always badger you to pass on my number to your friend." He taunts.

I can't help it; I laugh out so loud I see a few of the crews heads turn and smile and I feel myself blush.

"God you are insatiable." I grin.

I take a minute to just stare at him closely and I can see he knows I'm measuring up my next words carefully.

"Look, I'll be really honest with you, I get the sense that you've got a busy schedule, we've established you have 'baggage' and you haven't dated in a while. Me, I don't really have any intentions of settling down any time soon and am happy spending time with a beautiful lady and seeing how it goes. I am a one-woman man… well unless you beg for your friend to join us, then I mean I could possibly be persuaded." He pauses and I raise my eyebrows, "Worth a try." He laughs, "But seriously this doesn't have to be a big deal. Two adults, maybe a couple of nice nights, dinner, drinks, I might even let you see some of my ex-stripper moves." He wiggles his brows and I laugh. He makes it sound so easy.

"You make it sound so easy." I say aloud.

"It kind of is, but only if you're comfortable. The bulb thing, all part of the job ma'am, you really wouldn't owe me anything. We can part ways and I promise I won't make up an excuse to pull you over." he smiles.

I take a deep breath and say, "Ok."

"Ok?" he grins. "Yeah?"

"Don't sound so surprised, your very persuasive but I'm just going to tell you right now I may not answer. I might chicken out." I say being honest.

"Well, as long as you send me your friends number that's cool too." He laughs.

"Ha, Ha, don't push it." I say.

He laughs loudly and we begin to exchange contacts but I pause and look around, I have the weird feeling of being watched. I don't see anyone but the feeling stays.

"Ok, I actually have to get back to work." He says.

"Yeah, me too." I smile, I have no idea what to say now.

"Don't overthink it. I will call, I'll ask if you want to get a drink, on you, you'll say yes or no. That's it, no big deal. I'm gona wait a couple days though, let you stew. I don't want you thinking I'm a sure thing you know." He laughs and so do I.

"Ok, Officer Marks. You're on."

I wave him off and just stand there for a moment. That strange feeling doesn't fade and I look around again. Just as I begin to think I'm losing it, a movement in the Atrium windows catches my attention.

Sebastian is standing there at the window watching me with a look of unfiltered disgust spread clearly over his face and I can't help but flinch from effect. I have no idea how to react. He just turns away from me his whole body tight and his movements sharp.

Shoot!

Things were just starting to get a little better between us. I think it's time we get this "*Mrs. Chalmers*" nonsense out of the way. Sure, it's partly my fault for allowing this misunderstanding to carry on, I was angry and why should I have to explain myself to anyone but I can see Sebastian has a massive problem with deceit and he obviously thinks I am cheating on my husband. I need to just clear the matter up and hopefully he will stop looking at me like some harlot.

But as I walk around the site, looking in all the obvious then not so obvious places he could be, I come up empty. He's simply gone.

Which is crazy because he was just there. Maybe the stresses of the last few years or so have finally got to me and I'm losing it. I will just have to deal with him another day I think but it's such a shame, it really felt like we'd turned a corner earlier but now we are right back to square one. Lord at the look on his face, maybe were even further back than before. I pack my gear away and head home. There's no point in me hanging around here any longer.

CHAPTER 12

The next few weeks goes by in a blink of an eye and I am snowed under with the amount of work the project is taking. Sebastian has not returned to the site or the office once, well apparently some people have seen or spoken to him however he has been nowhere near any of these places when I have.

I haven't laid eyes on him in and it's the strangest feeling, even though I know his opinion of me must be horrendous and even though I shouldn't care what such a pigheaded ignorant insulting man like him thinks, I kind of miss him.

I miss sparring with him, I miss his rude and dismissive attitude and how it makes me feel alive when we argue, I miss his haunting stare and those brief glimmers of a smile.

But the man who I send daily updates is not the same person. He is always cordial, never casts any snide inappropriate remarks or curses. Nope, he just thanks me for the information and adds on more and more tasks or changes to my schedule or plans. To be fair his tweaks are mostly minor improvements that make sense, even if it does seem a little faster paced than we really need but Shelby did say he liked to work at a quicker time frame than most and as long as it doesn't impact our quality, which it isn't, then I see no problem so I reply with the same bland impersonal responses.

It's awful but the project is moving along so I can't really complain. I did send him my design draft ideas since it was obvious, he had no intention of scheduling a meeting to work on it together but I've had no response. I'm waiting it out at the moment, as whether I like it or not, I am going to see him this weekend and I don't know whether I am sick with nerves or some cruel form of excitement.

The Van Der Bilt's Anniversary party is this coming weekend and I am dreading it. I actually suggested they should think about cancelling, what with May feeling poorly but they both thought I was being ridiculous. Who cancels a weekend gathering at such short notice? They laughed. Apparently, I was worse than Sebastian.

So, on top of the mountain load of work I have been trying to get through, I have a weekend away to plan and prep for. The boys though are more than ready to get away for a weekend. They have been talking about it nonstop, which does not help.

I have appointments booked for the end of the week to get myself cleaned up a little and much to Shelby's disappointment, I refused the offer to be dressed for the weekend by designers. I know most people would be in their element but I would hate the feeling of being beholden to someone in such a way, representing their line and having my picture taken.

Not my plan for the weekend at all, I am hoping to stay as far out of the glare as possible. I mean it's not like I went to a thrift store and bought an outfit but I would rather stay a little more reserved.

I had hoped to attend just the ball and leave the next morning however almost as if they all knew that was my thoughts, they have included the boys in all the activities.

Sebastian's cousin Tabitha reached out to let me know her kids are roughly the same age as mine and we switched over contacts, so they have all been talking and making plans.

Apparently, her son Kye is into the same sports as the boys and they've been organizing meet ups after this weekend. And don't get me started on the boys thoughts on Kayla, Tabitha's daughter. Both boys seem to have a little interest in meeting her what with her being into as many sports as her brother and apparently, she's on some sort of baseball team that's pretty impressive.

So, I know I have no chance of leaving early but I am hoping to spend as much time in my room as possible. My only saving grace and the reason the whole weekend doesn't seem so terrifying is Shelby will be coming along. She and I are hitting the spa Friday morning, then we're grabbing the boys and her daughter Libby and driving up together.

And I am genuinely looking forward to meeting May in person. I feel like I've known her a lifetime from all the emails, phone and video calls but it will be great to actually meet her.

Sebastian though is my main worry. We haven't cleared up his misconception's and frankly I have no idea how to bring it up. Hopefully we won't need to see much of each other and we can deal with our work issues after the weekend.

The week is a whirlwind and I feel like the minute I close my eyes my alarm goes off and it's time to go all over again. Friday eventually comes round and I am so glad I scheduled the day off.

The crew know what's happening, so they all have their delegated jobs and until we finalize and agree the design modifications with the board which is scheduled for a few weeks, its mostly routine maintenance work. Shelby and I spend a lovely morning being primped, pampered and styled into submission and I start to feel a little less stressed about the coming weekend. Of course, I have also stalled enough and she will not let us go another day without hearing about my 'progress' with Officer Marks.

"I hate to break it to you Shell but I kind of keep letting him down gently." I sigh as we relax with a coffee.

"Oh Lord why? Why would you reject the man? I mean I get maybe you're interested in someone else just a smidge," She grins as I swat her, "But just think of all the things you could be doing with that gorgeous man!"

"I mean I'm not even touching that last dig," I stare pointedly at her and she grins over her cup. "It just doesn't feel right you know, but he is persistent I'll give him that." I laugh, "Although I'm not too sure if it's me he's actually interested in." I say as I peer closely at her.

To be honest, I've spoken to Jackson a few times over the last few days and although he does keep up the charming banter about how I still owe him a drink, he seems rather curious about my friend who is currently looking at everything else except me at the moment. I laugh,

"Aw c'mon Shelby, why would you reject a guy like that?" I grin, "Think of all the things you could be doing?" I replay back to her.

"Well, Mrs. Chalmers, if you can quite easily avoid the subject of a certain dashing devil, I am sure I have nothing to say about your stripper cop." she huffs, "I mean unless you want to talk about it?"

"Touché" I grin, "But I am serious Shell, if you're

interested, I can pass on your number or vice versa, if or whenever you're ready." I say softly.

"I don't know if I'll ever be ready to be honest." She sighs.

"I get it Shell, I really do and I wish I could just let go, have a drink with Jackson and not take it too serious but lord knows why there is a block. I just don't think I'm ready, although he is a very nice reminder that I am ready to start venturing out a little more. Maybe you and I are works in progress, eh?" I say.

"You betcha honey and we are going to have a fantastic weekend." She's so enthusiastic I almost get a little bit excited. Who knows maybe it won't be a complete disaster.

We pack up soon after, and head on over to pick Libby up from the dorms. She's all arms and long legs and looks but just as stunning as her mother. The same dark tresses and watchful eyes grace her youthful features.

Shelby is such a beautiful woman who seems to close herself in most of the time but when she relaxes and gets to know you the tension drops and she really is stunning. Like today, she's been pampered to the hill and looks all the more gorgeous for it. Her chocolate brown hair is down loose with a slight natural wave and her big almond eyes are clear and relaxed.

She looks at a peace I haven't seen in her other than when we had that drink and she seemed to lose a lot of the baggage she was carrying. It makes me happy to know she values my friendship as much as I her. I think we've found a kindred spirit in each other and long may it last.

Libby barrels in to the car and gives her mum a big

squeeze and I warm to see they have such a close relationship. It gives me hope for my boys and I, that even as they get older, they may still give me the odd cuddle here and there.

When we pull up at my house to pick them up, they are both sitting on their trunks filled with god only knows what. There looks to be every type of sport racket, ball, Christ is that a net?

"What the hell guys? You do not need all that sporting equipment!" I cry.

"Yeah mom, Kye said there's gona be all sorts of activities this weekend!" Noah grins. "Were like boy scouts again… always be prepared." he mocks.

"I already told him they would have equipment for us to loan but Kye said him and Kayla are taking their own as they want to win really bad. Apparently, it's really competitive mom and well you know…" he rubs the back of his neck.

"Yeah, yeah I know." I sigh.

"Dib Dib, mom." Noah smirks as he passes me to the trunk.

I just laugh my ass off, on the inside of course, when he rounds the car and catches sight of Libby sitting in the back, I'm ashamed to admit I may have smirked a little at his beetroot face when he caught my eye.

"Aw not cool mom, so not cool." He groans.

"Wow, that was harsh mom, a little warning would have been nice." Jacob sighs. He likes to pretend he's as confident as his brother but he takes a little longer to come out of his shell but Noah defiantly makes up for it.

"Hey, you must be Libby, I'm Noah the regular boy scout apparently." he grins. "And this is Jacob, he's not a fan of being called Jake or Jakey, unless you're a pretty girl… so I'm sure you'll be fine." he smiles.

"Doofus." I hear Jacob say, "Hi Jake or Jacobs fine Libby don't bother with this goofball." He laughs and they all settle in together talking about school and sports.

"Wow." Shelby says, "They are very enthusiastic young men."

"I did warn you." I laugh. "I just hope the Van Der Bilt's know what they're getting themselves into letting all these teenagers take over their home."

"Honestly the more the merrier with them. May's always had everyone from the family close, they spend almost every other weekend together, kids, adults of all ages. It's a sight I tell you." She laughs and off we go on the drive out of the city.

As we pull off the main roads a few hours later and start to head along a very secluded private driveway, I start to feel my hands get clammy. What was I thinking coming out here mingling with these people. The house feels like it's a million miles from anywhere and we're still only on the driveway.

As I think this, Shell pulls over towards the side of the road and at first it was hard to notice but now, I can see there is some sort of security code contraption and she leans over and punches in a load of numbers. She pulls away and I wonder what the point was. When the view opens up in front of us, she veers slightly to the left and before I know it, I can see the road curving off to the side behind a now opening security gate. Shells grinning like a fool and the boys are jabbering they feel like they're in a James bond movie. And so, begins the puns. I tune them out as we follow the curve in the road and slowly start to descend a massive tree lined stretch of road.

"Oh, Shell what are we doing here? What am I doing here? You, you belong in places like this... me?"

I drop my head to my hands.

"Now don't go getting your panties in a twist Leona it's just a house, a very large beautifully landscaped Billionaires mansion, but still just a house." She grins.

"You are so not helping." I sigh.

As I look up again, I try to take in the whole view but the building looks to be completely surrounded by greenery meaning as we drive up, we keep catching glimpses of the 'main house'.

We make a turn, coming to another tree lined road that drives us straight towards the entrance and as we travel further down, the trees bending and folding over us, the full building begins to come into view.

Oh lord what have we let ourselves in for!

"Aw man Jake, look at the size of this place." Noah says craning his neck forward to look through the front window for a better look.

"I mean, Mom this place is..."

"Yeah, it's something isn't it." Libby says, "Wait till you see it in full winter with the snow, it lights up like a fairy castle." She says dreamily.

I look to Shelby.

"What the hell Shell?" I start.

I don't get to finish the sentence because the next thing I know we're pulling out of the trees and following a grand sweeping driveway curving us all around to the left and we start to get a view of the building itself.

And my lord what a building. It's a beautiful mix of old and new, like an old Georgian plantation building but with subtle hints of modern. The dark grey roofing and large glass windows only make the sharpness of the pure white facade stand out more boldly. The surrounding greenery and lush foliage in an abundance of color make the place feel less stark and more homely. Which is ridiculous considering the place could easily home hundreds of people.

The gardens are picturesque and overflowing with flowers in every imaginable color and the ivy climbing up the tall pillars of the colonnade that runs along the front of the house only adds to the softening of the white building. It's simply stunning and I could stare at it for hours. I would love to walk around and marvel at the simple but effective design techniques used to create such a wonderful building however my Architects mind has to be pushed straight to one side, as the closer we drive, the more I notice the collection of people gathering at the main alcove of the home.

There is a massive central entryway with a row of heavy stone steps leading up from the drive way and as we pull to a stop in front of the building, they all begin to descend the stairs.

As I take a deep breath to steady my nerves Shell laughs and grabs my hand, "Remember it's just a house and they're just people, Just maybe don't picture everyone naked, That might be weird." She laughs and gets out.

The boys and Libby are already scrambling from the car, and my buffoon's are looking round in awe. I see Andy heading straight in my direction with his amused smile spread all over his handsome face and I grin back at him, "Well, you really are like Colonel Sanders aren't you old man?" I smile as he lets out that big hearty laugh which has everyone turning to look.

He grabs me in a tight friendly hug and rubs my

back.

"Oh, I've missed your spunk young lady. It's so good to see you again." He smiles.

The boys have made their way over and they both wait a moment to let us finish our hellos, then Jacob reaches out his hand towards Andy.

"Mr. Van Der Bilt Sir, it's great to finally meet you, Thank you for inviting us along for the weekend." He says and I stand a little prouder maybe these vagabonds will do me proud.

"Yeah, Sir this house is amazing!" Noah says still looking around. "I think I might need a map to get around though, so I don't get lost." He grins cheekily. Oh well, maybe not.

Andy laughs again as I see May make her way over after a very large hug from Shelby and Libby.

"Well dear, I was beginning to think we would never get together in person!" she laughs, "It's so good to finally meet you sweetheart." she says as she pulls me in for a tight squeeze.

"Yeah, I thought I was going to keep getting stuck with this troublemaker." I laugh and hug her tightly back. She is what I always pictured a grandmother would look like.

She is slightly smaller that Andy, and she looks exceptional for her age. Not in a botox-ed smooth face kind of way, no in that stunning growing old gracefully kind of way. She has shoulder length silver grey hair tucked behind her ear and beautiful dark hazel eyes with a lot of soft crinkles by their sides. Very similar to the man who is now pulling her close to his side and holding her like he still can't bear to not be beside her. They smile softly at one another and I feel their love envelope me.

"It really is wonderful to finally meet you May and again, thank you so much for inviting us along. I'm glad to see you looking so well and it's great to hear your feeling so much better."

"Yes, even if you slightly hoped we would cancel," she grins cheekily, "I appreciate it dear."

"What? Why would you want them to cancel this, Mom? C'mon it's gona be the party of the century!" Noah proclaims and I roll my eyes.

"Exactly young man," Andy says as he pulls Noah and Jacob towards them, "Who would want to cancel the great shindig I have planned for my lovely lady?" he grins.

"Ok, enough trouble from you." May laughs as we all head inside. "I will show you to your rooms so you can take a moment, hmm?" she says softly.

"Thank you that would be great." I say.

I turn to head back towards the car to grab our things when the car is no longer there, I look back around and Andy winks.

"It's all taken care of honey, bags will be in your room."

"Of course, they will." I groan.

CHAPTER 13

As we make our way inside, I get a slight introduction to the other few people who were standing outside. Of course, I've already met Shelby's father briefly before at work and he smiles kindly,

"Great to see you again, Mrs. Chalmers." he says.

"Leona, is fine Mr. Davies."

"Steve." he grins.

"Thanks Steve, you too." I smile. He introduces me to his wife Edith and they excuse their self's to go talk to their granddaughter. Libby looks ecstatic to be enveloped in the embrace and Shelby looks at ease. We catch each other's eye and smile.

The boys are jabbering away, asking questions about the house and the weekend's events and I quickly make my way over to simmer them down.

"Ok boys, let's get ourselves settled before we barrage the poor Van Der Bilt's anymore, hmm?" I say and Andy lets out a large chuckle.

"Excuse me Leona, do you think we're too old for keeping up with these young ones?" he grins.

I just smile back and am about to make a quick remark when two teenagers come barreling through the door.

"Told ya it was them, Kayla!" Kye, I assume comes charging at the boys. He looks to be built like an American footballer but not completely sure how to use his body correctly yet. He's all 'bull in a China shop', as he fists bumps both boys and asks if they're set for the weekend challenges.

The guys are both looking slightly stunned though as

they stare frozenly at what can only be Kayla. I'm guessing they haven't had a close look at her over there video calls as they look like statues.

Kayla is the complete opposite of her brother; she looks like an amazon warrior princess. She must be at least six foot tall; she has legs that goes on for days and a deep dark tan that makes her white blonde hair and piercing green eyes stand out strikingly.

I lean over and cough subtly to break the spell as I notice her cheeks begin to heat.

"Aw man! Guys please don't drool over my sister; I get this all the time." he sighs, "Kay, go take a walk or sumthin, please." he says as she blushes even more.

"Oops, sorry Kayla that was incredibly rude of us." Jacob says, as he shoves Noah who still looks like a deer in headlights.

"What. Oh, erm yeah… God sorry Kayla it's just… well… I mean your eh," he stutters and stammers as she breaks out a laugh.

"It's Ok guys, don't worry about it." She smiles showing her beautiful smile. "I hope you both know, just because of all this," she waves at herself so dismissively, she comes across as adorable rather than obnoxious, "I'm going to use it as a weapon to crush you guys in the sports this weekend."

That gets Noah all fired up.

"What, never gona happen!" he grins, "Nothing puts me off my game, not even a ridiculously pretty face." He grins and looks over at Libby as she laughs aloud.

"Oh, it's on." Kayla smirks and grabs Libby over for a hug.

"Good, now that's out of the way." The big oaf that is Kye says, "Wana go pick your bunk?" he beams.

The boys look to me for permission and I nod. I am

about to interrupt them charging off when they turn unanimously and thank the Van Der Bilt's again for having them. Andy and May smile at them and off they go, I hope to be seen again at some point.

"They are lovely boys Leona." May say's.

"Thank you, I just hope they behave this weekend. They get a little too in to competitive sports and it looks like your lot are similar." I sigh.

"Oh yeah, we have the biggest bunch of sore losers there is. There is always someone claiming fouls or technicalities, It's gona be great fun." Andy laughs,

"Ok dear, I'm going to let May get you settled in if that's ok? I have a little bit of work to catch up on and a few other people to greet." he smiles.

"Oh no, don't let me stop you two greeting your guests, just point me in the right direction and I will find my way."

Though as I say this, I look around the massive foyer with corridors running in every direction and when I follow the giant staircases directly in the center it also looks like it goes on forever. I reckon I could spend the weekend trying to just find my room.

"On second thoughts maybe Noah was right, have you got a map?"

They both chuckle.

"No need Leona, I'll leave Andy to his work and greetings and I will catch up with them in a little bit. Let's go get you settled." She says.

Andy comes over and gives me a massive bear hug.

"I truly am glad you came into our lives Leona, and we are both so happy you could spend this time with us." He smiles gently.

"Aw you're such a sweet talker when you want to be old man." I grin. "It's honestly my pleasure." I say and wave him off.

He reaches over and grabs May for a quick kiss on the cheek and a little squeeze of her bottom. God this man! He is a total charmer, I laugh.

"Wow May, how on earth do you put up with such a scoundrel?" I smile.

"Well, he has his moments." She chuckles with rosy cheeks.

We carry on talking and laughing as we make our way up the stairs and start to wander down the beautiful hallways. She walks me right along to the end of the hall were there doesn't seem to be too many doorways. The ones I did see, seem to be open leading to what looked like a massive library and another sitting area with a roaring fire. If I can, I plan on sneaking back and spending my time in there curled up with a book. It looks like heaven.

"I thought you would prefer to have a little more privacy away from the other guests Leona. I know you're not entirely comfortable here this weekend and I wanted you to be able to take a moment away for yourself if you become overwhelmed without bumping into every other guest." She says as she opens a door right at the end.

I am about to thank her profusely for having such a caring insight when I follow her into the room and take in the space.

"Oh, May this is, stunning." I say.

The room is painted in the softest shades of white and creams. The windows are almost floor to ceiling with little window seats covered in cushions and blankets draped perfectly. In the center of the room is the biggest bed I have ever seen. It's a white four poster with light translucent linens hanging gently from the posts. There are two ornately carved bedside tables at either side and a matching dressing table sits over to one side. There is a large log fire with two beautiful carver chairs situated in front of it and a door off to one side I assume is an ensuite. It's simply breathtaking.

"This is too much May," I begin, "Surely this room is better suited to someone else?"

"I don't know anyone it would suit more perfectly dear." she smiles.

"I mean honestly, I think I would happily spend the rest of the weekend tucked up here May! You will have to pry me out of this room." I grin.

"Well, hopefully that won't be the case Leona, I'm sure you will enjoy yourself, we may all seem a bit loud and overbearing at times but trust me it is all in good fun. My family are simply my proudest achievement in life and the people we choose to surround ourselves with have all been properly vetted." She winks.

I laugh out loud,

"I have no idea how I snook past but I am not going to complain." I grin.

"You dear have been welcomed by the most experienced vet-er there is… My husband. He has this uncanny gift at sniffing out a fraud. You my dear are no fraud. So, know this, You are stuck with us now. Once you're in, you cannot leave. We're like the mafia, only a little nicer, I would imagine." She laughs.

I laugh along with her and she comes over and sits down on one of the seats and motions for me to do the same. She reaches over and takes my hand.

"I know you probably feel a little overwhelmed Leona but please believe me when I say people only see what is on the surface. Not many people look below, but you dear, I believe you look a little closer than most. You have had some hard tasks thrown at you and you are still standing. I see something in you I saw everyday once. A pain. I know you don't know all of our story and I won't bore you with it just now but just know, All this…" she waves around, "All this came from hard work and grit, but it means little to us, without the people closest. What really means the world are the people who step inside with us. Family is the most important thing there is and I can see you've carved out your own Leona. I am so sorry for the loss of your husband; truly. But your boys are an absolute joy and you have done a remarkable job." She smiles so softly.

My throat is too tight to speak, I couldn't say a word without cracking but like she already knows she pats my hand and stands up.

"I will give you a little space to get settled dear, Just come a wander whenever you feel ready and Kye will show the boys where you are if they need you." She leaves me alone and I sit there staring into space.

How on earth did I get here and why do I feel like crying?

I have no idea how long I sit there just staring into the fire. My entire life, all I wanted was my own family to feel whole. Sure, I never had any plans to start one so early but for a while I had it, my own little family.

A lot of that time was spent just making our way through, the age old 'it won't always be this way' knowing that at some point all the hard work would pay off.

And it has in a way, you know. I am financially secure, my kids are happy and healthy, but I had always assumed me and Matt would be spending this time together, the boys wouldn't have had to experience that type of loss.

I lost my whole family myself when I was young, so I know how it shapes and molds you and I never wanted my kids to ever suffer that type of pain but life doesn't work that way. One day you think you have it all and the next your world comes crashing down with a bang.

I try to look at all the positives they do have in their lives. They have grandparents who love and spoil them, something I never had, they have a great group of friends who have been rocks through everything, making them laugh and dragging them out when they felt low. They have each other, this undeniable connection, knowing when the other is struggling or needs space and they have me.

I would give my life for them both and they are my whole world, the center of my gravity, they keep me grounded and make my life worthwhile.

Sure, I have my work which I adore. I am proud of myself for what I have achieved giving my beginnings. I have loved and been loved, which is something I won't ever take for granted and I am working on myself.

I have Shelby, a kindred spirit if ever there was one. She gets me, as I get her and I see our friendship staying strong and resolute. All in all, I have a good life, I decide to push my own boundaries a little further. Sure, this weekend isn't exactly the norm but I can enjoy it for what it is. And with that, I decide to take myself off on a stroll to find everyone else.

As I make my way along the corridor, I take a peek in some of the open doorways and sure enough there doesn't seem to be any people or even bedrooms in this area of the house so it puts me at ease. As I hear my phone chime again, I dig around in my bag and check it.

I laugh aloud, as I see I have a million missed messages from the boys already. Picture after picture of the cabins, their rooms and the lake, the basketball courts, it goes on and on and I chuckle at how well they adjust to their surroundings. They have no fear or feelings of inadequacy, which makes me proud. I am just putting my phone back in my bag when I round the corner and bump straight into a solid form.

"Oh dear, I am so sorry, I wasn't looking were I was going and I…" I start.

"No problem at all, Miss…?" I look up into a face that is so eerily familiar. He looks so like Sebastian, only with a lot less hatred or evil glares. His body is completely relaxed and at ease and he has a carefree look about him, it's so disconcerting it takes me a minute to realize he was asking a question.

"Oh sorry. Chalmers, Leona Chalmers." I say with a smile as I reach my hand out.

"Ah the elusive and maddeningly frustrating, Mrs. Chalmers." he grins wickedly and I pull my hand back.

"Excuse me?"

"I'm sorry, Mrs. Chalmers, I apologize it's just I have heard nothing but your name cast aloud for the last few months, I feel as though I already know you personally." He says as he reaches out and shakes my hand.

"Well, you have me at a complete loss Mr…?"

He grins so freely; I feel like this man doesn't know how to do anything else.

"Oh, I am Anderson, Anderson Van Der Bilt the 4rth but whatever you do please don't call me junior. Ghastly nickname and I will hold it against you forever." He grins.

This must be the oldest Van Der Bilt, I don't know too much about their backstory but what I do know is he's Andy's oldest grandson and the man who was supposed to take over the company but something about his playboy lifestyle and no interest in Architecture rings a bell.

"Ah I see you putting some of the pieces together Mrs. Chalmers, so let me help you out. My family mostly call me Anders, I have no interest in any form of Architecture or old buildings whatsoever. My father is Andy's oldest son and I am a deep disappointment to him for not following in the family business. I much prefer to spend my time fighting for the little man. Lawyer to trade but even that is sadly a disappointment to my father. Had I at least worked for some ridiculous corporate tyranny then maybe he could have moved on from the loss of another foot at the table but nope, not me, I have to work for the 'city'." He mock shudders and I stifle a laugh.

"Ok, that is a lot of information." I say.

"Yes well, I assume like most people you've heard the rumors of my 'party lifestyle' and figure I'm simply another trust fund tosser, not that I would normally mind. However, Andy and May have impeccable taste and they have a special fondness for you. Also, when you throw in the antagonist part of me that loves to wind my dear cousin up, yes, I think I would quite like to be your friend."

"Hmm, about that…" I start.

"Oh, he has a very quick opinion on most people Mrs. Chalmers, I wouldn't take it too personally. There was bound to come a time when that instinct of his was wrong and I think you my dear may be it." He grins like the god damn Cheshire cat.

"Look Mr Van Der Bilt, I…"

"Oh, call me Anders, please." He smiles softly.

"Well, to be completely frank, I am not comfortable you being so blunt about his obvious dislike towards me, I know I am a guest here but I don't need everyone thinking I am some sort of gold-digging freeloader or whatever else nonsense that cousin of your has been spouting…" I pause and glare at him, "Why the heck are you grinning like that?" I ask sharply.

"I see why he has such strong feelings in regards to you Mrs. Chalmers, you are an oddity in our world. You speak the truth and are very passionate about it, in a world full of lies and deceit. I like you and I do hope you will forgive me if I have offended you in any way. That, I can assure you was my last intention, in fact I was hoping you would allow me to escort you to join the rest of the group?" he smiles. He seems incredibly sincere so I simply shrug my shoulders and agree.

"I have no idea where I am going anyway." I say.

"Stick with me kid…" he laughs and I follow him down the hall.

He jabbers on all the way, as he guides me outside to a patio area surrounded by beautiful lush gardens, where there are an awful lot of people gathered.

He takes my arm as we step outside sensing my discomfort and I smile up at him, true to his word he does seem like the perfect gentleman and he has been filling me in on everyone who will be in attendance this weekend, so I at least have an idea the who's who's.

Fortunately, I already have a vague idea who a lot of the people are, what with them being work colleagues and such, although I can't say that I've ever mingled in any of their circles. And of course, it looks like most of the people here at the moment are family and selected close friends.

I spot Shelby sitting at a table with a face I recognize from her face-times, so when they wave me over, I don't feel too out of place.

When we get closer to them, Ander bids me adieu with a small nod, whilst Tabitha comes over and gives me a tight hug,

"Well, It's so nice to finally meet you in person!" she grins, "I was beginning to think we'd never meet." She laughs.

"Hello Tabitha, you too, thanks again for setting up the boys they seem to be having a great time already." I smile as I look out towards what looks to be a basketball court nestled over to the sides, partly secluded by trees but no matter what level of privacy there is I can still hear them over the comfortable chatter going on around us.

"Well, of course although I'm not sure how we're going to fair if these boys keep crushing on my daughter. Hanks about ready to lose his mind." She laughs, "Oh not just your boys Leona, Miguel brought a couple friends as well and my goodness it's like an Abercrombie and Fitch advert out there. Kayla and Libby can't wait for the rest of the girls to get here."

"Well, I'm just thankful I have boys, I can't imagine! You're poor husband." I laugh.

We settle into the patio seating and I begin to feel

relaxed, there is no awkwardness or uncomfortable silences, quite the opposite, they're a loud rowdy bunch themselves. They make jokes with each other in such a simple kind manner that I feel at ease joining in a little. Shelby gives me a big smile and the conversation turns to tonight's ball.

"So Leona, Do you want to get ready with us girls tonight or are the boys joining you?" Tabitha asks.

"Er, I think the boys are coming up to meet me when they are ready, so whatever easiest for everyone." I say.

"Well, you'll want to come dress with us, Tabitha is a better make-up artist than any I've ever seen and her supplies are phenomenal."

"Yeah, I'm actually pretty good." She kind of blushes a little.

"Well, I would love to join you as I quite simply suck at makeup, but I am pretty good at hair." I grin back.

"Ok, it's settled." Shelby squeaks out.

After a little more lounging and introductions to god knows how many more family members, I head back to my room to shower. The boys text to say they're doing the same and will come get me from Tabitha's room so we can all go down together.

I smile widely to myself, they seem really happy to be here and have fitted in quite easily. I only hope I can do the same this evening.

CHAPTER 14

Shelby was not kidding!

Tabitha's suite looks like a professional make-up studio! Every available surface is covered in a variety of instruments, with every type, shade and style of makeup, brushes, utensil's and god only knows what else.

I am so out of my depths but the girls are a whizz at making me feel comfortable. I am thrown into the bathroom with a dressing gown thrust at me and warned to get my butt back in a chair. I do as I am told and the next hour flies by in a blink of an eye.

I try hard not to spin on my seat and see what Tabitha is doing to my face, she asked to see my dress, told me to trust her and off she went since I had already styled my hair before I came along.

I kept it very simple and curled it into soft waves and pinned it up in a loose style twist at the base of my neck with a few loose tendrils framing my face. These are currently gently clipped away from my face so Tabitha can work her magic. I've told her I am not too keen on heavy make-up and I prefer a natural look but it feels like she's been at it for hours so when she exclaims, she is done I reign in the '*finally*' and smile politely.

"You have such a good poker face Leona but you can speak your mind here." she grins, "I know you couldn't wait for me to finish but I think it's worth it." she says as she spins me to face the mirror.

"Oh Leona… you look stunning." Shelby cries from over my shoulder.

Me, I struggle to speak. I have a little baby lump in my throat.

Tabitha has stayed true to her word and given me beautifully flawless, natural make up that makes my skin glow. My eyes have been shaded to give the illusion of a smokey eye which when I try to replicate makes me look like a racoon with a squint.

She has created a vision that somehow give a sultry look but still makes the piercing blue of my eyes sparkle, my cheeks have what looks like a natural soft blush, that I know quite literally took an age and my lips are a soft nude that gives the whole look a classic beauty. I don't think I've ever looked this good in my life.

"Wow, Tabitha! You have a gift, thank you." I smile. I can see her natural blush come through as she smiles back.

"Well, you gave me a pretty good canvas, just a shame about all the sighing." She smiles.

"Har, Har." I laugh.

"Ok, who needs help with their hair?" I say to take the attention away and just like that were back at it.

I style Shelby's hair straight and sleek down her back in a slick side parting and help Libby create a multi-faceted up do she snapped on her phone of some supermodel.

Thankfully it's not one I've already met!

We all head into the dividing rooms to get dressed and when I come back out, I smile at these lovely ladies. It's weird how easy a friendship has formed with these two and their girls are lovely young ladies. I am so glad we all met. It feels nice.

"Wow! Mom, you look beautiful." Jacob smiles softly as the boys lounge in the room.

"Yeah Mom, you look eh…" Noah grins as he rubs the back of his neck looking a little uncomfortable.

"HOT!" Shelby says, "Your mom looks hot." She laughs and both boys blush a little.

My dress is slightly more risqué than I expected it to be, because of the weight loss it hangs a little differently than I remember. It dips slightly lower in the back than I had anticipated and the deep V at the front is maybe more daring than I'm used to but it is still perfectly respectable. The color is a deep midnight blue which enhances the color of my eyes and the silk slides over my body with a quiet silky rustle. I feel a million bucks in it.

"Well, yeah." Jacob laughs.

"I mean we did say you should date Mom so yeah… you should get dolled up more often." Noah grins.

"Shut it you," I smile, "Now come over so I can get a good look at you."

Both boys moan and groan but my god do they look handsome. Looking like they've stepped right out of some designer advert in their smart tuxes, they're growing more and more into young men every day and so similar to their dad, it's startling.

Noah's left his hair slightly wild and untamed and Jacobs is as usual swept back neat and tidy. I can see the girls watching them closely from the other side of the room and I have no doubt these boys are going to break quite a few hearts over the years but if their own glances are anything to go by, they may experience a few of their own.

Noah folds over in mock bow, "Are you ready to go to the ball my lady?" he mocks.

"Very funny wise ass." I grin. His eyes dart to Kayla again and I can see Jacob gesturing to Libby that she looks very pretty, as she blushes at his kind words.

I smile over at Shelby and she grins back.

"What you think Shell?"

She laughs out loud, "No problem with me."

Both boys look confused as I put them out of their misery.

"How about Shelby and I make our way down together and you boys could escort these lovely ladies to the ball?" I smile.

They both look like they might wet themselves with excitement and I notice even the girls perk up at the idea but Jacob being his usual considerate self, sighs.

"Don't be silly Mom, It's your friends that are downstairs, we can catch up with the girls later." He smiles gently.

A few shoulders slump at his careful words but I notice Libby has a warm smile in her eyes and she nods her head at him as he comes towards me. Noah ever the instigator adds, "Yeah, Mom, what with you looking all hot and that, we need to keep a close eye out for any vultures on the prowl." He smirks.

We all laugh but I can see the little bits of disappointment, so I pull them off to one side and assure them that it would be nice for the girls and better if Shelby and I went together, since she's also flying solo. They don't look too convinced but agree to escort the girls down but come get me right away if they see any lurkers trying to steal my virtue! I have no idea what I did to deserve these two loonies but god I love them.

Kayla and Noah look ecstatic to be heading down together and as Shelby comes over, I hear Libby tell Jacob he was very sweet to refuse earlier to protect his Mom.

Seems like the age gap may be made up with his level of maturity. He's always seemed a little older for his age, so it's understandable she would see it.

"You sure about this Leona? I really don't mind even though the kids do all look very happy with the decision." Shelby smiles.

"Well yeah! You promised to show me a good night, Shell, don't go disappointing me but I'm just letting you know now, I do not put out on the first date." I smirk.

"Ha-ha, I totally could convince you." She grins.

"Well, ladies since my husband seems to have completely forgotten to come for me, I will be joining this little rag tag gang, if that's ok?" Tabatha grins.

"Wow a threesome! Jacksons mind will be exploding somewhere." I grin at Shelby.

"Yes, in his dreams maybe." She huffs at my smirk.

"Ok guys, we all ready?" Tabitha says.

Noah as usual plays up his part by bowing at Kayla and taking her hand in his for a gentle kiss, he then wraps his arm in hers and they head towards the door laughing.

Jacob looks affectionately at his brother, smiles then does the same for Libby. She laughs aloud, performs a mock curtsey and takes his offered arm smiling all the way.

As I turn to laugh at the girls, Tabitha does the same thing and offers her arm to both me and Shelby, we both grin, curtesy and all loop arms together.

What a sight we are going to be coming down that staircase.

The kids all drop behind and let Tabitha lead the way. She peels off towards a back annex that leads to an outdoor platform, with its own grand staircase cascading with fairy lights, leading all the way down to a massive outdoor terrace covered in white everywhere.

Artificial trees that look like the real thing, have sprung up from beneath the patio sweeping overhead with crystal white lights hanging from every branch, weeping willow wisp entwined amongst the lights give the illusion of a fairytale Forrest. Large ornate vases are planted all around, overflowing with a collection of white jeweled flowers and there are people everywhere.

Lots and lots of people everywhere. I try not to stumble as we begin to descend the steps and Shelby sensing my anxiety grips my arm tighter.

"They're just people Leona, who pee, get drunk and will probably make massive fools of themselves tonight, but people just the same." She whispers to my side and I laugh out loud.

I hear the boys chattering away excitedly behind me and I smile freely. This is a good thing, I am fine. That's my mantra I will chant and I am sticking to it!

There is an area sectioned off that I can't quite glimpse and there are patio heaters everywhere so there is a warm buzz in the air. As we arrive at the bottom of the steps, Tabitha's husband Hank is awaiting her.

"Ah, so I see you had a better offer then my fair lady?" he smiles and she smirks a little the bloody witch. Yeah, I know what you did there missy, I glare and she laughs aloud.

"Suck it up Leona." She grins sticks out her tongue and moves into her husband's embrace. I can't hear the tender words but their adoring glances are enough of a giveaway.

"You get used to how disgustingly lovey dovey

these two are after a few years." Shelby groans.

I just smile. No judgement here.

"Well, if you would ever decide to get that stick removed and started dating… you too could be that repulsively in love Miss Davies." purs Anders Van Der Bilt, over Shelby's shoulder.

Wow! He is a sight himself decked out in a very sleek sculpted tuxedo however unlike almost every other male in attendance wearing classic black, Anders is wearing a dark, almost blood red, crushed velvet jacket and looking very much like the dashing deadly playboy he is perceived to be and our very own Shelby looks ready to blow.

"Oh, piss off Anders, I am not going to let you and your little games ruin our girls night, why don't you go find another airhead to blow you in the library again and give me a break." She fumes and storms off towards her parents.

"Well, you just have a charming effect for a notorious playboy, don't you?" I murmur and he burst out laughing. I see Shelby's shoulders stiffen as she hears him but continues on her way.

"Why Mrs. Chalmers, may I be the first to say how simply ravishing you look tonight and I do hope you will grace a scoundrel like me with a simple dance later this evening?" he grins like the devil just came up from the depths below.

"I have no doubt, even a dance, is not simple for you Mr. Van Der Bilt, Sir." I frown.

He reaches for my hand and pauses, awaiting me to hold out my hand. I sigh dramatically and he grins up at me, as he turns it around and places a soft kiss near the pulse on my wrist. It's a weird gesture and he grins over my shoulder smugly; I turn to see what holds his eye but his dark chuckle has me spinning back around.

"I have no idea what games you are up to but I will not be part of it." I turn to march off, as an older familiar looking gentleman scolds him.

"Anderson, that's two enchantingly beautiful ladies I have seen you scare off in a matter of minutes, that has to be a new record, even for you." He glares sharply.

"Why father, I must get all this rakish behavior from somewhere… now which parent could that be?" he hums and taps the side of his chin theatrically.

The only sign of emotion at the dig is the twitch of a muscle on his father's lower jaw, Anders just sighs and his father simply stares at him and I'm left standing here feeling like a very weird spectator.

"Well now, no need to air all our dirty laundry in front of our esteemed guests, is there boys?" Andy chuckles. "And you, Miss Leona, look absolutely bewitching my dear, I hope these two haven't shown my family up as a complete disgrace?"

"Well, you Sir, are the biggest devil of them all, so what chance does anyone else stand?" I muse, attempting to break the tension slightly.

"She does have you there gramps." Anders chuckles as he starts to toddle off but swings back around and says very loudly, "Remember our rendezvous later Leona." he winks and off he goes laughing to himself.

"I am incredibly sorry Mrs. Chalmers, my son is quite simply a child in a grown man's body sometimes, he can't seem to help himself from creating mischief." His father says with a sad sigh.

"You know, I do believe he knows exactly what he is doing and isn't nearly the fool he pretends… however a scoundrel he is for sure." I laugh softly hoping he sees my meaning.

"Thank you my dear, I see why you have been welcomed into the fold. I hope you have a wonderful evening and manage to avoid any more dalliances with a rake tonight."

"Well, now I wouldn't go that far… some rakes are good for dallying with." May say's with a hearty chuckle, as she cozies up to Andy.

"Mother please." He groans and it's quite something.

He bids us farewell and wanders off to mingle with other guests. I can't help but notice his watchful gaze on his son. He seems to genuinely care for him and looks a little sad to see him play the court jester.

"Now my dear, you look beautiful, as always but also unchaperoned, where are those boys of yours?" she asks.

"Thank you May, you look an absolute vision." I say and mean it.

She is dressed in an exquisite, white beaded dress that drapes her figure beautifully. You would never believe she was an elderly woman. Must be the love of a good man and a happy life. A subtle cough beside me has me laughing.

"You too, Mr. Van Der Bilt Sir, you look very dashing, you almost can't tell you're a devil in disguise." I smirk, "My boys have the great honor of chaperoning those two lovely ladies over there next to the bar with the rest of the youngsters, although they don't look like they're doing much chaperoning, more like entertaining."

I smile as I see the girls crack up with laughter. Although it may look like they have abandoned me for their new friends, they have me very much in their sights, as confirmed with the salute from Noah.

"Ah yes, I see that, very fine young men you have yourself there." May smiles.

"Thank you and again thanks for having us… this is spectacular and I am very glad we came. Are you two ready for your night? You are feeling ok May?" I ask gently.

"Why you're almost as bad as someone else." she grins, "Yes, my dear I am absolutely fine. No need for worry, I have this old coot to keep an eye on tonight, lord knows what mischief he would be getting into if I'm not here to supervise." We all laugh and I ask what the plan now is.

"We are just waiting on the last of the guests and then we will head through to the dining area, have a lovely meal, hear a few spectacular speeches." he winks, "Then the party begins."

At that I see a couple move down the stairs heading straight towards us and I excuse myself to let them speak with their guests. I need a minute to gather my bearings, so I move off near an alcove just for a second.

I have that awful creepy feeling, like being watched again, as I lean back against the hard pillar and take a long steadying breath. It's been a while since I've ventured to this type of gathering, well a gathering of this many people.

Normally I'd have Matt by my side and he just thrived at these things. He seemed to always know what to say and could strike up a conversation with almost anyone. He would almost always find a way of persuading people to have a look at is nonprofit whilst doing it, always working.

I never minded; I was just as bad really. But now it's a little harder to mingle and it's worse when you meet people who you haven't seen since the accident. You feel like you're being dissected, then you get that look.

That half pitying look people give, when they just don't know what to say. I suppose that's part of the reason I never correct Sebastian either, hatred and disgust, seems easier to take than sympathy or pity. I am acutely aware that he is around here somewhere and I have no idea how to deal with him. It's like I can feel him near but when I look around, he's nowhere to be seen.

I spot the boys and notice their concerned stares, so I smile wide, give a little wave and begin to leave the little haven, when an older lady and gentleman stop me. "Leona dear, we thought that was you." She exclaims as she pulls me into a friendly hug.

"My goodness Eleanor, you were right, how are you sweetheart? It's been a while." Tom Hartley says, giving me an equally tight squeeze.

Eleanor and Tom Hartley where and still remain, on the board of trusts at the non-profit Matt helped run. It's an outreach program, which helps troubled teens get their self's back into work or education after all sorts of negativity in their lives.

Most of the kids come from broken or foster homes, some even from juvenile detention centers. It was one of Matts proudest achievements and the Hartley's are very kind people.

"Mr. and Mrs. Hartley, so very good to see you both. I'm so sorry, it's been such a long time since I've visited…" I start.

"Oh no dear, don't you be silly. It must be such a hard place to come, what with Matty's signature stamped all over the place. The kids still talk about him you know."

She says too kindly and pats my hand.

It's hard not to like these two but it's also stifling the level of pity. They both idolized Matt, so it's no surprise when Mrs. Hartley sniffles into a tissue.

"We miss him every day Leona, we just can't find anyone who cared as much as him." She sniffs a little.

"He is greatly missed." Mr. Hartley sighs.

"Why yes, *Mrs. Chalmers*, such a shame your husband could not be with us tonight, isn't it. What on earth would make him miss a great big party like this and leave his loving wife all unattended?" comes a devastatingly cruel voice.

My heart feels like it literally stops and even though I hear the sharp intake of Mr. Hartley's breath and Mrs. Hartley's loud gasp, I am frozen staring into the darkest most cruel taunting eyes I've ever witnessed but the heartache just keeps coming. I am just about to tear this man to shreds, when I hear the devastating words.

"Well, Mr Van Der Bilt, I am 100% sure if my dad wasn't six feet under Sir, he would have been here tonight living it up as well, probably even hitting up all these rich people for some heavy donations for the shelter, eh Mr. Hartley?"

Noah says and as I haven't taken my eyes off his, I can see the moment he realizes just what he has done. The abject horror that takes over his face as he looks at my boys, then the Hartley's, anywhere but at me.

"NOAH!" I exclaim sharply, "That is unnecessary."

"You said if we ever felt uncomfortable with those types of remarks…" he says, as he glares a little at Sebastian, "we should deflect using humor."

"I am not sure that's what she said, Noah." Jacob sighs.

"That is absolutely not what I said." I say.

As everyone attempts to begin speaking all at once, a loud bell rings and people start ushering us out of the room,

"If we can ask everyone to please keep moving into the dining room, food will now begin being served." A large voice booms.

Mr. and Mrs. Hartley still look incredibly stunned and rather insulted, but I abruptly turn the boys and start marching us away. I will not make a scene at this event. I will deal with that asshole later and he will god damn apologize to my bloody boys the minute I see him.

I can hear him murmuring behind me to the Hartley's and Mr. Hartley's very strong.

"You are apologizing to the wrong people Mr. Van Der Bilt, that young family have been through a horrendous ordeal and you Sir, should be ashamed of yourself, regardless of your awareness or lack thereof."

He storms off with his wife and I can hear him shuffling behind me but I will not deal with this in front of a god damn audience.

We rush in and grab an attendant and are directed to our seats. Thankfully, far enough away from the main table.

As we take our seats Jacob reaches for my arm,

"Mom, Are you ok?"

"Of course, kiddo, happens all the time." I joke. "Are you guys?"

"Yeah mom, happens *all* the time." Noah rolls his eyes and Jacob smiles softly. "Were fine mom, no foul, some people just don't know and to be fair, Dad would have found it funny and managed to squeeze a guilt check out of him." He laughs.

"Yeah, you're probably right." I sigh.

CHAPTER 15

Dinner looks magnificent, the food and wine are a massive hit and the atmosphere around us is full of laughter and joy.

The speeches seemed to create the right mix of oohs and aahs and the happy couple look so sickeningly in love, I actually have to rub the pain in my heart and wipe the tears from my eyes. They are incredibly lucky to have found each other.

The boys are having a great time and cannot wait to move into the party but me, me I am ready for a full-on nervous breakdown. Every time I look up, I can feel eyes on me.

If it's not Shelby's inquisitive ones pleading for me to fill her in, its Andy's soft watchful gaze, Mays sympathetic smile or even bloody Anders wicked winks but throughout them all I can feel him. I can feel him burning a hole right through me.

At some points, it feels like he seems sorry, then others, it's like he is a raging bull ready to charge me. Well, he will not get an easy ride with this one. I am sick of this man's push and pull and he will hear about it. When I'm good and ready.

As the loud clang sounds, the boys are almost bouncing in their seats.

"What has got you two so excited?" I ask.

"Seriously mom, this is gona be awesome. Once all the oldies are done with their waltzes and that the DJ comes out, I am gona rock that dance floor." Noah cries.

"And you?" I look at Jacob, he hates dancing.

"I promised Libby, I would show her a proper waltz." He blushes slightly. "She's used to only having cousins to dance with and was surprised I would know how." he smiles.

"Told ya those classes would come in handy." I smile and Noah ever the jokester adds,

"Yeah, Jacob, is that why you stayed in dance all that time? Nothing to do with Mrs. Markson the hot dance teacher? Hey come to think of it I might ask Kayla for a waltz, show off my multi-talented moves."

At that we both burst out laughing. Noah's classic dance is almost as bad as his singing and that is bloody awful.

"Yeah, you do that Casanova." I say and laugh again.

I feel lighter already as Jacob escorts me towards the dancehall with Noah whinnying behind us about how he's not that bad of a dancer… Is he?

As we enter a large white tented area with a sparkling dance floor, again in glowing white, there is a full-size classic orchestra set up in a faraway corner and through the arched alcoves you can see the outside gardens in full bloom, twinkling lights are shinning everywhere and it simply feels magical.

But just as I am about to sigh at the simplistic understated beauty of it all, someone grabs my arm,

"Ok Leona, let's send these wild ones off to enjoy their selves and we will go have a large glass of this extremely delicious champagne or maybe a strong shot of jack, eh?" Shelby says.

Noah is like a horse in the traps.

"Can we mom? You're, ok? You sure you're, ok?" he rushes.

"Yes, of course, off you go… but behave." I warn

Noah mostly.

Jacob hangs back a bit, "You sure that guy didn't upset you earlier mom?"

"Aw honey, don't be silly; it happens you know. No harm done. You go enjoy your night and I want to see that perfect waltz." I smile and give him a quick hug.

"Aw man your kids are a dream but I thought they'd never piss off!" Shelby smirks.

"Don't, do not even start."

"What the fuck happened over there? I swear I could feel the tension from across the room?"

"Oh yeah… a bit like that tension with another Van Der Bilt, eh? What was *that* about?"

"Touché bitch… let's get a drink." She says wisely.

As we wait at the bar for our drinks, I turn to scan the room, I can see the boy's step away from their dates but can't see where they are going but the dark head towering above them is hard to miss.

I follow their every step and observe every second of the interaction, if he so dares to make my boys uncomfortable, I will throttle him with my bare hands, just as the tension is starting to escalate through me, I see Noah lean his head back and laugh out loud and Jacob offer a weary smile.

I watch as Sebastian reaches out his hand and both boys take the offered shake and accept the apologetic look, he's throwing them; it almost disarms me, then he looks up and catches my eye and the soft smile that graced his face disappears. It's no longer a glare, simply a perfectly blank expression. I turn and gulp whatever god-awful drink Shelby has placed down in front of me and try my hardest not to cough up a damn lung.

"What the hell was that?" I screech.

"Sambuca." she grins, "Maybe it will loosen you up."

"Yeah, right back at you, I see a special red coated devil lurking in the shadows with his creepy eye on you, care to explain?"

She downs two drinks she has in front of her, takes a deep breath and rolls her shoulders and faces me square on, "Well, that red coated devil was supposed to be my husband, in some sort of twisted nineteenth century arranged family marriage and that prick, took one look at me and refused point blank, right in front of my face,"

Oh no, she sees the horror on my face,

"Oh, don't begin the pity party just yet, it gets better… He said, And I quote, *'No fucking way am I marrying some petulant child brat.'* Then, he very graciously asked me if I wanted to fool around on the side?" She spits it out so fast it's hard to keep up. "So, what did I do? I ran out and married the first bastard who spoon fed me a fairytale of lies and well, you know how that part of the story ends."

"Aw Shell, honey I didn't know, want me to accidentally push him down the stairs or something." I have to bring a little humor. I can see she hates that pitying stare as much as I do, so I give her my own humiliating saga.

"Well, Sebastian asked me why my dead husband stood me up tonight, in front of his old bosses, who thought Matt hung the fucking moon by the way and my charming son proceeded to tell him how his dad would have come but… and *I* quote, *'Is six feet under'*. What the hell kind of pair are we?" I grin.

"We, my bestest friend, are the most awesome pair of badass chicks this little corner of the world has ever seen and you and me honey, we are never going to get trampled on again." She grins and pulls two glasses of champagne from god knows were, we clink and I really know I shouldn't but I join her in drowning it like a god damn shot.

Well shoot!
Now I'm a little drunk.
I am a total lightweight when it comes to mixing alcohol, so I ask the barman for a glass of ice water as Shelby goes off for a dance with a friend, after me reassuring her a million times that I'm fine.

I see the boys out on the dance floor, Jacob is performing a perfect waltz and Noah, well god only knows what he is dancing but Kayla looks happy just the same.

Mr. Davies approaches and asks me if I would do him the honor of taking a spin with him so off, I go.

"I want to thank you Leona." he starts, "Shelby has had a really rough time the last few years but ever since she joined your team, I can see my daughter coming back to life before my eyes. She's thriving and my wife and I are so thrilled to know she has someone like you for a friend, as well as a boss."

He is so sincere; you can see how much it must have hurt him, to watch his daughter be in so much pain and feel helpless.

"Mr. Davies, I appreciate the sentiment Sir but honestly Shelby has brought just as much to my life, lord maybe more than I can ever repay. Her work ethic is impeccable and honestly, I don't know how I managed anything before she came along. She is an asset to the company in so many ways and I honestly think at this point, it won't be long until she's, my boss."

I laugh and he laughs along with me.

"But even if she does leave me for another department, I can assure you sir, I am going nowhere. She has brought so much joy into my life that I had no idea what I was missing. I know you're my boss and this may overstep but I'm not too proud to say I had my work, my kids and little else after my husband passed. Shelby is bringing me to life, she's showing me how to be a friend and a woman, I am forever in her debt." I say passionately.

"You, Leona, are a remarkable young woman and everyone at the firm can see how hard you have worked through such a devastating time and for that my dear, I am sorry, you are as special a person as my daughter and I can see why you both get on so famously. You are both so strong, yet you just don't see it. It's an honor to have you as part of my daughter and our lives Leona, and I do still thank you." He says softly.

We carry on dancing in a comfortable silence and it's really nice.

As usual though the peace doesn't last long.

"Mr. Davies, Sir, I hope you don't mind but I'd quite like to cut in for the next dance?" I hear from behind me. Mr. Davies must feel my body tense, as he looks me directly in the eye and asks if that's ok with me?

Shit! I cannot make a scene, so I simply nod and thank him for the dance. As he moves away, I keep my head down but the minute I feel his hand reach for mine, I begin to turn away...

"I actually have to sit this one out, I need to excuse myself..." I start.

"Do not even think about it, the whole bloody room

is watching with baited breath. My grandparents are already terrified I have disgraced our family name and are adamant I make a very public groveling apology."

He stares down at me, those penetrating stormy eyes glaring, as I look behind him, I indeed see a collection of Van Der Bilt eyes following our every movement.

"May doesn't need to be getting anymore worked up." he says stiffly.

Andy looks apoplectic and May looks a little distraught, so I put on a fake smile, give them both a little wave and turn to face towards the man of the hour. I do not look at him. I can't.

He seems just as tense as me, as he again reaches for my hand, this time I let him take it and move towards him. I still can't bear to look up, so of course he growls slightly.

"This isn't exactly a pleasure for me either sweetheart but you could at least try and not look so constipated." He growls.

"Are you serious?" I start as my eyes flash towards his. He holds my stare and his gaze softens slightly.

"Ah, so the fire is still in there, not sure I could tolerate that meek version you've had on display tonight."

"You know what? Screw this and screw you…" I start, as I turn to move away but he pulls me roughly towards him and leans that scandalous mouth of his towards my ear,

"Now, now, people are watching, wouldn't want them all to see your true colors now, would we… *Leona*?" he growls snidely.

I lean further away from him, attempting to create some sort of distance. My traitorous body is far to comfortably molded into his,

165

"You are a bastard, you know that? What in the hell is your god damn problem? You really are the most ridiculously infuriating man." I fume.

"Well now, that is some potty mouth you have on you," he grins bloody devilishly, as he moves me effortlessly around the dance floor. "And here you have everyone convinced you're a lady, tut tut, whatever would they say?"

"I'm sure they would give me a damn medal for not smacking you in the bloody face." I glare.

My body is on fire, as I feel the heat pour through him where his hand is placed, just a smidge, lower than necessary, on the base of my spine. His warm firm grip clasped in mine, his strong chest chafing roughly against the silk of my dress. I hate that my own damn body is betraying me, I can already feel my nipples tighten, my flesh become flustered and my core is on fire.

The only consolation, is he looks in just about as much discomfort. His jaw is tight and his body is rigid, every part of him tensed and coiled, ready to be sprung and I pray I can make it through the dance and get as far from him as possible. I can feel the alcohol barreling through me and my palm starts to tremor.

He lets out a painful sigh and I tense, I can't do this here, there is no way can I let him sweep me through the dance floor, as he throws out some sort of pathetic apology.

"Leona." he starts.

"No… Don't you dare, Do not even attempt to say another word, just finish this god-awful sham of dance and then leave me in peace." I say through gritted teeth.

"That's not really realistic now, is it?" he mutters

deeply, as he stares down at me, those damn penetrating eyes drilling into mine.

I stumble and he pulls me closer, flush up against him, as I get a brief press, against his obvious strain. Oh, dear Lord, This cannot be happening.

He groans slightly, as his hand slides caressingly over the bare skin at my lower back, when I feel it, the spark, the burning heat, that tingle of sexual awareness and it's all too much. Too damn much, I feel like I'm about to burst into flames.

"Christ, Leona, I'm sorry, it's…"

The music begins to slow down and I am ashamed to admit it but I run. I up and flee, sure I make it look like I thank him for the dance but I can't escape his presence any quicker and he lets me go just as easily.

I am almost at the escape, when Andy stops me, "Leona sweetheart…" he starts,

"It's ok Andy, honestly, That bloody Shelby and her Sambuca is making a reappearance and I need a little air." I say as believable as possible.

"I am so sorry for Sebastian," he starts and I again interrupt.

"Andy don't, It was a simple mistake. He meant no harm and I assure you that I have been in far worse situations."

He glares at me with a little heat himself.

"Now Leona, that's a pack of bullshit and you know it!" he says.

"Look, it was a genuine mistake that we both should have dealt with, way before tonight, it's fine, he apologized, I accepted, we will move on."

He raises his eyebrows.

"I mean sure, we're not going to become bosom buddies but we are adults and we can move on, all in the past, I swear. Now will you please go back and enjoy your evening? If not, I'm going to have to make a scene for getting a little drunk and that is not a good idea for anyone." I smile tightly.

"You my dear, are the worst actress I have ever seen however I also see you are going to deal with this your own way and for now I won't interfere however if you need me, know I am here for you, family issues or not, you hear me?" he glares.

"Yes, Sir." I salute, with a cheeky wink.

"You kids will be the death of me." He groans. "Ok, off you go but don't dare go scurrying off to your room all night."

He sees me look towards the boys.

"Don't worry about them, the DJ will be setting up soon and your Noah has already challenged a few people to dance off's. And Valerie wants to introduce you to a few people." He says with a smirk, knowing just how to compose me.

"Yes Sir." I lean over and give him a soft kiss on the cheek. "Thanks Andy." I turn and walk away quickly so I don't have to look at him.

CHAPTER 16

Great, now I'm lost.

I have wandered back through the building inside and after using the appointed restroom and trying to spend, what felt like a lifetime, regaining my composure and calm my traitorous body, I've walked and walked and have no clue where I am.

I begin looking in doors and find myself in what looks to be a library, similar to the one next to my room. There is a roaring fire and a well-stocked bar over to the side.

I muse over Andy's words from earlier, that the private rooms were all locked up, so with the doors being open, it seems safe to pour myself a shot from the decanter and sit my aching body down by the fire for just a second. Weariness seeps over me. How on earth have I landed myself in this position?

I don't know how long I sit there, letting the heat from the fire and the sips from the now awfully low glass, wash over me. I keep telling myself to move but somehow never actually doing so.

I hear a door close sharply, as I feel him in my being. I don't move a muscle, hoping I'm wrong.

"You can't hide forever you know." He says bursting my bubble.

"Nope." I hiccup. Shit, that's not good.

"We need to talk." He says so stiffly, I can't help but let out a small laugh.

"Nope." I snigger.

"Are you drunk?" he asks astounded.

"Nope." I chuckle.

"For Christs sake, give me that." He says as he storms over and snatches away the glass and decanter.

He leans down in front of me, as I sit curled up in the softest chair I've ever sat on, wrapped up in the coziest blanket and stare off into the fire.

He reaches out a hand and clasps my chin gently.

"Did you drink all of this by yourself?" he groans.

"No, Sebastian, I just shared it with some random guest and then we had a very hot sweaty fuck and I sent him on his way… now piss off your ruining my bliss." I say.

He looks furious for a moment.

"That's what you think isn't it? That I'm some god damn… tart, who wants to bed some rich man and screw him out of his money or god knows what you think! Who the hell knows what goes on in that twisted mind of yours." I screech slightly.

He thinks I am a lot more drunk than I am, so I assume someone else paid the whiskey a little visit before me. I have drunk way more than I should have, but I'm not *that* drunk.

"That is not what I meant." He says tightly.

"Sure, it's not, you've said it almost every-time we've spoke." I sigh.

"Yes, because I thought you were bloody married!" he snaps.

"Well, if you had…"

"Don't you dare say 'If I had asked', you knew fine well I thought you were married, why didn't you ever correct me? Why would you keep that to yourself? After everything I said? What the bloody hell type of game were you playing?" he roars.

"How dare you…"

I fly up from the seat and stumble a little, my legs

have pins and needles from sitting in the same position for so long, I don't get the chance to right myself, as he grabs me, pulling me upright.

"How dare I? How dare you? Why didn't you tell me about your husband?" he shakes me a little.

"I… I tried."

"You tried? How hard is it to say 'I can fuck around with as many stripper looking cops as I want, because I'm not cheating on anyone', why let me believe you were the worst kind of person, why let me say those god-awful things to you?"

"Honestly, I have no idea. Maybe it was simply better than having your pity." I sigh, as the fight slowly drains out of me. He's right, I knew all the '*Mrs. Chalmers*' shit was an issue.

"Jesus Christ." He shudders.

"Your right, Sebastian, I should have corrected you. I am sorry."

His body tightens and tenses, the heat radiating from him, building.

"You have got to be kidding me? Why the hell are you apologizing to me?" he shakes me, almost violently as he grasps my chin, forcing me to look up at him.

"Tell me this is all real. Tell me *you* are real, Leona. I can't keep fighting this anymore!" he roars before pulling me to him, crashing his mouth to mine and devouring me.

I can't catch a breath, my whole body responding instantly, like I am trying to climb my whole being inside of him. He reaches his hand around cradling my scalp, tilting my head to force me into submission, as if I am fighting him.

But Lord, it's the opposite, I want to draw in every

single piece of him I can. His tongue delves deeper into my mouth and mine dashes out to meet his. I feel starved, my hands struggling to find any purchase, as I claw at him, feeling the moment his tightly controlled restraint snaps.

My dress is dragged up around my waist, as he pulls my core harshly against his rock-hard erection. I groan in to his mouth, as he moves us fluidly, placing me on top of a desk or table.

I would love to say it was like a scene from a movie, where the dashing hero sweeps all the items off the desk uncaring of the mess but I am so blinded by lust, I couldn't tell you where I am, never mind if there was anything to be swept.

I feel his hand slide up my bare thigh, as he wraps my legs firmly around his waist, my fingers reaching upward, I pull sharply on the soft hair at the base of his skull, as he lowers his lips to my neck. That sinful mouth makes its slow way downward, sucking and kissing, as he pulls my hard peaked nipple through the silk of my dress, into his mouth.

My hands are tearing and pulling at the layers of clothes, with an almost desperate need to feel skin. One hand slides down the back of his shirt and reaches down to claw at his back. His hand tightens on my breast and his teeth tug sharply on my nipple.

I let out a soft startled gasp and he freezes, like a spell has been shattered, he's frozen in time.

He pulls back sharply and stares directly into my eyes. The depths of his lust overwhelming, his eyes are black like coal. But I see it, the color seeping back in, like the reality around us. He doesn't move a muscle though, just stands there staring.

I blink hard, nothing.

"Er, Sebastian…" I start.

"Fuck!" He groans and tugs on his hair. "What the hell am I doing?"

I just hang there half clustered in his grasp.

Yeah buddy, what are you doing? That was way too hot and heavy, far too quickly, but truthfully, I was loving every minute of it, so why on earth are we stopping?

My whole body and soul feel alive for the first time in lord knows how long but I am also aware this is slowly becoming real awkward by the second. I am still entangled in his lap, my dress is bunched up around my waist and Sebastian, Lord Sebastian, looks like he has been savagely attacked by a wild animal.

"Er, maybe we should…" I say as I start to climb of his lap. Yup, I am as red as you can get!

His grip on my waist tightens sharply, he doesn't push me away, yet he also doesn't pull me any closer. He just grips my bare skin and lowers his head slightly.

"Just, give me a minute." He grunts.

I wait a good minute; I need more than a minute myself but I feel like this is getting a little weird, so I begin to slowly ease my body away from his and lower my feet back towards the floor.

He stays rigid but doesn't stop me, which if I am truly honest… sucks! My own overwhelming urge to hang on to him slips and I slow my movements even more.

"It's okay Leona, I'm not a colt ready to bolt, you can climb off me." He says.

It sounds almost insulting but the strain on his face shows he thinks I am afraid to spook him, not that he's totally repulsed by my body mounted on his.

"Eh ok, so I…" I start, having no clue how to finish,

thank the lord he interrupts.

"Christ Leona, that was, well, I shouldn't have taken advantage in that way, you're drunk and…"

"I am not drunk!" I say sternly.

"Yes, you are, and I was out of line, it's been a shitty night, well month or so and I suppose I'm more stressed out than I realized, I shouldn't have taken my frustrations out on you. That was not my intentions when I came in here." He doesn't blink, as he roughly runs his hand through his hair and attempts to fix his elegant tuxedo back into place

"Oh, so what where your intentions, Sebastian?" I say sharply, as I stand upright and glare at him, folding my arms tightly across my body. I am pissed, possibly un-necessarily so but yet, I am.

"Well, I came to talk to you in a civilized manner, apologize for my behavior and ask you why the hell you didn't tell me you were a widow! Not molest you, a drunken woman!" he snaps, "For fucks sake, I am not an animal! I can control myself… but you… you just keep getting under my skin on a bloody daily basis, I will not fall victim to this shit."

He is mumbling now under his breath and I get the very clear impression that Sebastian Van Der Bilt does not lose that cool calm exterior very often and for some reason it pisses him off that he lost his control, with me.

I do try hard, I swear I try so hard but as I stand here flabbergasted at him as he rants, mostly to himself, whilst he fixes his clothing in a quick and brusque manner, I can't help it.

I laugh.

Not a quiet little giggle or even a simple guffaw, nope, me I go and let out a hearty loud chuckle, which freezes him on the spot.

Those penetrating black orbs snap up to meet mine and he growls.

Growls like a caged animal. Rough and volatile under his breath.

"Are you laughing at me?" He snaps tightly, shaking his head, "And you're not supposed to be drunk! Why am I even bothering with this bloody conversation, you'll no doubt forget all about it by the morning and I'll have to go over this whole damn thing again!" he mutters.

"Like I already said, I am not drunk and I can bloody assure you, I won't be forgetting anything in a hurry!" I stamp back.

Shoot! Why did I say that? Ok deflect.

"You know you really have a filthy mouth when you're all enraged." No, that sounded way more seductive than I meant. He raises his eyebrow. Just that one.

"What I mean is, I don't think I've ever heard you curse so much." I stammer.

"Well, it appears you bring out my heathen side." He glares at me as if it's my fault.

"How the hell is that *my* fault?" I glare right back.

"Well Leona, It seems you simply allude some sort of enchantment that makes sane minded men, turn blood lusty! I have no intention of losing my mind or my money over some crazy spur of the moment fuck!" he swipes.

"Are you serious right now? I don't want your mind or your bloody money! And I sure as hell don't want to 'fuck you' as you so eloquently put it! What the hell is wrong with you?"

He grins at me. Not a sweet charming grin that you

could swoon over, nope he throws out a full-blown devils smirk, that makes my panties damp and forces me to clench my thighs tightly together to stop me from slapping the damn thing off his gorgeous face, before I try and jump his bones, again.

"Well now, as much as I would love to believe that snippy little statement, your body unfortunately gives you away. Your nipples are pebbled, your face is flushed and if you clench those thighs any tighter together sweetheart, you're going to give yourself a wet patch on that fine silk." He smirks.

"You know what Sebastian; you are a total prick! Yes, you're absolutely right, my body cannot hide the fact that a quick fuck does sound pretty good…" I start, as he stares at me, "But you know what else, I would not fuck you if you were the last man on earth, want to know why?" I don't wait for an answer as I can see his own temper rising. "Because no matter how sane and well put together you may seem to show the rest of the world, I see you! You are an absolute bastard through and through! You have had a problem with me from day one and I will be fucked if I bend over and take your bullshit anymore. No, I am not fooling around on my husband, No I am not interested in bedding a man who is old enough to be my grandfather. No, I am not trying to seduce my way to the top of the firm and No fucking way will I sleep with a prick like you, no matter how much my stupid body betrays me! So, you can piss right off with your self-righteous shit elsewhere. Stay away from me from now on and I will do the same."

I turn away from the heated gaze he is throwing at me and stomp over to the chair were I left me heels. I snatch them up and don't bother attempting to put them on or fix myself, before I march out of the room.

Nothing can be worse than looking at his stupid face any longer. I really wish I wasn't so immature but unfortunately, I can't say that's something I've ever been, so naturally I slam the door on my way out, as I stamp down the hall.

Of course, my life sucks donkey dick because not only is there someone else walking down the hall at that same precise moment but it is none other than Valerie Van Der Bilt floating towards me.

MY OTHER BOSS.

With a huge smile on her face. There is no way to hide the fact that I have obviously had some sort of raging altercation with someone. My hair has come undone, My dress is half bunched up at the back and I have no shoes on. Valerie on the other hand looks like sheer perfection. She is of course wearing a fabulous silver jeweled outfit that looks like it's a dress but upon closer inspection is actually a pantsuit. Her make-up is simple and sophisticated and her hair is gathered in a loose knotted style at the back of her head, not un-similar to how mine had looked pre-Sebastian!

"Leona my dear, I have been looking for you, but I see you had moved onto your own little party maybe?" she smiles softly, "Or you had the unfortunate task of meeting with my pigheaded nephew and it went slightly askew?" she hedges.

"Something like that, Valerie, yes." I admit, frowning. "Is there somewhere nearby I can freshen up?"

"Of course, follow me." She starts walking towards the way I had just came and I stay stock still. "Oh, don't worry Sebastian will not come out of that room any time soon I can assure you, my nephew will punish himself for a lot longer than the time needed for us to waltz on past that door I assure you." She grins softly.

Again, I just stare after her.

"You know we could just hang around here and wait for someone else to come past, maybe spread a little gossip?" she gives me a pointed look which gets my feet moving sharply.

I walk as quickly and as quietly as I can past the offending door and don't look once. We both startle a little at the loud crash but Valerie just keeps on going and I trail after her.

I mean what else can I do? There's no way in hell I'm going to check on him. We take a turn at the end of the hall that I never noticed before and Valerie pulls out a key from her purse and unlocks the door. She moves into the room and I follow. It's not unlike the previous room only more feminine, softer colors in paler neutral tones, again with a warm fire burning away.

"There is a bathroom through that door, you can give yourself a little moment," she smiles, "Whilst I pour us both a stiff drink eh."

"Thank you, Valerie, that would be great." I say.

"A little suggestion though, you have magnificent hair, maybe you should let it down once in a while without repercussions hmm." She says softly with a smile as she turns to fix the drinks.

I walk into the opulent bathroom and sink down on to the small chaise that's placed in the corner, in front of a large window.

What have I done now? How do I keep getting into predicaments with this man, he infuriates me beyond belief and all rational thought, yet I can't deny how much I wanted him. How alive every part of me felt in his arms. Then he has to go and open that damn mouth of his. Every time, he seems to say the wrong thing. It makes me want to punch him or bloody kiss him and I honestly don't know what's worse.

I take a deep steadying breath and set about repairing the damage. My face thankfully isn't too bad, quality make-up huh! My dress, I smooth out as much as I can but Valerie's right my hair may be irreparable.

I seem to have lost the most of my Kirby grips and it's too heavy to stay up with what I do have. I settle for pulling some of it back from my face and letting the rest hang loose, some tendrils fall forward but it's the best I can do. I take a long look in the mirror before I brace myself to go out and face my boss.

I mean seriously, Fuck my life!

"That looks so much better Leona."

She smiles softly at me as she hands me a large glass full of maybe brandy. I probably shouldn't drink any more however I need something to calm my nerves, so bottoms up. I thank her and take a large sip.

Oh wow, it's like hot liquid honey.

"And that's why the doors kept locked, wouldn't want anyone drinking my good liquor."

"That's divine, what is it?" I ask.

"100-year-old honey bourbon brandy. It was a gift from a great lover from my past, every time I drink it, I think about hunting him down just for another bottle but alas it wasn't to be." She sighs softly.

"Well, I can see why, It's delicious. Thank you for sharing."

"I gather you need something after your latest encounter with Sebastian?" she just watches me.

"Well, yes it seems we really do bring out the worst

in each other and I have absolutely no idea how to resolve it." I hedge.

"Leona, I am going to be very honest with you dear and I am saying this as Sebastian's aunt and not your boss or friend. My nephew is a remarkable young man, who is also deeply disturbed, with a very cynical view of the world." She pauses. "He truly is one of my most favorite people and I would never betray him in any way however on this occasion, I feel it's only right you get a little better understanding of how he came to be the man he is. Normally I would never interfere, but alas its becoming glaringly obvious something has to be done."

She motions for me to take a seat opposite her as she lowers herself into a chair in front of the fire.

"Sebastian's father was an exceptional man." she starts softly, "He was such a very sensible and serious young boy who was determined to take his place in the family business. He idolized Andy and followed him around everywhere; he knew that as the second son he would have to put in double the work to earn his place in the firm and he was more than up for the task." She smiles fondly. "His creativity brought something totally different to the business and he had an artistic flair that couldn't be imitated. He thrived at University and even worked in another firm; to really prove he was more than just his family's name, more than just a shoe-in to the firm. He was on track to take over as a partner, just like his brother when he met Sebastian's mother." She pauses and I can sense this isn't easy for her.

"You really don't have to confide any of this to me Valerie, I am sure your family, like most have things they would rather not re-hash." I say.

"Yes, well I really think you need to hear this and I have no idea if Sebastian is even capable of anything more than he already is but I think it's worth the shot to give him every opportunity." She smiles at my frown; I have no idea what she's talking about.

"You'll understand soon enough Leona. When Archibald met Sylvie, his whole world imploded. They were the worst possible mix for each other. Sylvie wanted to live the high life and she saw Archibald as her golden ticket. A typical cliche really." She sighs sadly, "He lost himself in her and he lost his future in the process. Everything he had worked for, was gone in a blink when she came along." She shakes her head gently as if banishing the thoughts.

"Of course, in the beginning they at least tried to keep up with the work schedule since it afforded them both the wine and dine party lifestyle Sylvie craved and she was a remarkable hostess. Always throwing extravagant parties and gatherings. She thrived when she was hosting but unfortunately the more, they partied, the less he worked, the less income they had coming in and Archibald started squirrelling through his inheritance money faster than sand through your fingers. He became a different person in such a short space of time and it really looked like we were losing him."

She pauses and takes a moment to compose her thoughts, I reach out almost instinctively and clasp her hand. She smiles and it's almost painful to watch.

"Then Sylvie fell pregnant, she was devastated. She had absolutely no intention of carrying a child but Archibald was elated. He made a very sordid deal with her to keep the baby." She sighs and takes a large gulp off her drink.

I simply wait, she seems, almost lost in thought and as much as I hate to intrude on Sebastian's personal life, it is starting to make sense why he is the way he is. His loathing of social climbers and gold diggers.

"Sylvie agreed to keep the baby as long as she was sent off to a private retreat were no-one, god forbid would see her 'fat' as she put it. She sequestered herself away and kept herself healthy and birthed Sebastian. He was the perfect baby. All dark hair and eyes." She smiles genuinely.

"But Sylvie had no maternal instincts whatsoever. She had her own plans and no interest in a baby. She agreed to stay for the first years of his life but sadly didn't even last six months. She filed for divorce and took Archibald for every penny. He gave her it all willingly, for custody of Sebastian. But he was so lost after that, he had sunk too far to climb out of his despair at the state of his life and over losing what he still regarded the love of his life. He was blinded by her for so long, yet he worked hard to get himself back together and he almost did. He was a good parent and taught Sebastian so much. He loved him with a deep ferocity but warned him severely off the pitfalls of love. He convinced Sebastian, work should always be your first love. For years Sebastian watched his father lust over multiple women, they came and went nothing more nothing less until Cheyenne." She looks up with such a wretched look on her face, that I have that horrible sinking feeling in the pit of my stomach.

I really don't want to hear anymore. I know enough.

"I think I've heard enough Valerie; I understand what you are trying to convey but I still don't think this is any of my business, though I appreciate the gesture. It does help understand Sebastian's reactions a little more but I feel a tad uncomfortable knowing so much of his personal history. His childhood is really none of my business and I think he would despise me even more if he thought I knew any of this."

"Your damn right I would!" He barks from behind me and I startle, I knew nothing good would come from coming here this weekend but this is too much.

CHAPTER 17

"Sebastian, this is for your own good. You need to stop…"

"Enough Val!" he all but roars. "Hasn't this woman already burrowed her way into this family way more than is necessary?" he doesn't even look at me, he is too busy glaring at his aunt.

"For goodness sake Sebastian, I have said nothing that a little digging in the media wouldn't show up, I would never betray our family secrets but this hatred for Mrs. Chalmers has gone on long enough. Your opinions are misguided by your fathers stupid mistakes and they are destroying your life." She says passionately and I squirm in my seat.

I should not be witness to this. I start to edge my way slowly across my seat and out of their eye-line, when his roar freezes me.

"I said enough. How I live my life is my own decision, no-one else's… and you do not move another damn muscle!" He turns so sharply and pierces my heart with the look in his eyes.

He looks both devastated and furious.

"Sebastian!" Valerie scolds but now his eyes are on me, he just glares.

"As I told your aunt, I appreciate the gesture but your personal life is just that *yours*. I have no interest in it." I start as I stand up and his eyes tighten.

"I told you not to move a damn muscle." He growls.

"For goodness sake Sebastian, she is not a dog to be ordered around, you need to get control of yourself."

Oh dear! Why would she say that? I mentally slap

my forehead, like a red flag to a bull, he grows more enraged by the second. Yet he still doesn't take his eyes off me.

"Val, you need to leave us, now." He says as he holds my eye.

"Well, I do not think that is a good idea." She glares right at him but he pays no attention.

"Mrs. Chalmers and I need to have a talk once and for all and you… need… to… leave… now!"

He speaks with such barely controlled restraint; I feel like I should be terrified but somehow, I'm not. I just glare straight back. You know what, maybe a good old shouting match is just what's needed to put this nonsense to bed.

"Sebastian, I…" she begins

"It's fine Valerie," I say, "Sebastian is right. We need to talk." I glare right back at him and do not blink.

See who you intimidate you prick. Not me but as he grins ever so slightly, I get a small spark of fear and like a bloodhound he smells it.

"Lock the door on your way-out Val, I would prefer there was no-one else around to hear any more of my personal life tonight, if that's not too much bother." He still won't look at her and she looks deeply hurt at the tone.

"Are you sure about this Leona?" She says gently, staring directly at me.

"Yes, It's fine." I square my shoulders.

"Ok, but I will be just down the hall if you need anything." She says as she throws a glare at him. "I am truly concerned about you Sebastian and I love you; I would never intentionally hurt you; you know that and I look forward to your apology, when your temper has settled. But mark my words do not make more of an ass about this situation or you will find yourself in my bad books and I can assure you, it's the last place you want to be." She says sternly.

He stands immobile for a few seconds, then nods his head, "Duly noted."

She moves to the door without a backwards glance and I hear the click of the lock as the door closes.

What the hell have I done now?

We both stand there staring at each other, yet its oddly not as weird as it should be.

I refuse to show him any emotion though, I have hated the pitying looks I have received over the last couple of years, so I will not throw any out into the world myself, let alone to this man who looks like he is seriously about to crack.

If only my heart didn't hurt at the thought of him, if only he wasn't so damn handsome my chest aches and if only, he didn't make me feel so suffocatingly hot that I still want to jump his bones, prick or not. It's infuriating.

"That's a mighty lot of serious thinking you're doing over there *Mrs. Chalmers*." he mocks slightly, "But I've got to give you props for not putting on the waterworks or dishing out any pitying looks." He looks a little puzzled by that and I decide to just get this nonsense over with.

"Look Sebastian, I have been on the receiving end of enough pity looks and sympathetic smiles to last me a lifetime." I sigh, "Life sucks. But I assure you, I will not be dishing any sympathetic glances out to anyone; it doesn't help and is often de-meaning, no matter how well intentioned." I state firmly. "I am sorry, however." He growls as I ignore him and carry on,

"I never corrected you, when you sneered your '*Mrs. Chalmers*' shit at me and I should have. Maybe we would have avoided that embarrassment from earlier on but I didn't and I should have, so for that I am sorry. It was unfair of me. I am also sorry if I gave you the wrong impression of me but let me assure you here and now, I have no interest in your upbringing. I have no interest in how its affected your character and I sure as hell have no interest in your family's money, fame or whatever you want to call it. In the case of being transparent, I am fairly well off myself, not anywhere near your elaborateness…" I wave my hand around as if that explains my meaning and carry on,

"But I am financially comfortable enough off that I can afford to put both my boys through University, I own my home and have a simple life. I have no damn interest in any fortune or fame. I hate everything that shit represents, as for your personal life…" I pause and shake my head; he almost holds his breath.

"Yes, go on… what about it?" he glares.

"I really don't give a fuck about it, to be perfectly blunt. I couldn't much care whether you had a happy Von Trap family upbringing or you were bloody Oliver! It's none of my business, *you* are none of my business. Honestly, I think you're simply a prick to me because you choose to be but that is really neither here or there. I've said my piece, I've apologized for any wrongdoing and I would quite like to get back to check on my boys, so if you have nothing more to say I will be off." I stare.

"Well, that's quite a lot to take in now *Mrs. Chalmers*…" he starts.

"Oh, piss off with that snarky *Mrs. Chalmers*, you had your bloody tongue down my throat not half an hour ago and it was not *'Mrs. Chalmers'* you were saying then so knock it off." I growl.

"You really are something when you lose your temper, you know that." He smirks.

Me, I merely glare and my foot involuntary starts tapping.

"Your boys are fine," he sighs, "I spoke to them not five minutes before I opened that door and assured them you were ok and they could head on down to the fire with the rest of the kids." He says a bit too softly, "Before you start bitching, I spoke to both boys this evening and apologized profusely for the scene earlier. I would never hurt anyone intentionally, let alone children, and the loss of a parent is not something I would ever mock or sneer about." He says sincerely.

And because I swore, I would never give 'that' look I simply stare.

"I must say Leona, you really are something, I know you are desperate to cave a little, '*aw poor boy lost his parents too*', '*he must be so lost*', '*he knows how it feels*', and yet you stand there like some stoic ice queen." He grins. Actually, grins like some insane sociopath.

"What the hell is wrong with you? You are giving me whiplash Sebastian!" I groan.

"Honestly, I have no fucking idea, because of you! I came in here listening to Val spout all that nonsense and all I can think is how manipulative can someone be, to peer so intrusively into someone's private life,"

"I did not!" I start ready to tear him a new one…

"Calm down, I know that. I heard you tell her that, twice. You baffle me on so many levels, All I came to do earlier was apologize and yet again you beat me to it. You confuse me to no end Leona, and quite frankly,

I have no idea how to deal with that."

"Yes... well... still, you shouldn't be telling the boys it's ok to go off goodness knows where, now it will take me an age to find them." I sigh, "And whether I 'beat you to it' or not, I needed to apologize regardless."

"See, that is exactly what I mean... Yes, you should have corrected me but that does not excuse my behavior towards you. I treated you appallingly and I am sorry for that Leona. I have no idea why you irritate me so damn much." He says it so simply I know I should be offended but he genuinely seems to have no idea why and it's almost laughable, yet I refrain. I know where that got us last time and I fear it won't help.

"Well, I must just have that effect on some people." I shrug.

"That's not what I mean, I won't give Val's nonsense any credit but I think it's pretty safe to say, we both know I do not trust just anyone with my family and you already know I have no time for social climbers or gold diggers."

"Might want to get a new girlfriend who's not a stuck-up publicity whore." I mumble and slap my hand over my mouth.

Shoot! Where did that come from?

"Er, sorry that was totally inappropriate and way out of line. Sorry." I grumble.

"Well firstly, Melania, is not my girlfriend and yes, that was incredibly inappropriate but you are right on her character though, hence why she's never met my family and nor will she ever. I do not cross those areas of my life for good reason however all my lines seem to blur when I am around you."

Aw that was almost a compliment.

"It's fucking infuriating and I really don't have time for it."

Ok, back to being a prick. I glare at him.

"That's not really an insult, although I know it sounded like one. Look let's just get this out in the open. You and I both know there is some sort of… chemistry thing going on here. I never cross the line with married women, ever, that's why you pissed me off. I hate cheaters above all else and I hated myself more for wanting you regardless of your marriage. It's not something I am comfortable with but you have been honest with me and I guess I owe you the same." He says it so roughly, as if it still pisses him off, even now he knows I am not technically married.

"I want you Leona, married, widowed, single, I don't really give much of a damn, I just know I want you in a way that feels toxic to me and I don't know how to get rid of it." He fumes.

"Wow, and they say romance is dead." I mutter dryly.

"I can assure you one thing Leona; you will get no romance from me. None. I have no time for soppy sentimentality, nor have I any intention of dating, having any form of a serious relationship and god forbid, anything close to marriage. I am not made for it. However, I would very much like to fuck you into next week and then move on with our lives." He says it so seriously I can't help it; I laugh gently.

"You cannot be serious! In the space of the last few months or so, you have called me a gold digger, cheater, tart, lord only knows what else and now you're telling me you would like to maybe fuck me for a spell and then we can go on with our lives, as if that's a normal conversation."

Unfortunately, I wish I was as appalled as I sound but all I can think of is how good getting fucked by this man sounds. I have officially lost my god damn mind.

"I said that I *want* too Leona, not that I will." He sighs, "I sincerely apologize for molesting you earlier. It was inexcusable and you are more than welcome to press charges or report me, but I can assure you from here on out, I will not lay another inappropriate hand on you."

His face is so tightly controlled, determined, I can see he truly believes deep down, I could lure him into some dastardly trap.

"I will deal with my own disappointing urges myself…" he squints at me, as he spots my childish smirk. "That is not what I meant and you know it, for goodness sake grow up." He glares. "I am trying to deal with this in an adult manor but if you are still drunk Leona, we can leave this to another day?" he frowns.

"Nope I am fine, I apologize." I smirk a little.

"Yes, well let's get this dealt with and move on." He pauses and takes a steadying breath, bolstering courage or reciting his awful apology in his head, then he begins. "Leona, I am truly sorry for the genuine mistake I made of thinking you were stepping out on your husband. I offer you my sincerest condolences for your loss." He carries on not fully looking at me, so he completely misses the daggers I am throwing directly at him.

"It was a genuine mistake and I promise to keep my opinions on how you live your personal life to myself moving forward. I have accepted that you and I will have to close out the Montgomery deal together and I will be more civilized in the future. I have also been made fully aware that you are now a welcomed addition to this family and I will do my best to deal with that. I will try and accept that your intentions are genuine in that regards and I am sure we can avoid each other as needed." He finishes and looks at me expectantly.

Is this guy for real?

"Sebastian, you had my breasts in your mouth and your hand up my dress, not half an hour ago and now you're speaking to me like, some sort of stunted robot! What in the hell?"

"I can assure you right now, that will never happen again!" he says darkly.

"So, you want to just forget about it?" I ask, as I cross my arms.

"Already forgotten." He glares tightly. He is nowhere near as controlled as he pretends. I shouldn't tease, I know this but screw it.

"What if I don't want to forget it?" I ask.

"Tough shit!" he snaps.

I simply stand there and look at him. He is fighting it so hard; he wants me but he hates himself for it. I would normally be unsure why but ultimately; I can see he has made up his mind.

"Ok Sebastian, I get it. Are you sure though? You know fine well now I am a widow, I am not a cheater and I have honest intention in regards to this family. Are you positive you have no interest in taking this…" I wave a hand back and forth between us, "Chemistry or whatever it is any further?" I ask and watch him closely.

His whole posture is rigid, his jaw is tight and he seems to be clenching his teeth.

"Positive, regardless of my earlier actions I can control myself." He replies through gritted teeth.

"And you are sure we can move on and work together without ripping each other's clothes off?" I smirk. I know I can't help myself.

"I am sure!" he snaps.

"Ok then," I say, as I hold my hand out to his, "Friends?"

He stares at me for so long, looking at my hand like I am Eve offering him an apple, but eventually, like I knew he would, he takes my hand in his and shakes it.

"Colleagues, Mrs. Chalmers, only colleagues." He groans slightly and pulls his hand back sharply.

"Fine but enough with the *Mrs. Chalmers* shit, Leona is more than fine. Otherwise, we will have to go back to the whole SIR debacle." I grin to lighten the mood.

"Fair, Leona it is." He says and moves as far away as possible but still watches me intently.

"Now if you could be so kind as to point me in the direction of this fire, I would like to check on my boys and get myself to bed." I smile softly.

See we can be civil. The heat in his eyes when I mention bed doesn't dim though but I decide that will be his problem to deal with, not mine.

"Sebastian?"

"Yes, I can show you where to go." He says a little stiffly.

"No, it's fine you can just send me on my way and I will get out of your hair. You must want to get back to your family. I've taken up enough of your time." I say.

"It's fine, there is no way you won't get lost. The trail to the woods is well lit but it's far too easy to veer off." he sighs.

"Honestly, I can go find Shelby, or Tabitha even." I am grasping at straws here; I've put on a brave face long enough. I need my own breathing space. But as usual, he senses it right away.

"Now Leona, surely, you're not scared of a little walk in the dark with me? I thought we were going to be *friends*?" he grins.

Oh dear, I'm positive nice Sebastian, is going to be a hell of a lot worse, than dickhead Sebastian.

"Colleagues." I snap automatically.

He laughs, actually laughs out loud and as I gape at him, I know I am already in major trouble. He is just so devastatingly handsome; he looks like a completely different person altogether, when he eases up. I'm not sure, I am going to be capable of fighting this.

"Ok colleague, let's go." He offers out his arm with a sarcastic smirk on his face and I freeze.

He's getting his own back for the hand shake, I'm sure of it. I keep looking and when he raises his eyebrow pointedly, I know I am right. This weekend was a terrible idea.

CHAPTER 18

"Mom, this weekend was a great idea! Thanks for letting us come. These guys are a blast!" Noah screeches, when he sees me come through the woods.

The whole place has fairy lights twinkling in almost every tree but it casts a soft glow and the light from the fire gives enough illumination to give you awareness but it is still a little creepy if I'm honest.

"It's perfectly safe," Sebastian says behind me, "This is all private land and although you can't see it there is security everywhere. The boys will be fine. I would never let my nieces be out here otherwise." He says softly.

"Thanks, that makes me feel a little better I suppose." I grumble.

Sebastian has been the perfect gentleman on the walk here and he was entirely correct I would never have found it, or Shelby who seems to have disappeared off lord knows were. Just as I have that thought, I see her storm towards me.

"Stay the fuck away from these Van Der Bilt men Leona!" she says and throws an awful glare at Sebastian as she passes. "Nothing but rakes the lot of them!" she carries on as she heads back up the path towards the house.

"Shelby, wait." I say as I go to follow her but Sebastian reaches out and grasps my arm.

"I would give her some space just now; she tends to need to vent to herself first after she's been in Anders' company for too long."

"How do you know…" I start and just like that he

comes waltzing up the path.

"You owe me a dance missy." He croons.

"Yeah, and you owe my friend an apology I think!" I say crossing my arms. I hear rather than see Sebastian's soft chuckle next to me and I look up at him. His eyes soften a little and I catch my breath, God he's beautiful.

"Ahh, I see you two have kissed and made up?" Anders smirks.

"Fuck off, Anders. Leona's right though you better not have pissed Shell off too much or Gramps will be on your ass." He says half sternly, half mockingly. He almost looks... relaxed. It's incredibly weird.

"I can assure you, it's her who should be apologizing to me! That woman will be the death of me." He rolls his eyes dramatically.

Before I begin to give him an earful, I see Jacob coming up the path towards us with a familiar face in tow, "Miguel?" I say in a shocked tone.

"Hey there again Mrs. Chalmers, good to see you." He smiles gently. "Unc." he smirks.

"Punk!" Sebastian says as he ruffles his hair.

"Mr. Van Der Bilt's," Jacob says. "Thanks again for letting us attend, it's been great fun."

Aw these boys making me proud. And here I was worrying.

"Yeah, it's been a blast! And the weekends only just begun!" Noah grins bringing me right back down to reality.

As I look around, I notice it's mostly just teens that's hanging around down here and they seem to have settled right down, laughing and joking and I can see the boys are eager to talk privately, I excuse ourselves from the men and walk a little distance away.

"You good Mom?" Jacob asks immediately. "You and Mr. Van Der Bilt sort out your issues?"

Yeah, kiddo like that's going to happen in this century.

"Of course, just a simple misunderstanding, we're all good. Are you guys, ok?" I ask pointedly.

"Yeah, he explained earlier that the 'Mrs. Chalmers' around the office confused him, makes sense you know." Jacob says understandingly.

"I'm sure someone mentioned before that could happen..." Noah grins.

"Yeah, yeah smart Alec, I hear you." Noah made a wise crack about how I would never get a date if people keep calling me Mrs.

Little shit nailed it.

"Ok, so this is pretty cool huh?" I say changing the subject. "You guys having fun?"

"Aw mom it's so cool! Tommy and Marco are well jealous, and Kayla is so chill. She's like almost as good as us at sports."

"Almost Noah? She just whipped you at Table Tennis." Jacob laughs.

"That my friend was me giving her a win, it's all part of my plan." He winks.

"Boys I am warning you both right now... Do not toil with these girls." I give them a stern look. "I brought you up to be gentleman and if I catch either of you disrespecting any female, you are going to be in serious trouble, you hear me?" I glare.

"Mom, don't be ridiculous, we would never be inappropriate. The girls are cool and if I can persuade Kayla to give me a shot, I will treat her like a princess, though to be fair I'm not sure she'll let me she's kinda fierce." He grins sheepishly. Maybe she can keep him on the straight and narrow. I glance at Jacob.

"Libby is nice too but she has made it perfectly clear she is too old for me." He rolls his eyes, "She's actually a little immature for me but I won't point that out, me being a gentleman and all." He huffs a little and I settle.

"Okay well if you guys are going to behave, I think I will head back to my room. You sure you're ok in the cabins? The girls are in different ones, right?"

"Aw mom c'mon! You think the Van Der Bilt's are throwing some wild teenage orgy?" Noah laughs.

Ok he's got me there but I was a horny teen once so I think it's a fair question.

"Yeah, yeah but boys will be boys and all that!" I say. "Okay off you go, best behavior and I will see you both in the morning." I lean over and give them a quick hug, so not to damaged their reputations. Cue my eye roll. Noah charges off towards Miguel, who has been chatting nearby with Sebastian, as Jacob pauses.

"Sure, you're ok mom?" he asks.

"Yeah kiddo, you?"

"Yup, taking it all in." he grins. "You want me to walk you back?"

Shoot! I never thought of that.

"It's ok Jacob, I'm about to head back as well. If its ok with you both, I can escort your mom back?" Sebastian says gently. The prick from before has done a disappearing act and the man in front is far too charming.

"As long as it's ok with you mom." Jacob says watching me closely.

"JAKE! C'mon we need you for the dual!" Noah and Miguel shout.

"Off you go, I will be fine. Have fun." I give him a

glare.

"Gotcha, fun!" he smiles. "Thank you, Mr. Van Der Bilt, Sir."

"Sebastian is fine."

"Thanks Sebastian, Night mom, love you." He says as he runs off. I stand for a moment and watch him go.

"They're great kids Leona." He says softly coming up beside me. "I really hope they forgive my earlier transgression." He stares after them.

"It's already forgotten for Noah, you apologize sincerely, he accepts it and moves on. Jacob will too, just takes him a little while longer to test your sincerity." I sigh. "I can find my way back fine; you go enjoy the rest of the party." I shoo him away.

He lets out a loud hearty laugh that tingles up my spine.

"Did you just shoo me?" he grins.

"Eh, well I just meant…"

"Oh, I know exactly what you meant Leona but unfortunately its later, darker now and there is no way I can let you toddle off in the dark alone. Bloody Anders has sulked off and I wouldn't put it past him to hop out and give you a scare. He bores too easily that one." I start to try again and he sighs,

"I am heading back that way anyway, what's the harm?"

"Are you sure you don't want to stay longer?" I say as I rub my arms. We're a little further away from the fire now and my wrap is not that warm. I really do want to get back inside.

"As much as it pains me to say, I think I am a little too old to be hanging around teen beach fires anymore." He grins, "and to be quite honest I'm bloody freezing now."

He's right.

"Okay, kind sir, if you don't mind, please get me back to warmth." I smile and turn to head in what is obviously the wrong direction, as I almost smack right into a tree. Typical the only one without bloody lights.

He lets out a soft chuckle and I think that alone heats my body temperature a couple of degrees.

"This way, sweetheart." He says it so softly, I choose to ignore the pang in my chest and his muttered curse.

"Thank you." I say and swing round with a fake smile.

It feels like the walk back takes double the time but apart from the chill in the air, I honestly don't care.

Holding onto Sebastian's arm as we walk through the sparkling trees and listening to him talk so easily about his nieces and nephews is perfection. He asks a lot of questions about the boys and reassures me that a couple of the older kids will be on night watch. Apparently, Hank, Kayla's dad has some sort of security perimeter set up around the cabin which is kind of overkill but as I said, 'teenagers'.

I shiver slightly and pull my wrap more snuggly around me and Sebastian immediately stops walking.

"Damn it, Leona you're frozen." he says as he starts shrugging out of his jacket.

"Goodness Sebastian no, it's fine honestly."

He moves me off the path slightly, under a sparkling tree and pulls his suit jacket around me tightly, he tugs my wrap off and ties it around me like a scarf, whilst all I can do is stare deeply at him. He looks so handsome under the softness of the lights and he is almost like a different person when he acts this nice.

"I'm sorry I was talking too much and didn't notice where we had walked, Come on I will get you back inside quickly." He says staring down at me.

"Honestly, it's fine. I enjoyed the walk and the company." I smile softly.

He looks a little strange for a moment, "Yeah, me too." he sighs.

"Sebastian..." I say as I stare at him, and because I'm watching so closely, I see it, the moment he thinks I am going to push things. "Thank you for putting our differences aside and walking me back, I would have frozen to death just wandering these paths. It really is beautiful though." I say softly.

"Yeah, it is..." He says quietly and I look up at him. "C'mon let's get back." He says and pulls me a little closer to his side, as he guides me through the gardens. Now that I look around, we're not actually that far from the main house and I can see the lights from the marquee.

As we approach the tent, I feel him start to discreetly pull away, so I turn to him and start to take off the jacket,

"Leona it's fine, wait till you're warmed up." He says but I can see him watching around us.

"Lord no it's fine, Wouldn't want to start any wild rumors now, would we? I don't think my reputation could take it." I say to lighten the tension but he frowns down at me.

"Leona, if there was any other way..."

"There you are! I'm claiming that dance my lady." Anders bows in front of me. Wow, his timing is terrible but probably also perfect. I don't need to hear the rejection so I pull up my big girl pants and grin.

"Now that's a sure-fire way to warm me up," I grin,

"But just one, I'm off to my bed after I say goodnight to the happy couple." I turn and he's staring at me like he can see into my soul.

"Thank you for walking me back, Sebastian, have a good night." I say and turn away sharply. No reason to prolong the moment.

"Come on you scoundrel, did you apologize to Shelby?" I frown.

"Oh, I never got the chance she's been avoiding me all night and prancing around with that idiot over there." He shrugs his shoulders casually but he also keeps a close eye on them both.

Sure, enough Shelby is sitting beside a handsome man who seems to have her in hysterics but it also looks a little forced, so I shrug and go in for the kill.

"Oh wow, he's very handsome." I grin.

"You Mrs. Chalmers are trouble! You and I both know he is not *that* handsome! Not as handsome as my dear cousin or I." He leers.

"Well Anders, I haven't met all these handsome cousins yet so how could I possibly judge?" I grin.

He lets out a loud bellow that has people turning to smile and pulls me onto the dance floor.

"I knew we were going to be best friends Leona; I just knew it, now let me show you how to dance." He grins widely.

And he does, for way longer than is appropriate but he is a great distraction and I do indeed warm up quickly.

I also feel emptier than normal, I miss his touch, his heat and that beautiful laugh that he rarely gives out. I feel like I can still sense him near, even though I can't see him but I sigh and put it down to exhaustion. It's been a long tiring night and I decide my bed is calling.

I thank Anders profusely and beg off any more dances.

He chides me for being old and boring and I laugh him off as I head over to the happy couple to bid them goodnight.

I pause at the edge of the dance floor and simply watch them both sway to the music, enclosed in their own personal bubble.

Andy stares adoringly into Mays eyes and she snuggles up even closer, he leans down and places a tender kiss on her forehead and then the old rogue whispers something, no doubt inappropriate, in her ear which has her giggling like a schoolgirl.

Lord these two show me what true love, what real soulmates look like and for a horrible moment I feel my eyes well up. I want that.

I wish I could say I've at least experienced it once in my life but I recognize that what me and Matt had was love and friendship but maybe not just quite as deep, or maybe it's simply something you earn with age and longevity.

I subtly try and wipe my tears but as I look up my heart aches to see Sebastian standing just out of sight alone, watching them both with a soft almost wistful smile on his face, when he turns that full stare on me, I can't look away. I can't move, I am frozen in place by his hauntingly beautiful face and I feel another tear slide as he lowers his gaze, turns and walks back into the shadows. I take a deep steadying breath and wipe at my eyes gently as I make my way towards them both.

"Well, you two are the definition of true love and I think you may have ruined my make-up!" Expensive or not, there is no such thing as waterproof mascara so I am not taking any chances. If I look like a panda I will brash it out.

"Leona dear, Are you having a good night?" May asks kindly.

"It has been wonderful, thank you again for inviting us, the boys are having a great time but I am simply exhausted! That is one crazy grandson you have."

I motion to Anders who is dancing some poor eighty-year-old woman around the dance floor. To be fair she looks like she having a whale of a time but she will feel every bit of it in the morning.

"Yes, he is a live wire that one. And I hope everything is resolved with my other grandson?" She asks.

I smile softly. "Of course, just a simple misunderstanding. We are all good."

"I do hope you didn't let him off too easily Leona? His behavior lately has been appalling." May sighs.

"Well, he has had a lot on dear." Andy hedges.

"That is no excuse, he has been running his own company and yours for years now and I've never seen him so tense, maybe if he settled down."

"Now May do not start." He grins at me. "More grand babies are all she's after." He chuckles and I feel acid in my throat.

Lord, the thought of Sebastian settling down and having a family is an odd sensation to say the least and I do not like it one bit. Rationally, I realize that is the sole reason we are not in the middle of what would have undoubtable been some very hot sex but just the thought of him actually taking that step leaves me feeling oddly hollow.

"Well fine, as long as it's not with that harlot he sleeps around with, she is trouble that girl... Sorry Leona. You have probably had enough of this lots family drama to last a lifetime." She chuckles and I try to catch my breath.

"I am sure Sebastian will find whatever it is he is looking for when he's ready, now if you guys don't mind, I am pooped! I have checked in on the boys and I am going to head off to bed. I hope you both enjoy the rest of the evening." I say as I try to make a swift exit.

"Of course, Leona, thanks for coming and we will see you in the morning my dear." Andy says and May smiles along.

Me, I bolt, As fast as I can. I just need to get away from all these people. I wander around aimlessly for a bit trying to get my bearings, when I eventually find my room. I get inside, lock my door and sink into the bed without changing or even taking off my make-up. I just need this day to be over.

As I lay there, I am haunted by visions of Sebastian's face across the dance floor, the loving look as he watched his grandparents share a tender moment and then the sadness when he saw me watching.

He won't allow himself to feel that type of love, it was written all over his face. He will refuse it no matter what. But lord the thought of him having any type of family, especially with that superficial witch Melania, almost made me physically sick.

I have no idea how it has happened but in such a short space of time, I have fallen for the most unattainable man I could possibly have chosen and I have to work with him.

FUCK MY LIFE.

CHAPTER 19

BANG, BANG, BANG!

"LEONA GET YOUR SCRAWNY ASS UP!"

I shoot upright, Argh my head!

BANG, BANG, BANG!

"For lords sake Shelby I'm coming!" I screech and hold my head again. As I slowly open the door, I want to strangle her perky smiley face.

"Rise and shine ladybug!" she smirks.

I loathe happy sunny morning people. I am not that damn cheerful until I am on at least my second coffee, well to be honest I don't think I am ever that cheerful.

I linger at the door staring at her, words are not so easy this morning.

"Are you just going to ogle my fine ass all morning or let me in?" she grins.

"I'm thinking option C, Slam the door in your face, go back to bed and sneak home later on when no-ones watching." I say seriously.

"Wow, I owe Tabitha a twenty, I was dead sure you were a morning person." She frowns.

"Not without a heavy dose of coffee." I groan and wander into the room. She follows closely behind and takes a little bit too much pleasure in slamming the door closed.

"Bitch!" I grumble not looking round as I flop onto the bed.

"Aw I was sure you were going to be kissing my feet when you saw the goodies I brought." She smirks, I hear it in her tone.

I very gingerly raise my head and notice a dining

cart littered with steaming covered plates and what looks like two very large decanters of coffee!

"I always knew there was a reason I befriended you, Shelby!" I grin.

"Yeah, well I can't say the same about you, you look awful and I would prefer you not put me off my food, so want to hop that skanky butt in a shower whilst I plate up?" she smiles sweetly.

"Sure, then you can tell me all about that display you were putting on with the blonde in the corner last night." I smirk as I pass her and grab a coffee as I go.

"Sure, thing doll face!" she says as she clatters every plate, teacup, god every damn item on the table together as I head to the bathroom and grab a couple of Advil and take a large gulp of my coffee.

Heaven.

I make it out of the shower double quick and pop on a robe that's hanging on the door, slide my feet into the slippers and head on out to devour food, coffee and gossip. Yum.

But when I walk out of the bathroom Shelby is not alone.

Valerie and Anders are both seated at the table alongside Shell and her close proximity to Valerie and her distance from Anders lets me know these two have not kissed and made up.

However, it does leave me the dilemma of there being a weird tea party going on in my bedroom. Anders and Valerie are bickering over something and Shelby is throwing death stares at Anders whilst he pretends to be oblivious. It would be funny really if I wasn't bloody naked under my dressing gown.

"Ah Leona, I wanted to come and check in on you, make sure you weren't ready to bolt after witnessing our dysfunctional family." As she says this, she swats Anders hands away from the food on the table. "You have already eaten breakfast Anderson, stop being a nuisance." she swipes.

Shelby smirks and he sticks his tongue out.

"Honestly you two are as bad as each other!" she glares at Shelby. She begins to respond but Valerie just keeps on talking. "Come sit down and eat something Leona, we don't bite."

"Well, that's not necessarily true now Aunt." He grins devilishly.

"Why exactly are you here again?" Shelby glares.

"I wanted to check on my new favorite girl. Do you have a problem with that as well Shelly." He grins.

"You…" Shelby starts but Valerie cuts her off.

"Don't you two bloody start! Anders say goodbye, Shelby makes Leona a plate up. Leona sit." she says sternly.

"You are really losing your fun edge Auntie Val, Ronnie's gona overtake you shortly if you don't stop being a spoil sport." He frowns.

"Yes, that is not likely." She grunts.

He leans down kisses her cheek and pulls out a seat at the table for me. As I hedge my way over, I pull my gown closer together and he grins wildly. As I sit down, he places a gentle kiss on my head from behind.

"I really do hope you stay the rest of the weekend Leona." He says softly as he passes towards the door.

Shelby doesn't look round once, so she can't see him come up behind her and smack her with a big kiss on the cheek.

"Wouldn't want you feeling left out Shelly." He grins and rushes out the door as she throws something off the table at him.

Valerie just raises an eyebrow and carries on drinking her tea.

"So how did it go last night?" she cuts straight to the chase. They both look at me expectantly.

"Yes, all sorted." I say as I reach for a fresh cup of coffee.

They both just continue to stare. I try to ignore them but when I look up, they are just... waiting.

"What?"

"Leona, when I found you running down the hall you looked like you had just escaped a burning fire and I have never witnessed Sebastian, so uncontrolled in all my life, so please excuse me if you think I am going to believe there was no repercussion's from our chat." She states.

I look to Shelby who just munches on a piece of toast like she's watching a damn soap opera! No help at all!

"Well as I said before, our chat did make Sebastian's behavior more understandable and he was very upset with you sharing that information but we accept that we had both made some mistakes thus far and we have agreed to put our issues aside and... well... get on with our jobs." I say simply.

They are both frowning at me as though I have failed a test spectacularly and have no idea how to tell me.

"Leona, you do realize Sebastian is attracted to you?" Valerie asks bluntly and Shelby scoffs into her teacup.

"You dear are not helping." She says sternly and Shell sits up straight.

"Well, I don't know what that has to do with anything." I start.

"Aw for feck's sake Leona! You both want to jump

each other's bones; we could all see it from the looks you were both throwing back and forth. How in the hell did you two not get it on last night?" she cries and slaps a hand over her mouth.

Lord! Was I that obvious, does everyone think I am some weak female pining over an unattainable man?

"Well, I wouldn't quite put it like that," Valerie frowns at Shelby, "But Leona we all had hoped after the rendezvous in the library, you two would see how you both feel about each other."

"What rendezvous?" I grimace.

"I may not be married dear but I have been seduced and ravished a time or two and I can bloody well tell when it happens to someone else and you my dear were thoroughly ravished in that library." She tuts.

Jesus! How is it even possible that I had not noticed this bunch have been scheming, manipulating and playing bloody matchmaker. I have to put a stop to this immediately.

"Look, I appreciate that you think I may be desperate enough to need help in securing a… What a date… a man? But I can assure you both, I am more than capable of doing that myself and the exact same can be said for Sebastian! If he chooses to date or not, then that will be his decision and quite frankly, it's none of your god damn business."

"Leona…" Shelby starts.

"No Shell, this is not a joke! I will never have any relationship with Sebastian other than professional, so just back off!"

"Well, I'm glad to hear we're both on the same page." I hear drawl from behind me and I simply sigh.

"Why the hell is everyone in Leona's room?" Andy says and I've had enough.

"Apparently there was some family discussion about setting your grandson up with a would-be wife and I've been selected as the unlucky lady."

I see Sebastian stiffen at that but he can take it whatever way he god damn wants.

"Your grandson Andy is a big boy and if he chooses to mess around with questionable women that is quite frankly his choice, I would appreciate if you all left me the hell out of your matchmaking schemes. I have no interest in being pitied or set-up in anyway so if you all don't mind, please leave my room and let me pack in peace."

"Leona that is not what happened here." Andy starts, "Is it?" he glares at the room.

"Look, Sebastian and I are not remotely interested in each other in that way and we have finally agreed to put our differences aside but this..." I say with a wave of a hand, "This is incredibly intrusive and quite frankly bloody weird." I say.

"Welcome to the family." Shelby grins.

"Shut up, Shelby." Sebastian says but she just continues to grin. I can't though, I cannot even look at him. I feel him staring but I ignore it.

"If you don't all mind, I am in a damn dressing gown, could you please just take you discussion elsewhere." I say and walk towards the only other room, the bathroom.

I hear a muttering of "sorry" and "I only came to help" as I close the door.

I sink to the floor and lower my eyes. What the hell kind of family is this and why do I so desperately want to be a part?

I wait for what feels like a good fifteen minutes and when I am positive, I hear no movement, I slowly creak open the door. As I begin to think I am safely alone I spot him. He's so still and quiet, if it wasn't for the fact, he is over six foot and standing in front of the window I probably wouldn't have even noticed him.

"I asked *everyone* to leave." I say stiffly.

"I know."

"And yet you didn't think that applied to you?" I ask.

"No, I gathered it applied specifically to me." He responds still staring out the window.

"Okay, so you're just as ridiculous as the rest of your family then?" I surmise.

"No Leona, I am about as far from my family's ridiculousness as you can possibly get but sometimes… just sometimes, I wish I could be more like them." he sighs so forlornly.

I want to touch him, soothe the tension in his neck. Comfort him and it takes everything in me to stay still.

"Why are you here Sebastian?"

"I apologize for them. Their behavior was appalling."

"Yes, it was."

"You can't choose your family I suppose and normally they are relatively sane in front of guests. We seemed to have reached an… understanding and I would hate for this to ruin it."

I simply stand there; he still hasn't looked round and he sounds so, dejected or something, that I have no idea what to say, so I don't say anything. He continues staring out the window and my feet itch to go see what he is looking at.

"Why where you crying last night Leona?"

"Why did you come here Sebastian, really?" We both ask at the same time. Damn, he went straight for the jugular.

"Honestly? I came to ask if you would like to take a walk with me in the gardens." He laughs sadly, "Even though I know I shouldn't, even though I can't give you anything you need, even though my crazy family is trying to push us together, I still came, because for once in my life, I wanted to be selfish."

I don't know how to respond but when he turns and looks at me, I am even more lost.

"I heard you clearly Leona, I won't make you the unlucky lady." He smiles falsely. I know it's false because I've used that smile too many times.

"That was not a dig at you Sebastian." I start.

"No need to explain, I just want you to know I will be having a very strong word with the lot of them to drop this. They have no right to make you feel uncomfortable and Andy has already made it very clear you have not to be bothered, so I would ask that you don't run off just yet. Your boys are having a blast by the looks of it and I would hate to ruin their weekend as well." He motions outside the window to where he was looking.

I take a moment and then move closer, when I look outside, I see the boys in a large group, all tossing around a ball.

They look happy and carefree; I watch as Noah charges Kayla and sweeps her up off her feet and runs down field with her so she can't steal the ball. They are both laughing hysterically but it's when I see Jacob move towards Libby with a huge smile on his face that stops me stock still.

He looks so young and for a moment, I feel my eyes well up. He has really struggled to find that easiness again and to see him look like he's actually enjoying himself makes any decision for me. I am sticking this weekend out. No way am I stealing those smiles.

Like he senses the change in the atmosphere, he laughs softly.

"Ah young love. What it would be like to go back to a time when things were that easy." He says gently.

I blink hard and refuse to let any tears fall, I will not even dare go back to that time in my life. Fighting tooth and nail, working three jobs, whilst keeping up my grades to try and get into a good college, all to get into student accommodation so I would have a clean bed to sleep, only to fall bloody pregnant and almost lose it all. Yeah, I don't think I was every that carefree.

"Leona... Are you ok?" he asks scarily close.

"Oh yeah sorry, miles away." I say watching my whole world heal out there on a garden lawn.

"Did I say something wrong?" he asks peering too closely.

"No Sebastian, just wondering if I've ever really had a carefree moment in my life you know? Sorry, that was a bit too pathetic." I laugh it off. "Look you're right, the boys are having a great time and I won't spoil that. I'm a big girl though, you don't have to make any speech, I will tell anyone who asks to mind their own business. You shouldn't have to put up with matchmaking at this point in your life if you choose not to Sebastian. I hope you realize I was only trying to make your family see we would not be a... thing." I motion.

"Oh, we all got that loud and clear I think." He says brusquely.

"That was your choice Sebastian, It may have sounded harsh but I will not be pitied. You made yourself perfectly clear that you have no interest in a relationship and I was only trying to point that out without them badgering us both. I was not rejecting you. I did not reject you." I say.

I turn away from him and continue to watch outside.

"I didn't reject you either Leona," he starts and I raise my own eyebrow. "Not in the traditional sense anyway." He sees my expression and carries on,

"I have never had a relationship in my life, I refuse to let anyone have that type of power over me, I am simply not capable of that type of thing and you Leona, I think that's exactly what you're looking for."

"I never said that." I say.

"You didn't have too; I saw you perfectly clear last night when you watched my grandparents and your heart almost broke right there on the dance floor. You want romance and chivalry and love Leona, and that is something I do not have to give. Add into the mix we have a very complicated working relationship on top of the fact that it seems my whole family has deemed we would make a 'wonderful couple'."

He glares at that last bit as if it's been remarked on and I can totally see his point. I completely understand, yet my whole heart feels like it's breaking because as much as he says he is not capable of these things, he already showed he was more than last night.

"I understand." I say softly.

"Do you?"

"Yes, Sebastian I do. I wish I could say you were wrong and I don't want those things but I've never played the field. I have never sown my wild oats! I'm not sure I'm made for that type of thing. I wish I was." I say and let it hang in the air.

"And that Leona would be a crime. You deserve more than a casual affair but it would be all I could offer. And I couldn't even offer you that until after the Montgomery deal is over. I would never allow myself to mix business. I couldn't."

"I really do get it Sebastian; You don't have to explain anymore." I smile.

"If there was ever anyone who could tempt me to throw away all my beliefs and morals Leona it would be you, but I would only hate myself for it."

He says it so devastatingly, I know deep in my soul this man would break my heart so easily, for someone who thinks he is incapable of love, I see he has simply too much and has no idea how to use it. He saves it all for his family and that's part of what makes him truly remarkable.

"You would resent me and I would hate myself right along with you." I say sadly.

We simply stare out of the window and watch the group play down below. I stop myself multiple times from agreeing to some casual affair but I just don't think I could do it with him. I know I've already fallen too hard; I don't think I would get back up after it.

He leans over and pulls me towards him. I feel my body react instantly as I curl into him. He places a soft tender kiss on my head and I ache when I hear his gentle whisper,

"I really do wish I could give you more Leona, I am sorry."

He kisses my forehead, lingering for a brief moment and then pulls back and walks out of the room without so much as a second glance and me… I crumble. How on earth can I already feel so broken over a man I've hardly known for any length of time.

CHAPTER 20

After hiding out in my room for the remainder of the morning I head outside to check in with the boys. They have been keeping me up to date on the scores of the apparent 'Van Der Bilt Games' and as far as I am aware they are all just as competitive as each other.

I head towards the basketball courts were I have been told Noah is kicking serious butt so far and prepare to face everyone after this morning's little tea party.

"Leona, over here! We saved you a seat." Shelby and Tabitha wave me over and I follow their direction.

"Hey, I saved you one of the best seats in the house and you are just in time for the show." Tabitha says as she starts to fan herself.

I look to Shelby and she is grinning from ear to ear. She hands me glass of orange juice and I take it with a thanks.

"So, what am I waiting for?" I say.

The sound of a loud ringing buzzer going off has me looking towards the court and it quickly becomes evident why the girls are just sitting here.

As I adjust my seating, I watch in morbid fascination as most of the men start to head over to a table set up with refreshments just outside the court and proceed to strip off their jerseys.

I mean not all of them but you can clearly see Hank, Tabitha's husband, pull off his shirt, along with a few of the men I sort of recognize from yesterday and begin toweling off their sweat.

Tabitha wolf whistles at her husband and he puts on

a ridiculous little dance tease show, lord who knows what that is, for her and we all laugh. Anders not being one to miss out calls out,

"Ladies, how would you like to a see a real man strip?" then proceeds to give a very decent rendition of a Chippendale.

Just as I am about to laugh out loud with the others, I see Sebastian fooling around at the back of the court with Noah. And lord, he already has his shirt off and I think I forget to breathe.

His light grey basketball shorts are hung ridiculously low on his hips and his abs for days are on full display. It's so much skin! I feel myself begin to color and immediately regret my earlier decision. I could totally do casual if it means I get to play with all that he has going on.

"Eh here," Shelby says passing me something.

I don't think I even blink as I take it,

"What's this?" I say eyes still glued on the naked torso of my boss.

"For the drool!" she says and laughs aloud.

"Aw don't tease! It's a lot to take in." Tabitha says with a grin.

Anders who seems to be watching the full interaction cusses out loud. "God damn it, Sebastian! We made a deal! You were supposed to keep that stupid six pack covered up!" he groans. Not that he has anything to groan about, he is almost as buff as Sebastian, maybe a little less definition but not much.

"Bugger off Anders, maybe if you worked out more and stopped drinking as much, you wouldn't be so out of shape!" he grins as he takes a gulp from his water bottle.

He catches my stare, smiles and goes back to his

tactics talk with Noah. As soon as Noah spots me however he grins and heads over my way. Please don't bring him along, I grumble internally.

Yeah, it's really not my day as they both head straight in my direction.

"Do not lick his abs! Do not touch his abs! Do not look at that fucking V." I chant to myself.

"Might wana stop that chanting now honey, not sure your boys are quite ready for that level of filth from their mom." Shelby laughs aloud and I color. Bloody hell, I said that shit out loud and now I have to look up as they approach.

"Mom did you see the score? We are top of the leader board! Seb's bloody awesome and we've not even played baseball yet. We have this in the bag."

"Hey Sporto, I'm pretty sure we were clawing it back in that last game." Anders calls as he walks over to join us.

"Aw man, Seb whipped you on defense, you guys don't stand a chance. Jake come tell mom how we're gona win this thing with the most points in… like ever!" he calls.

"So humble." Sebastian grins at me.

"What… eh, yeah sorry, he's a bit too competitive and gets carried away. Noah, cool it or I will tell the boss to dock you points again for un-sportsmanship!" I glare at him and he groans.

"Mom, you need to knock that off, it wasn't fair in junior league and it's so not funny now." He cries.

"Yeah, well no-one likes a show off." I say sternly as Jacob smiles at me.

"Well, some people find show off's rather endearing." Anders pipes in and waggles his brows.

"Yeah, you never used to complain when Dad got all

'*Chalmers are winners*' on us." Noah groans.

Before I even get a chance to respond Jacob cuts in, "Eh yeah she did Noah, like all the time, that's why she made old man Bueller deduct points from Dad as well, remember his face?"

He actually laughs and I can't move. They say it all so blasé but it's been such a long time since they've spoken about Matt in such a casual manner, especially in front of other people, I am a little shocked.

"God Jake your right! Dad was fuming!" he laughs aloud.

Anders being way more perceptive than he portrays looks me dead in the eye, "Leona, are these boy's saying you got involved in an adults game and made the referee deduct points from your own damn husband?" he says it so incredulously, "Wow, you are evil! I knew it!" he grins goofily.

"Aw man Anders, you should have seen it, Dad was all gloating about being so far ahead and mom shouted him out in front of the whole town, she was like, '*Mathew Chalmers you are an adult who is setting an example for two impressionable young boys, get it together or I will make you!*' and he was like, '*Aw honey, what are you gona do?*' with this big goofy smile, remember Jake?" He is grinning so widely and I remember it all too well, I was so pissed at him.

"Yeah man, she stomps right over to old Mr. Bueller in front of everyone, whispers something in his ear, next thing you know the whole town is in an uproar as old Man Bueller walks over to the score board and deducts ten points. Even Dads teammates were laughing." He smiles widely and everyone around us is in hysterics. I don't know where to look, stuck firmly in the past, when Sebastian lightens the mood, who'd have thought.

"Well, I don't know about you guys but I'd like to keep all our hard-earned points on the board so there will be no gloating from us, will their Noah?" he grins at him and Noah grins right back,

"Well, I don't know, who's in charge of the scoreboard?" he smirks a little.

Sebastian pauses for effect and everyone looks directly at him... "Andy." he says with a full wide smile and a series of laughs and 'aw mans' ring out around us.

"So, what you think Jacob?" he says as he puts his arm around my sons shoulder and they both look at Noah. "Can we reign this guy in or we gona have to cut him loose, can't have us losing any points and I don't know about you guys but I'm pretty sure your mom may easily pull an 'Old Man Bueller' on Andy?" he says it so easily with a huge smile, the boys are all laughing and even Noah who would be, well for no better choice of a word crapping it to get kicked off a team, is laughing along.

"Aw man you guys are so harsh!" he laughs. "Yeah, yeah, I'll keep the gloating to a minimum, but man when we win, I wana see all you guys bowing down. I mean baseballs almost next and well we all know who rocks that bat." He grins.

"We will see punk!" says Anders as he grabs him in some sort of manly tussle.

It's just all so easy. We could slot in to this family with so much ease that it shocks the hell out of me.

Shelby reaches over and squeezes my knee and I realize I'm sort of freaking out, thankfully the boys are all hyped up and Sebastian and Anders have them in fits of laughter. A loud buzzer rings out and Hank shouts for them all to get back to the game.

"Mom your gona stay and watch, right?" Noah cries as he starts to run back to the court.

"Yeah of course," I shout, "I need to keep an eye on your sportsmanship!" I grin and he laughs aloud.

"You watch me mom, I'm gona get bonus points for being such a good sport." He smirks and runs off.

"Again, how is it possible we are twins?" Jacob laughs and leans down and gives me a quick squeeze.

"We're all good mom." He smiles and runs off to join the rest of the team. I can feel Sebastian and Anders eyes linger a little as they slowly walk off, talking deeply to each other.

"You gona watch my sportsmanship Leona honey?" Anders calls with a saucy grin.

"I am pretty sure you do not need any more encouragement Anderson Van Der Bilt… plus I hate to break it to you *honey* but I am all in for the other team." I smile but realize how it sounds as they all laugh.

Anders frowns at me, places his hand over his heart and mocks devastation, then grins at Sebastian, "Guess she's watching you guys then eh cuz?" and off they go with Sebastian clipping him round the head. He gives me a soft smile and they get set up for the next round.

"You doing ok, sweetie?" Tabitha ask's and Shelby gives my leg another squeeze.

"Wow, I mean that was like a lot!" I blurt.

"Yeah, you seemed a bit spooked there for a min hon, I take it the boys don't talk about their Dad that much?" Shelby says eyes full of understanding.

"Not really like that, we talk about Matt all the time, it's more they don't really bring him up in front of other people that often and not with, forgive the expression, strangers." I say.

"Yeah, they seem so comfortable here, they've really slotted in with the rest of the kids." Tabitha says and I crack a little.

"Yeah, but why? How am I supposed to even deal with that? It's like the whole lot of you have opened this big space to welcome us into and all I can think of is well, why? Where do we even fit? And I pray to god no-one even dares to try set me up with another member of this loony family." I vent.

"Thanks!" Tabitha grins.

"You know what I mean."

"You have no idea how embarrassed I was coming back here after the whole 'EX' disaster Leona. I was mortified, all I kept thinking was, why should I come back to this crazy dysfunctional lot and let them judge me and find me severely lacking. But as much as they are mostly all insane," she grins at Tabatha, who takes a sip of her drink and shrugs, "They didn't, they helped me heal and they just accepted me, no questions asked. I mean other than that damn asshole Anders who continues to try and make my life a living breathing hell but I love the rest of them. You don't have to bring anything to the table, just be yourself that's why we all love you." She says softly.

"She's right and we have all been thoroughly warned about the matchmaking. Sebastian tore everyone a new one for making you feel so uncomfortable, we know we are a bit much to take and we threw you right in at the deep end but Andy has warned us all. Dating any family member or not, you are part of the mad bunch now whether you like it or not and those boys of yours are going to be coming back here a lot, I fear so you may just have to suck it up honey." She smiles.

"You're stuck with us."

She passes me a glass of what looks like orange juice but most certainly has a little top up inside and as I sit here and watch my boys play so freely, I think she's right. They've always lacked a large family and they look to be thriving here surrounded by fun and laughter.

FUCK ME!

I AM STUCK WITH THESE LOONYS.

As I sit with the girls and enjoy the company, I am so thankful that they haven't pushed or prodded me about my situation with Sebastian because honestly, all I can think about is how much I want to throw caution to the wind and ask him for that casual affair.

I catch his eye on more than one occasion and he smiles so easily, he is like a different person altogether out there with his friends and family. He includes the boys so easily in their banter and I feel a pang in my heart that we couldn't have more. He is so good with them and he makes me crave things I thought I had long stopped thinking about.

As the game comes to an end, I watch Noah carefully and sure enough other than a gentle back and forth ribbing with Kye and Anders over their lack of precision he has reigned in the goading which makes glad. He can be a bit much at times. He high fives Sebastian and they all start to make their way from the court. Hank swoops down on Tabitha's seat and grabs her in for a sweaty hug.

"You are going to pay for that!" she screams at him as he wraps her up in his sweaty grasp.

I notice the blonde from last night that was chatting up Shelby stroll over, shirt off, slung over his shoulder, eyes gleaming as he makes his way straight for her.

"Oh crap." I hear her groan under her breath and chuckle.

"Flirting seemed like a good idea in the moment honey? Never looks half as good the next morning but he is kinda hot." I grin.

"Not funny, I can't get rid of him now, he's like a bloody boomerang, I keep sending him away and he just keeps coming right back around." She groans.

Anders crashes down on the bottom of my lounger,

"Here comes your toy boy Shelly."

"Fuck off Anders." she growls.

"Hey Shelby, we still on for a walk through the gardens later?" he asks smiling. He really is quite good looking but in a young pretty boy type of way.

"Hey Maxwell, eh I'm not sure what the plan is for later," she hedges, "Don't you guys not have another game coming up?"

"Yeah, we have the swim race but I thought we could maybe take a walk before it since you girls have opted out of the swim." he smiles.

"We haven't opted out Maxwell, we are just saving our skills for were they are better needed, although now I am thinking maybe joining in the swim race could be a good idea." Tabitha muses. "What you think girls? This lot seem to think we're just here to look pretty?"

"So not cool Hank!" Anders cries. "You definitely put her up to that! You bloody know Shells in my set and a darn crap swimmer who just gets in the way."

Maxwell looks as lost and confused as me.

Shelby looks pissed. Hank smirks.

"You know what Maxwell, sorry no walk for me, seems I need to go look out my swimsuit." She glares at Anders. "I am not a crap swimmer! You are just a damn cheat but you're on!" she fumes.

He grins like the Cheshire cat and I swear if I didn't know any better, I would say he manipulated that whole situation. He confirms it with a saucy wink and a, "Ooh can't wait to see this!" he grins. Yeah, I bloody bet you can't, I think. "It's almost worth the loss of points with the Olympic swimmer over there." He motions to Tabitha, who has the decency too blush.

"What!" I screech.

"I was not a damn Olympic swimmer Anders, knock it off." She looks to me. "I was picked for the Olympic team many, many years ago. But alas my dreams of gold were dashed by this punk and his own super swimmers." She grins so lovingly at Hank you can tell she is not in the least bothered.

"Well thanks for clarifying that." I say sarcastically and everyone laughs. Well maybe not Maxwell he still seems a little confused bless.

"So, you in, Leona?" Anders taunts.

"Me, hell no! I don't even have a team but I will of course come along and cheer my girls on." I smile.

"Of course, you have a team silly, everyone does whether they participate or not." Tabitha says.

"Oh, who's am I in then?" I ask.

"Mine." I hear Sebastian murmur. "But you don't have to join in if you're not a great swimmer. We're already so far in the lead even Tabby couldn't make up the difference." He grins.

"Hey, how is that not gloating?" Noah cries.

"You know what Noah; I think you might be right." I smile, "maybe I will join in and strategically lower your average." I grin.

"Hardly mom," he starts but Jacob nudges him and

they both smirk. "Yeah, I suppose we can add you in." he says almost convincingly but Sebastian's watching the encounter a little too closely.

I'm not that good, totally not Olympic good but I can more than hold my own so I just smirk.

"Ok troops, I guess we're all heading to the lake, and I must say, I for one cannot wait to see all you beautiful creatures get crushed by my gorgeous wife." Hank says as we all get up and head back to the house.

CHAPTER 21

THIS IS NOT A LITTLE POOL RACE!
What the hell was I thinking joining in this crazy game. I thought it was for sure just a simple swim. I really should have known better. Damn crazy rich people!

"Breathe Leona, it's not that long a course." Shell says as she does some sort of warm up stretches.

"Are you serious! It looks like a ten-mile stretch!" I cry.

"You'll be fine they don't really count our points in anyway, and Tabitha's gona whip this one, so just enjoy it for what it is."

The boys are of course buzzing and Kayla looks like she is in a zone of her own. Kye is psyching himself up with some sort of chant and Maxwell is simply watching Shelby rather closely. Sebastian is lounging over by his grandparent's, the Davies and the rest of their company, everyone seems in good spirits.

I am gladly not in the first set of races so I can get a good watch of how it all goes. Thankfully it doesn't look as bad as it first seemed and a few people's races look more fun than competitive. Of course, the boys line up and they are up against Kayla and Kye, Libby and Miguel. I can hear the trash talk from here and I have to laugh at how serious Kayla and Noah are.

Libby is trying to make Jacob laugh and Noah keeps telling him to keep his head in the game.

The Claxton sounds and they are off.

Shoot! If Kayla is anything like her mom, we are all screwed, she is off like a shot. They are all pretty evenly paced for the first stretch but as they barrel back Kayla just up's her pace and give herself a good distance with Noah pretty hot on her tale.

Kye and Jacob are pretty evenly matched and in a blink of an eye it's over. Kayla of course won with Noah a not too far behind second. Jake and Kye were pretty tied and Libby just pipped Miguel at the post. They all take it in good fun though and I see Noah congratulate Kayla, Libby is shouting at Jacob for not going easy on her and he laughs in her face.

"I thought you said not to treat you any differently Lib?" he grins.

Miguel is claiming cramp and Kye just laughs at him. It actually looks quite fun.

"You sure you want to do this Leona? There's no pressure." Sebastian says behind me.

I turn around to laugh and stop still. Those abs up close are truly a sight to behold and I pause to take him in. He's wearing dark navy shorts, not knee length loose, basketball shorts like before but football style, tighter, cut a lot higher on the leg, giving me a good glimpse of the firm muscles corded in his thighs.

He reaches out and tips my chin up.

"Don't want to swallow any flies." He grins.

Lord. I must be glowing.

"Eh yeah, sorry about that." He chuckles softly.

"Aw for Fu... Fecks sake Shelby! Are you serious!" we hear and turn to see Shell strip of her kaftan, showing off her swimming costume.

"What?" She grins. She has gone all out! She is wearing bright red skimpy thong bikini bottoms with a bikini top that looks molded to her breasts. Her fabulous figure is on full display and the men gathered around look ready to crawl at her feet.

"You darn well know what." He starts adjusting his shorts and I burst out laughing. Sebastian laughs at my side and we head over to the start line.

As I line up, I look along and see my group. Of course, there is Tabitha, swimming goggles on focused on the waves, Maxwell and Anders both staring directly at Shelby, and me and Sebastian.

"Leona," I hear and turn. "You won't get very far in that sundress." Libby says and I frown.

Oh, I was paying too much attention to Shelby I forgot to take my own dress off.

"Shoot here Lib." I say pulling the dress over my head and toss it towards the sand.

I hear a sharp intake of breath and look up into Sebastian's blazing eyes as he takes in my simple black bikini. It's nowhere near as scandalous as Shelby's but it does scoop my breast's up a little and makes my ass look, well amazing, if I do say so myself.

"OH, FOR THE LOVE OF GOD! WHO PUT US IN A RACE WITH ALL THESE DARN…!"

Anders shouts as I hear the Claxton sound. I shoot off and focus on the task. I can hear a lot of noise going on around me but I zone out and focus only on the swim.

It's been a while but it feels great to be back in the water. I see Tabitha up ahead and Shelby and Sebastian are pretty close by, when I pass the finish line, I look round to see where I came and feel myself enveloped in a hug.

"Wow, Leona you were great!" Tabitha says. The boys are cheering and Noah screams,

"That's it mom! You show them us Chalmers are awesome at everything!"

"Noah!" I warn and he laughs.

"Yeah, yeah, I'm humble but you rocked." He grins and Jacob gives me a cheesy thumbs up.

I see Sebastian come up behind us and I turn to smile but he looks a little dazed. Shelby crashes up behind him shouting,

"God Damn, lunatics!"

"REMATCH! That must be cause for a rematch. That's blatant cheating." Anders sputters, as Maxwell follows behind.

"NO FREAKING WAY!" Shelby shouts, "That's your own damn fault for being so easily distracted." She grins.

"Easily distracted are you serious. You did that on purpose." He cries as she smirks and saunters off up the beach. "And put a darn cover up on." He growls at her.

I turn to Sebastian and laugh.

"Those two really need to sort their issues out."

"We need to take a walk." He says darkly.

"What?" I say shocked at his expression.

I look around and see we're pretty much alone. Tabitha is off cheering her win and everyone else has filtered away to watch the rest of the races.

"Please take a walk with me Leona, and for the love of god grab your sundress." he groans.

Well for that I send him a cheeky smirk.

"You know Sebastian I have no idea where it went." I say saucily.

"You are trouble." He groans and takes my arm, as he guides me away from the group.

I look around to check that no-one is watching, especially the boys but everyone is focused on the next race. Sebastian is kind of dragging me along anyway so it doesn't really matter.

"Hey…" I say as he rushes a little more. "My legs aren't nearly as long as yours."

"Shit, sorry but I need to put a little distance from all those damn perving eyes."

He fumes. What perving eyes?

He sees my confused look and laughs aloud.

"You cannot be that oblivious Leona surely?" he slows and stares down at me.

"Er…"

"You look like a fucking bond girl crossed with a playboy bunny strolling up that beach! There wasn't a comfortable pair of shorts in sight." He grunts.

"I think I appreciate the *compliment*?" I say as I raise an eyebrow, "But I'm fairly sure Shelby's little show was what caused all that… straining." I grin.

"Oh yeah, care to explain why *I* have to take a mile walk away from the group to try and get *my* shit under control." He glares.

I swear I fight every single urge I have to not look but I can't help it.

"Oops!" I smile at his very large and obvious strain.

"Oops, What the hell do you mean, oops? I have a raging hard-on, in the middle of a damn beach, with my full family and your god damn son's in the vicinity and all you have to say is '*OOPS*'."

At this point we are so far away from the rest of the group I am confident if he calls my bluff, we would have no way of being spotted.

"Well, I'm not really sure what else you would like me to say Sebastian. I think asking if you need a hand might be outside the perimeters of our '*friendship*'?" I sass while finger motioning air quotes.

"Lord help me, Leona! I am trying to keep my word

here… but you are testing my god damn patience." He pulls me flush up against him and I get the pleasure of feeling the evidence of his so called 'patience'.

"Well, I never proclaimed to be smart Sebastian, I'm not quite sure how to fight this myself." I say grumpily.

He moves us back slowly off the beach and towards the trees skirting the sand.

"Nothing has changed sweetheart," he starts.

"I know." I say as I lick my dried lips. God, I hunger for him.

"I don't want to hurt you…" he says gently.

"Oh, for fucks sake Sebastian, I am a big girl! Either kiss me or not, but you asked me to walk with you, you want this as much as I do but I won't bloody force this." I say heatedly.

He looks down at me for a long moment, so long I think he is going to walk away but the next thing I know I am being tossed up in the air and his hands are on my ass, spinning me to press firmly against a tree as he kisses me with a wild animalistic roar.

Shit! What have I done. He's snapped.

He thrusts his tongue inside my mouth as he presses his hard length against my core. I fight the temptation to cry out in case I spook him again and he stops because quite simply I am burning up.

He keeps a similar pace, darting his tongue in and out as we grind against each other. There are no barriers this time so I run my hands all over his back and arms, anywhere I can really. I can't get enough. I thrust my tongue out to meet his and he pulls away sharply, tasting at the skin, following his own trail down to my aching breasts. My nipples ache as he rips aside the scrap of material covering them and pulls one into his mouth. I bite down on his shoulder to avoid making any sound and I feel him chuckle.

"What is so funny?" I glare.

I mean he has my breasts exposed, I have my whole body wrapped around him like a vine and I am ashamed to say are still rocking back and forth over his groin.

"You are, no need to keep quiet sweetheart, I couldn't stop this if a nuclear missile was launched directly at us." He grins.

"Huh." I mumble.

"Yeah huh." He tames his pace and begins to slowly use his erection to push me deeper against the tree. I am aware of the bark digging into my back but I honestly couldn't care. As he pulls his head back and looks down at me, he reaches a hand up and strokes away some of the hair that is plastered against my face to the side.

"So, damn beautiful." He says softly and I melt.

He lowers those perfect lips down over mine and continues to kiss me into oblivion. I can feel my body heat climbing with his steady rocking against my core and I am trying my darnedest not to explode as he keeps up a steady pace, his hand reaches slowly into my bikini bottoms and I cringe, knowing he is going to feel just how much I want him, because I am soaked.

Just as he reaches inside, we both jump. A Claxton screeches way to close, I startle and start clawing my way out of his grasp. He stops me immediately by pulling me closer and hushes me.

"I am not sure if there is anyone hiding out in those trees who may have been spotted missing and should maybe think about taking the private path back to the house before they happen to get caught in a compromising position, but if there is, I would advise them to walk fast." Anders chuckles to himself and as much as I want to punch him in the fucking throat, he just saved my skin.

"Shit!" Sebastian says and lowers his head to mine. I start to scramble again and he jerks me a little.

"Please stop squirming sweetheart, it's having the opposite effect of what's needed here." He groans deeply and I immediately freeze.

He very carefully peels me off his body and sets me softly on the ground. He avoids my gaze a little and I stand stock still and fold my arms. I must look bloody ridiculous because as soon as I do, I realize my breasts are bloody exposed and I quickly rectify it.

"Thanks." He grumbles but I just refold my arms and wait. The foot tapping must give me away as he slowly looks at me. I raise one eyebrow and wait.

"We, really should get back." He says, still not facing me fully. He turns to lead the way and I wait.

"Leona… what?" he says.

"Look at me Sebastian." I force.

He does but looks away quickly.

"For Christ's sake Sebastian, Are we going to do this every time?" I rage.

"That's not what this is…" he waves a hand.

"Well, what the hell is it and why won't you even look at me?"

"I swore to you I wouldn't do this again, only mere hours ago and all I want to do right now is fuck you so hard against that god damn tree, I couldn't give a damn that your sons could walk over and see us! How the hell is that me not losing my damn mind." He shouts.

"I'm not sure it's you losing your mind," I start.

"I like your son's Leona." He says making me

pause. "A lot, they are good kids and I've been where they are. They are just starting to warm up to us all, finding a space for themselves in this ridiculous group and I will not mess that up for them by screwing their mother like a cheap whore." He cries.

Shoot! How am I supposed to respond to that!

"I'm sorry but it's the truth. I see it in them both, they want to belong here, feel a part of something bigger and I won't destroy that for them. They've already lost enough."

"Wow, and you said you don't know how to love." I say carelessly, as he pales.

"Not me," I smile tenderly, "You Sebastian Van Der Bilt, care about everyone else around you so deeply. You put far too much pressure on yourself, but you are right. I would be devastated if they caught us in that type of situation. So, thank you for putting them first. Nuclear missiles and all huh." I grin to lighten the mood.

"Yeah. Just, can you give me a minute." He says and turn his back to me. I guess he has to try and hide the evidence, shame on me though, because all I can think of is, what a damn waste.

I attempt to fix myself but realize there is nothing that can be done, I look a state. My hair has come loose and is a riot, I fix my costume as best I can but I can't hide the scrapes on my back, as I turn around, I see him simply watching me. He reaches out a hand and pushes my hair away from my face, as he removes a twig. We both laugh and he leans down and kisses me softly on the lips.

"So damn beautiful." He takes my hand and guides me through the trees.

It's ridiculous, there are rocks and bark and lord

knows what else everywhere and I am still too caught up in a daze, that I don't even realize how badly my feet hurt until I curse a little as my foot scrapes over another rough patch.

"Christ, Leona where are your shoes?" he glances down and I notice he has bloody sliders on his feet. Well, no wonder he was marching on through!

The next thing I know he sweeps me right up into his arms and I cry out.

"Sebastian, What the hell?"

"How on earth do you not have shoes on? I have been dragging you through a damn forest you lunatic of a woman." He glares.

"Well, I didn't think I was about to go on a bloody bush hike when you asked me to take a walk!" I shout back, "Put me down I look ridiculous."

"I think you look perfect right where you are sweetheart." He says softly and I almost bloody swoon. "I am not letting you down to scrape anymore skin off those bloody feet." he moans.

"You cannot carry me back to the house like this!"

I fume, even though if I'm honest, there really is nowhere else I would rather be. Wrapped up in his arms feels like heaven.

"Watch me." He smirks.

"People will see." I try.

"Fuck them."

Well with that I rest my head against his chest and feel him press a tender kiss to my head, as he marches straight through the damn woods.

CHAPTER 22

I jerk awake, startled that I fell asleep.
In Sebastian's arms.
Walking through the woods.
What the heck? And where the hell am I? I sit up cautiously looking around, relieved to see I'm back in my room, tucked in under my covers. I roll over and draw in a sharp breath, my bloody feet ache. I throw back the covers and see I have bandages wrapped around both my feet.

"What the…?" I ponder.

"They're just a precaution, you were moving around a lot when I lay you down, I figured you may do more damaged, so I bandaged them up. They should be fine just a little sore I would imagine." Sebastian says from the window seat.

"Oh, thank you, I am so sorry. I can't believe I fell asleep." I say mortified. "Did anyone see?" I ask tentatively.

"No you're good, I texted the boys and told them you got lost wandering the beach and cut your feet. They said you are known for being a little clumsy so they didn't seem overly worried." He says with a soft smile.

"Thank you for that, and well for this." I wave a hand at me and my feet.

"How are you feeling?" he hedges.

"Eh…"

"Your feet Leona, how are your feet?" he smirks.

"Well now you mention it they do feel a little tender." I frown.

"Yeah, you may get to hide away in this room for a little longer." He says.

"I mean it's no hardship." I say as I look around the room. There's a soft knock at the door and I stare towards it.

"Nothing to worry about, I asked for some lunch to be brought up for you since you missed it."

He heads toward the door and I watch his every move. He's changed into a fresh pair of dark navy slacks and a slim fitted t-shirt that shows of the curve of his biceps and the tan covering his forearms. His dark hair gleams dampness, like he's just stepped from a shower, and a fresh woodsy scent lingers in the air. I hear him thank whoever is outside and he pulls in a fully stocked table. He moves it over next to the seats at the window and proceeds to set the table with care. I can't take my eyes off him.

"Do you think you could manage sitting at the... what?" He says as he looks round and catches me starting.

"Huh, nothing, just watching." I smile, "Yeah, I'd like to get up from the bed."

"That makes one of us." He mutters under his breath.

"Hmm well..." I grin.

"Food Leona." He laughs.

I start to move from the bed and am about to just hop down when he swoops over and grabs me around the waist, "For Christ sake Leona, your feet." Shoot! I was too busy ogling.

"Oops!"

"You and your bloody oops." He grunts and moves in closer and places an arm around me, taking the most of my weight but as soon as I put my feet down, I can't help the yelp.

"Christ! That sting's." I cry and see him frown.
"Hey, this isn't on you." I say sternly.

"Of course it is, I dragged you into the trees with no shoes on and mauled you, then marched you through a bloody forest." He says roughly.

"Sebastian do not make this a big thing! The boy's told you their self I do this kind of thing all the time. Are you doing all this because you feel guilty?"

"Of course, I feel guilty!" he curses.

"For Pete sake, it was an accident, if I wasn't so bloody distracted, I would have noticed."

"Yeah… why were you distracted smart ass?" he fumes!

"Oh, piss off, I was as wrapped up in you as you were in me. We are both as bad as each other here so drop the penance crap. Be here if you want to be here but do not stay here out of fucking guilt!" I shout.

"Believe me when I say there is nowhere else, I want to be." He says it so viciously I have to laugh.

"Wow, you don't have to sound so ecstatic about it." I glare at him and hate that my body moves in closer.

"Yeah, well I'm not!" he says and lowers me into the seat.

"I honestly have no idea why you're making this so complicated."

"Let's just eat, shall we?" he growls and starts moving plates towards me. He places a teapot in front of me and I tell him I can manage. He takes a seat across from me and we sit in silence for a while as I drink my tea and eat a corner of a sandwich.

"Do you know where the boys are?" I ask.

"Yeah, they're all out at the batting cages, practicing for the softball game tomorrow." He replies.

"And everyone else?"

"The rest of the group headed out for a cruise around the lakes." He says as he watches me.

"I'm sorry you missed out." I say meaning it.

"I'm not." He keeps watching. "Can I ask you something?"

"Eh sure…"

"What spooked you earlier when the boys started talking about their Dad?"

"Wow! Straight for the kill, huh?" I groan.

"You don't have to answer I'm just curious."

I sigh, "The boys were always outgoing, the life and souls of a party. Noah's just… well Noah. He's actually still a little more subdued than he was before the accident," I grin, "But Jacob, he was so much more outgoing. Never as much as Noah but way more than he has been the last few years or so. We talk about Matt, my husband, all the time around the house and with their grandparents but they keep it at that. They don't normally share things with other people and I '*spooked*' because… well honestly," I hesitate,

"They never had a big family, they had Matt, his parents and me. That was it. They used to watch all those ridiculous movies with the big family Christmases or gatherings and would cry out for more… cousins, a long-lost aunt, anything really and when I saw how comfortable they are slotting in here, with this dysfunctional lot, yeah, I got spooked."

He watches me intently.

"You can ask." I smile softly.

"Your family?" he says gently.

"Yeah, I don't really have one of them… My mom had me when she was really young, she kept me on and off for the first few years, she never spoke to her parents after she fell pregnant. My father was her high school boyfriend, they were both bitterly disappointed with their lives after they had me, so were on and off for years. I floated between them both but they were unstable most for the time, then they just spiraled." I pause to take a small moment,

"My dad died after being out drinking too much one night when he came to pick me up from my moms', we were walking along the side of the road back to his place, when he tripped and fell in front of a truck. He died on impact. My mom disappeared for a while after that. She overdosed the following year. I tried to contact her parents for her funeral but they were in a retirement home, her mother had Alzheimer's, she never even remembered having a grandchild. Her dad wasn't interested, said he had no whore daughter… I don't think they were very good people." I say.

"And your fathers parents?" he says simply. No pity, no sad looks, which helps me carry on.

"I met them once after their son died. They never came to the funeral but when social services found out my mom had passed away and I had been living alone in her house they got in touch with them, they came met me, took one look and walked right back out the door. They said I looked far too much like the women who destroyed their sons life." I pause and he just waits, patiently.

"They did sign the certificate to say I could receive my dad's inheritance, apparently his grandfather had left him the house he was living in, so I got the money from the sale of the house, which is how I managed to avoid the system for too long. I got shipped about a few times but because I had good grades and kept my head down, I managed to get into a decent college, went on to University, mct Matt in my first year, fell pregnant with the twins and the rest they say… well you get the drift." I smile. "And that is my happy childhood, I suppose I owe you that anyway after Val…"

He shuts up my blabbering by crouching down in front of me, he takes my face in hands when I won't look at him and forces me to make eye contact.

"Thank you for sharing." He says and kisses me. Not a hot and steamy one like we've shared before, this time he moves slowly, takes his time and kisses me so softly my eyes well up and I pull away.

"I don't talk about any of this stuff."

"I appreciate that, it kind of makes sense you know." He says.

"What does?" I ask.

"This pull I feel towards you. I know on the outside it looks like I should have had the perfect upbringing and I won't even attempt to compare. But I see in you the same thing I saw in myself for years. An obsessive need to carve out your own way in life. A fixation on proving you were capable of looking after yourself, not needing anyone to take care of you. Of proving we are not our parents." He says and I feel it, this connection, that as different as our worlds may be we both have a lot of the same insecurities.

He leans back into his chair and I'm almost scared what's next.

"Can I ask about your husband?" he says gently.

I laugh.

"I never have any idea what you're going to ask next… Yeah shoot. What do you want to know?"

"I'm not sure to be honest, was it some grand love affair, were you soulmates? Do you think you could love again?" he looks a little confused with himself to even be asking.

"Honestly, yes, no, maybe." I sigh, wondering where even to begin.

"We were crazy young, I craved stability and Matt was that in abundance. He was an only child, his parents were older than most, he was so handsome and charming, he came in and swept me off my feet." I smile to myself.

"I kept mostly to myself when I started University, had no friends and was just happy to have a decent place to crash and study. I worked in a diner during the day and a bar at night near campus and Matt was the all-star sports guy. He spoke to everyone and he used to talk to me most nights. He always asked me to join them after my shifts or offer to walk me home. I think he had a bit of white knight syndrome you know." I glance at him and he just nods.

"I could never understand why he didn't give up. He started showing up at the end of my shifts and would walk me back to the dorms. He was persistent and wore me down. We dated for a little while and next thing you know I'm over halfway through my first year and pregnant. I'm ashamed to say but I was devastated. Matt was ecstatic. His parents were over the moon. They never imagined having Matt so late, so a grandchild was a bonus. Then we found out it was twins and well my world just flipped."

"You had to drop out?"

"Yeah, I stayed as long as I could but the pregnancy was tough. My grades were good though they let me move online. I used the money from my dad to buy a little apartment, moved in and began working like mad to get my degree whilst battling every kind of sickness there was. Matt moved in and well we just lived. He got his business degree; I got my architects and we both got two bouncing baby boys."

I pause and take my time.

"It's okay Leona, you don't have to carry on."

"It's fine, I loved Matt, so much. We were great together; we both had the same goals with work and he was a fantastic father. But we were always just muddling through, barely getting by. We never felt this overwhelming need to make time for us as a couple you know."

He smiles softly.

"You asked me the other day why I was crying watching your grandparents. I stood there thinking '*I want that*', I want someone to look at me like Andy does to May, even Tabitha and Hank. They have this bond, this spark that shines between them and I realized for all I loved Matt, we never had that. And maybe life stole it, maybe if he hadn't been taken from us, we would have had it in time but I'll never know."

He smiles sadly at me.

"Yeah, I know… that's why we can't date. I get it Sebastian and lord knows I wish I could have a causal relationship but you were completely right. I am not made for it. Not with you. I would always want more."

"You make me want more Leona, way more than I ever thought I could want for myself but I would end up hurting you and your boy's in the end and that would hurt me more. I think they really need to be part of this… '*dysfunctional family*' I think you called it and I would never ruin that for them."

"Well, we really are a pair eh! Maybe we can be friends though? I will just never watch you play basketball ever again." I grin and he laughs.

"Yeah, and I won't be held accountable if you show

up in an obscene bathing suit again!" he groans.

"Friends?" I say and hold my hand out with a smirk.

A loud bang on the door has us both jumping and in walk the real loves of my life.

"Hey, hey! What's going on in here?" Noah says and wiggles his eyebrows.

"Noah quit it!" Jacob punches his arm. "How you feeling mom?"

"Yeah, I don't think I will be doing anymore dancing anytime soon." I say and show them my bandaged feet.

"Aw man that suck's, there is another party later." Noah says with a frown. "We can keep you company though; save you being bored out your mind up here." He says.

I can see they both look a little disappointed at the thought of missing the party but before I get the chance to decline their offer Sebastian steps in.

"I was actually going to ask if you guys would be ok with me setting your mom up in my office and her and I getting a bit of work done on the drafts for the Montgomery job?" he says it so easily I almost believe him.

They both pause a little and look Sebastian over, sensing his sincerity.

"Do we have to ask what your intentions are with our mom Mr. Van Der Bilt, Sir?" I almost automatically scold Noah but realize its Jacob who spoke.

I look at him sharply and see he has stood a little taller and is watching Sebastian with a sharp eye. Noah looks, dare I say it, angry.

"Dude?"

"It's fine Noah, Jacob is well within his rights to ask

my intentions." He smiles. "Your mom and I had a pretty rough start."

He hears my snort and pauses… "Sorry, carry on."

"We did not see eye to eye at all but we have cleared the air and are slowly becoming friends. I assure you boy's both, I respect your mother immensely and think she is a remarkable lady, I will not disgrace her in any way."

Well fuck a girl could've hoped! Cock blocked by my own children!

"And I assure you if that were ever to change, you two would be the first people I asked for permission." He says.

Wait what?

"That sounds fair, huh Jake?" Noah says looking back and forth.

Jacob takes a minute and turns to me, "Are you ok with all this mom?"

Shoot, what do I say to that?

"Sebastian's right we had a bit of a time getting past our differences but we are building a friendship and we do have a lot of work to get through, so it could be a good idea to try and make a crack at some of it while I'm off my feet." I say ignoring the obvious.

"And if his intentions change?" he asks straight out, no flinching no judgement, just stares me straight in the eye.

"Well, I'm sure that's not what he meant and…"

"It's exactly what he meant mom." He says still standing ram rod straight. The tension in the room goes up a fraction.

"Well, I think I will start with the working friendship first and like Sebastian said, I would speak to you guys first before anything like that but boy's that is not what is happening here. Please don't get carried away." I say looking directly at Noah who is already moving his furniture in his head.

"I'm sorry if I made this more awkward than it should have been Jacob, Noah, but I won't lie and pretend if I ever manage to get my shit together, I would not ask your mom on a date."

What in the hell is he doing? I am glaring daggers at him and he is refusing to look anywhere in my direction but keeps a close eye on the boys expression.

Noah takes a deep breath and Jacob just waits.

"We appreciate the honesty Sebastian, and if it's ok with our mom then it's cool with us if you guys want to hang out working." He says very diplomatically not agreeing to anything else I see and so does Sebastian.

"So does that mean you don't want us to hang out with you guys tonight and we can go to the party?" Noah wiggles his eyebrows and Jacob laughs and slugs him around the head.

"Yeah, that's fine, you two can go, have fun but keep me posted and come say goodnight before you disappear tonight."

"Cool."

Sebastian excused himself and left me with the boys and we had a good chat. They both like him and apparently have no problem with me dating him at all and I have no idea how to tell them he is not interested that way. He was just covering all his bases.

I settle for telling them not to get their hopes up. I'm not sure either of us is ready for a serious relationship but they will most definitely be the first to know. Christ how is this my life.

They head off for the party and I just take it easy keeping off my feet as much as possible. The girls,

Andy and May all pop by to check in and I apologize for being such a clumsy fool and awful guest. No-one seems to hold it against me so I begin to relax until Sebastian comes by and wheels in a damn wheelchair,

"Your chariot awaits." He grins.

"No way." I frown but when he points out the alternative is for him to carry me, I quickly subside. So, I am wheeled through this maze of a house and find myself sequestered away in the most beautiful library I have ever seen.

It's all dark wood paneling and leather-bound books on almost every wall. There is a roaring fire flaming away in the corner and a large table has been moved close by. It is littered with all sorts of blueprints and sketches and my fingers itch to get a closer look.

"Calm your pants missy or I will wheel you right back around." He says as I almost topple out of the chair trying to peer over.

He helps me into a seat and we get straight to work. His sketches are flawless and his design ideas impeccable. We actually work well together and have a lot of similar ideas. We both make slight adjustments to each other's designs and agree that we have only enhanced the work. The time flies by and I am delighted to be getting on with the project.

We come to a sticking point when it comes to the Atrium. Sebastian agrees with some of the board members that we should just pull it down and re-build something more modern. I am aghast.

I explain my hopes for the space and he agrees it has its merits but would be a greater expense and create a longer time frame that he's not sure he can commit to. He then lets me in on the fact that as well as working for his family's company, he also has his own!

"How the hell do you have your own firm?" I ask shocked.

"Well, it's not that big of a company, when I left University, I didn't want to just walk into a job," he smirks at me, "So, I became an apprentice. I stayed there for nine, ten years learning everything I could and when Mr. Donaldson decided to retire after a mini heart attack, I decided to buy in. It's a great family run company and I mostly do the design work and the Donaldsons still hold the majority shares. They know they can buy me out anytime but right now it's going well."

"For goodness sake Sebastian do you sleep?" I cry.

"Well as I said before, I don't have much time outside of family and work." He smirks.

"Yeah, it all starts to make a little more sense now, although I have to be honest…"

"Go on." He grins.

"A lot of time or not, you can do way better than that nasty woman you've been seeing. If you don't mind me saying." I just made myself angry even thinking about her.

"You can drop the scowl; you were completely right about her character and she has been removed from my…" he frowns.

"Your what? Oh god please don't tell me you have some sordid list of horrible women to hook up with?" I groan.

"I may not *date* Leona but Christ I still have needs." He says stiffly.

"Wow, ok yeah, thank goodness I didn't inadvertently decide to become part of some secret harem of filthy women." I fume.

"Trust me Leona if you and I went there I wouldn't

have time for any other women. It's a constant struggle to be in the same god damn room with you and keep things platonic never mind if we were... well..."

"Sleeping together." I provide.

"Yes, now let's get back to work, I made a promise to your boys and I for one intend to keep it."

"Yeah, about that..." I frown deeply at him.

"I won't lie to them; I've been on the other end of the lies myself and I won't do that to them. If I ever do get my shit together Leona, you are the only person I would want to make that type of effort for and your boys will be the first to know about it, and stop with those moony eyes! I said *if* and that's a big fucking *if*."

"Yes sir." I salute just for good measure and grin.

"God woman I think fucking you may be the only thing that will shut you up!"

"Wow Sebastian! Now I know why you don't date... such a charmer." Anders remarks with his impeccable timing.

"Where the bloody hell did you come from? And that was a private conversation."

"Like the one from earlier at the beach?" he turns to me, "You owe me my dear, and well played in the race." He bows gallantly.

"Aw now don't be a sore loser... and thank you for today." I smile.

"You are welcome." He says to me, "You are not!" he looks at Sebastian.

"Do not even start Anders."

"I will only say it this once... You are a fool. You are not your father and Leona is not bloody Cheyenne! Do not fuck this up!" He says so seriously, the joker completely gone and the lawyer in his place.

I do not move a muscle.

Sebastian glares at him and he turns to me and takes my hand,

"If he does mess this up, which we both know is highly likely, I am always here as the better replacement. For you gorgeous I would give up the philandering." He says it so seriously I actually don't know how to respond.

"OUT NOW ANDERS!" he shouts and I startle as he gets up to leave but not before I see his wink. Trouble maker.

He wanders away and Sebastian storms off for a few seconds, coming back with two glasses.

"You are getting a smidge of this since you are such a lush."

"I am not! Well… I'm not that bad." I say.

"One drink and then bed." I chuckle and he slams his drink back.

"Yeah, yeah I heard it too." he smiles.

The boys come by just as were finishing up and ask to take shot's each of wheeling me through the house. By the time I slip into bed, I feel like I've been on a rollercoaster. I say goodnight and send them off to the cabins and swear to Sebastian that I will manage getting to bed perfectly fine. I mean I don't but other than a broken vase who will know the difference?

CHAPTER 23

Thank the lord it's the last day of this weekend.

As much as everyone has been great and Sebastian and I are in a somewhat better place, I really am desperate to get home and decompress. The boys though never want to leave.

My feet are still pretty sore but it's bearable if I wear flats so that's what I stick to. I get dressed and head downstairs to join everyone. As I enter the room Andy rushes over and takes my arm,

"Hey there girlie, what are you doing walking around?" he huffs as he steers me over to a massive dining table full of familiar faces.

I say Hi to everyone as I pass and take my seat beside Shelby.

"Hey sweetie, you doing, ok?" she smiles.

"Yeah, more embarrassed than anything else." I sigh.

"No need dear." Andy laughs, "We've all been there or made nearly as big a klutz of ourselves. May do you remember when Anders fell down the garden hill into your ivy bush?" he laughs.

"Hey, that was that darn cat's fault! I was bloody itching for days and you all said I had to lie in a bath of tomato juice. It was years later before I found out that was for skunks spray, not poison ivy."

He glares around the table and everyone laughs and starts regaling all their own mishaps at the house. I feel Shelby's hand clasp mine as she whispers,

"See, just normal people in a fancy house." She smiles and I beam back at her. She's right. The breakfast carries on in the same vain, they're loud, shouting over one another, taking pops at themselves and everyone else but overall, there is smiles all round and I love every minute.

The boys are popping into the conversation so easily and as I catch Andy's eye as he gives me a warm smile. This crazy, dysfunctional, family. How did I get so lucky to find myself with a seat at the table?

The talk turns to the last game of the tournament and excitement buzzes round the air.

"Well thanks to the girls points in the swimming race, it's anybody's to be won." Andy declares.

"Bloody Leona was a ringer and everyone knows Shelby's a cheat!" Anders exclaims.

"Oh, shut up, you were bet fair and square! Get over it and yeah Leona was a ringer." She grins at me.

"Yeah, she was!" Noah shouts and I laugh along.

Everyone starts heading out and I wave the boys off with their friends to get set up.

"Need me to grab your wheels?" Sebastian grins as he helps me up from my chair.

"Har, Har."

"Seriously though how you doing today?" he says as he takes my arm supporting my weight off my worst foot.

"Much better, thank you."

"And how did you manage last night?" he grins and I pause and look up at him. He keeps a straight face but I can see the cracks at the side of his mouth.

"Fine, why do you ask?" I say cautiously.

"No reason." he grins now. He couldn't know, could he?

"You know May decorated this whole house herself," he says conversationally as we begin slowly walking much further behind everyone else due to my baby steps.

"Oh yeah, she's done a wonderful job."

"Hmm yes, her favorite pieces are the things she went out and sourced herself." he goes on, what the hell is he talking about now? "Some special painting here, an ornament there, even some family heirlooms."

Shoot! Why would there be a bloody family heirloom in a guest room? Of course, there wouldn't be… right?

"Her favorites are… the… vases she dots around the place." He finishes but I can see he's about ready to crack.

"You asshole! That was cruel… It is a joke, right?" He's too busy laughing and I take a moment; he looks so young and carefree.

"SEBASTIAN!"

"Yes, yes it was just a joke but please tell me how in the hell you broke a vase?" he laughs.

"I will not!" I grunt.

"Ok then, care to tell me what you whispered in old man Bueller's ear?" he dares to ask.

"You sir will never know!" I try to stomp away and almost fall over the rug and take out a… yup you guessed it a bloody stupid vase.

He can't help himself; he laughs so loudly people turn to see what's going on and I punch him in the side.

"Knock it off you, everyone's staring." I grimace.

"Let them." He continues laughing and I join in… eventually.

The Van Der Bilt's of course have their own mini baseball park in the garden, so us ladies who are not participating get to sit behind the iron link fence on the bleachers. Although Shelby and Tabitha are still bitching about how Sebastian has moved me to a perfect spot and covered the hard bench with a soft blanket and cushions for me to prop my feet up.

"And you're sure you are not sleeping with him?" Tabitha asks for the millionth time.

"Knock it off, his grandmother is right there!" I grit through my teeth.

"It just seems weird how attentive he is for someone not getting the goods, you know?" she looks seriously confused.

"I told you he felt bad for not noticing I had no shoes."

"Hmm." Is all she says.

The game gets underway and everyone is on the edge of their seats, well mostly everyone. I know my boys and they are not losing this game no matter what happens.

Noah has put on a good front so far but he is a cert to bust his ass. This is one of his favorite sports and he's really good, like major league good and Jacob, he's right up there with him.

So, it's no surprise they knock it out of the park, I sit there and watch them embrace Sebastian and the other teammates and parade around with their cup and medals like they've just won the Super Bowl with a huge grin on my face.

Noah accepts his grunted congratulations from Kayla with a big easy smile and hugs her right back. It's nice but worrying, as I can see Hank glaring in the corner. That's going to be one to watch.

I see Libby smile at Jacob and he tells her better luck next time. At first, she looks ready to bitch him out but she just shrugs it off and tells him she will be practicing for next time. He offers to give her some pointers if she wants to catch up sometime and I hold my breath. Jacob threw it out all cool and calm but I can see he is unsure if she will take him up on it. I feel Shelby grab my leg as she watches alongside me.

"You know what Jake that sounds good, thanks." She smiles at him and they go off chatting.

"Well, I'll be damned!"

"Shell don't make it a big deal!" I grin and she smiles right back.

"Aw we could be in-laws..." she smirks.

"Piss off you." I laugh right back.

"Hey mom, we're all gona head down for some celebratory drinks at the beach before we head home, that cool?" Noah says with Kayla close by his side.

"Yeah, that's fine, I'm going to head upstairs and get packed." I say as I give him a big hug.

Jacob, Libby and Miguel all wander over,

"You guys all set?" Miguel says. And off they all start to go, Jacob doubles back at my cough and accepts my congrats, then runs off to catch up. Shelby heads over to chat to her parents and I just sit back and enjoy the peace.

"Hey, Do I get one of them?" Sebastian says as he towers over me.

"One of what?"

"A congrats hug?" he grins, "I mean I did carry your boys out there." He grins.

"Yeah, sure you say that now they're out of the way!"

"Yeah, they're something else! Are they on a team, being scouted because if not you really need..." he pauses at my laugh, "What?"

"Of course, they are, there fricking awesome and have had multiple offers. You're getting a bit too…" I tail off.

"Aw yeah sorry, it's just you know they're really good and…"

"It's fine Sebastian I know what you meant."

"Well about that congrats then?" he says as he sits down and I lean over and hug him.

"Well done, I'm sure you helped out in some way." I grin and we talk for a little bit.

"So, are you heading home with Shelby this afternoon?" he asks.

"Yeah, I want to get back and get set for tomorrow. What about you?"

"I'm not leaving till later tonight; I have a conference call in a bit so I'm going to take it here and settle up a few things before I head back. I have a meeting next week with the Montgomery investors and I would like you to come along. Pitch them your idea about the Atrium, they may not go for it but I think it's worth giving them every option." He smiles at me and I'm stunned.

"Seriously?"

"Well yeah, it's a good idea Leona but it's totally up to the board if they want to pay the extra expense." He says.

"Wow, well thanks and yeah I will have a proposal made up right away." I smile back.

As I look around, the field has emptied out and it's just so nice and peaceful.

"Ok, well I may not see you now again before you head off but I want to thank you for an… enjoyable… weekend." He grins.

"It was something all right!"

He leans down and kisses me softly, not the rip off each other's clothes type of kiss, just sweet, heartbreaking because we both know that after this weekend it's back to a working relationship.

"Leona…" he starts softly.

"It's fine Sebastian, we both know where we stand. We don't need to make this a big thing; it could have been great but we're just both too far apart on what we want. No biggie. At least we can work together properly and get this project done well." I smile softly.

"Yeah ok, well I'll help you back to your room." he says.

"I think I'm just going to sit here a bit longer; I will text one of the boys to come help me back." He frowns and I stop him,

"Honestly, It's better like this, Sebastian."

"Ok, well I guess I'll see you at work?"

"Yup." I smile up at him, "Now off you go." I shoo him.

"You and your shoo-ing." He smiles, leans down and kisses me softly, turns and walks away. And I know in that moment I will never have that all-consuming, devastating, soul crushing love because the man who is walking away holds my heart now. Sad but true, so I lay back and look at the sky and will myself not to cry.

Not ten minutes pass and I hear him slide onto the bench with me.

"Hey gorgeous, need a hand back to the house?" he smiles.

"Sure Anders, thanks." I say as I heave myself up and head back to pack.

"Aw c'mon Noah! Shelby is waiting and Libby has

to get back to the dorms!" I call.

Noah is currently saying his farewells to Kayla and Kye but mostly Kayla, as if he is a soldier going off to war.

Jacob and Libby are chatting away in the back of the car and Shelby is ignoring Anders poignant stares or glares I can't really tell anymore. I bid a tearful goodbye myself to Andy and May but we really do need to get on the road.

"Noah!"

"Coming! God mom." He eventually strolls over looking like someone kicked his puppy.

"Hey!"

"Sorry," he grumbles, "Kayla's going off to camp for a few weeks so we won't be able to catch up for a while." He frowns. Ahh.

"Okay well at least you'll still be able to txt and call."

"Yeah, I know. Sucks but."

"Yeah, buddy it does." I say and pull him in for a hug. I kiss the top of his head and shove him towards the car, "But other people gotta move!" I grin and eventually we are on the road.

CHAPTER 24

The rest of the day flies by what with the unpacking, washing up, getting school stuff ready before I know it, I am falling into bed and the morning light is poking through the blinds.

Since my feet are still a little sore, I avoid my morning run and pour a coffee and decide to catch up with my emails.

Right at the top is a message from Sebastian, I open it right away and frown a little. Unfortunately, the Mandarin conference didn't go as planned and he has to fly out to Singapore this morning and Isn't sure when he will be back. He is confident he will be back before the board meeting for the Montgomery but as a backup plan can I be prepared to take the lead if needed.

What the heck!

I email him back right away but realize he will be airborne, so I will have to wait to speak with him. He has left a brief outline for the week but I sigh when I read *'he knows I am more than capable of handling it… he trusts my judgement…'*

I mean lord a week ago he was trying to have me fired and now this! But he is right, I am more than capable and I will not let anyone down, so I set about getting to work. I bid the boys goodbye, Noah still seems a little down but I hear Jacob say that Libby was thinking of taking a drive up to see Kayla in the next few weeks and offered them both to come along. He immediately perks up and as I leave Jacob rolls his eyes.

"What have I done!" he laughs.

The week speeds by with all the work to be done and things run smoothly, we have a few hiccups but nothing major and we are still on the correct timeline.

I send Sebastian an email thanking him for his trust in me and I give him daily updates on where we are. I send him my design drafts and my pitch for the Montgomery board and he responds he approves. Our interactions are friendly but not much else and I cannot help but miss him.

The beginning of the next week he lets me know negotiations have gone well and he will be back in time to make the meeting but I will have to meet him there as he will be coming straight from the airport. I assure him that is fine and work goes on.

The day of the meeting I am up way too early and have gone over the pitch so many time that the boys could probably recite it word for word.

I head to my office and gather up my gear and wave the boys off to school. They are both doing great and Noah and Kayla seem to be keeping in touch on a daily basis now.

As I start to load my things in the car, when I notice I have a flat tyre. I do not need this today but it's not a total disaster, right?

Wrong! As I remove all the crap I just carefully loaded into the trunk, I take out the spare wheel only to find a bloody nail sticking out of the side wall.

SHIT! I grab my phone and immediately call the car service. Unfortunately, there is a burst main on one of the roads and they are backed up for miles it will take another thirty, forty minutes to get a car to me.

I phone Shelby and she tells me she is stuck in the traffic herself so she's out but she spoke to Jackson last night and he is off work today, why don't I give him a shout? I warn her I will be wanting way more information on how she knows Jacksons schedule but she just rushes me off the phone. I have no time to waste so I phone him and he answers right away.

"Hello gorgeous, calling to tell me when you're taking me out for that drink?" he sings down the phone.

"Eh no, I'm calling for a favor actually."

"Aw darling you're breaking my heart. That's gona be two drinks now or maybe we can come to another arrangement." He laughs.

I tell him my predicament and he tells me to hold tight he will swing past he's only a few minutes away.

When he pulls up in a sleek black sedan, I don't even question it, I just start loading things in his car. Within a few minutes were on our way downtown to the meeting and I try to fix myself up a little.

I dressed really nice this morning, of course for my meeting but also because it's the first time I will have seen Sebastian since his grandparents ball and I wanted to look nice. I know I'm pathetic but it is what it is.

"You look very sexy today Mrs. Chalmers." he wiggles his eyebrows.

"Piss off you, where is the panda car and what's going on with you and Shelby?" I glare.

"Well, hello to you too! The *panda car* is for work only missy, and I am off duty this morning."

"And Shelby?" I stare.

"Well, I figure since you seem to have no interest in buying me that drink, I could ask for a favor instead." he looks almost bashful.

"So, I happened to run into the lovely Miss Davies last night and she quite simply refused point blank to go on a date with and I quote *'A stripper looking sexpot playboy like me'* apparently and I again quote *'she has dealt with enough of my type to last a lifetime.'* Care to elaborate or do me a solid and talk her into a date?"

"I can't see why she would have said that, what on earth would have given her that impression?"

"Har, Har you know fine well I am upfront and honest but like I told the fine Miss Davies last night I am still a one-woman man and I would very much like to take her out."

I watch him and he does look incredibly serious. We pull up in front of the building and he gets out and helps me grab my things.

"Well?" he pouts.

"Ok, I will talk to her but I am not making any promises you hear. If she says no, my duty is done." I say as he smiles widely, pulling me in and kissing me on the cheek.

"You are an angel; I will call you later ok." He grins as he jumps behind the wheel and spins off. I laugh at him waving like a loony out the window and turn to enter the building when I see Sebastian standing there.

Literally just standing there, watching me.

"Hey you! You look exhausted!" I say as I walk towards him. He doesn't move, doesn't smile, simply keeps on staring.

I put my hand on his arm and he pulls back.

"You, ok?" I ask concerned.

"Yes Mrs. Chalmers, are you prepared for the meeting." He says stiffly as he holds open the door.

"What's with the *'Mrs. Chalmers'* shit again?" I stare sharply.

"I think we should keep this professional; I wouldn't

want to give off the wrong impression." He says firmly and I frown.

The building is busy, so we load into the elevator and don't speak another word. As we get off at the conference floor, he practically ignores me but I won't hassle him, he looks exhausted and I want to get set up right away so we go about our business. I hear the door open and Valerie comes in.

"Leona, I just wanted to wish you good luck with your pitch," I frown I hadn't even told her about it yet, "Sebastian sent me the outline of your design and I must say it's beautiful dear. I really hope the board go for it; I agree with Sebastian they would be foolish not to include it." She says kindly.

"Thank you, Valerie, I really hope so too." I look to Sebastian but he is talking to someone on the phone.

"Well, I won't hold you up any longer, Good luck." She says and heads out just as the first members of the board start to arrive.

Sebastian begins welcoming them and the meeting gets under way. As the updates starts to wind down, he pauses and ask the board if they could give him another few minutes of their time.

"Mrs. Chalmers here has been the lead designer on this project alongside myself and many of the design changes you have all been awed by are mostly her additions. She is a truly talented architect and she has a proposition for the board that has the full backing of the Van Der Bilt firm." He hands it over to me and I try to not dwell on the statement he just made otherwise I could kiss him. I thank him for the kind words and pitch my ass off.

As the board members begin to leave, they ask a few more questions that I am happy to answer. When the room has emptied, I see Sebastian is getting ready to leave.

"Hey," I say as I stop him, "That was very kind of you to give me your backing."

"Not my backing, the boards backing, everyone was wowed with your design and they would be fools not to go for it." he says simply as he starts to leave again.

"Sebastian, is there something wrong? With us I mean?" I ask.

"There is no us." He states plainly.

"Well, yes I know that but I thought we were getting along, friends, I'm sure we said." I smile softly.

"Colleagues Mrs. Chalmers, just colleagues, now if you will excuse me, I have a lot of work to get too." He turns and walks to the door and pauses, "I do hope they agree to include your design, It would be a wonderful addition." He says and walks out the door leaving me wondering…

WHAT IN THE HELL JUST HAPPENED?

The rest of the weeks carry on in the same way. Sebastian is polite but distant.

He seems to avoid me on site and in the office as much as possible and I miss him like crazy.

Since everything is finalized and the work is well underway there really isn't much need for him to be here and he has been back and forth on his other projects. He still checks my emails daily and adds any notes he feels are needed but mostly he lets me run it. We are awaiting the decision for the Atrium and I am starting to think it may not happen.

As another week begins, I am called to Valerie's office. As I head up, I ask Shell if she has any idea what's going on but she's as in the dark as me. When I arrive, I see Sebastian making his way out of Valerie's and heading to his own.

"Hi," I smile, "Any idea what this is about?"

"Sorry, no clue I'm afraid." He says.

"Eh… How've you been?" I say as he says,

"Good to see you."

And walks on past.

OKAY THEN!

As I enter Valerie's office, she comes around her desk with a huge smile on her face.

"Congratulations Leona, The board have accepted your proposal for the Atrium at the Montgomery and have asked that you oversee the development. Well done." She grins and I am shocked.

"Seriously? I really thought since it was taking so long, they had rejected it." I say.

"No need to worry now, it's all systems go." She smiles, "You should be really proud of yourself Leona, it's a beautiful design."

"Thank you, Valerie. Oh, I'm so excited. Did the board say if they were going to take up my idea of the opening ball?"

"Well, I'm not entirely sure, let's get it built and take it from there hmm?"

"Yes, yes of course. I want to thank you Valerie for giving me this opportunity and sticking with me." I say.

"You earned it all by yourself dear, your dedication to this company has been impeccable and I am so glad that it's finally paying off. Now go get Shelby and you girls go out and celebrate. Enjoy it because you now have to back up all those big plans you have." She smiles and gives me a quick brusque hug.

"I am genuinely pleased for you Leona."

"Thank you, it really means a lot."

"Ok, of you go now." She smiles.

As I leave her office I almost dash into Sebastian's but as I look in, he is standing observing every inch of my face, he must have already been watching how it went with Valerie and he obviously knows the deal went through, yet he stands stock still behind his desk simply watching, keeping himself apart.

I study him closely and he gives me a sad smile, then turns away as I force my feet to move, otherwise I will charge in there and force him to tell me what the hell went wrong. But I made a promise to myself for both of us not too push him, he needs to make the choice himself and if he doesn't, then I have to accept that.

The time flies by and before I know it the Atrium build is almost complete. I have worked day and night to keep the project on track and to fit the deadline.

Ironically the date for the build to be finished coincides with the time the original build was opened and I take it as the perfect sign to approach the board with my idea to re-open in the same style as the original.

Shelby has been working nonstop beside me through it all and has made her own list of ideas for the proposed opening night. She has sourced some magnificent artefacts from the original building which she has been getting restored on her own time and I ask her to make up a rough pitch to give the board a feel for the idea we are going for. Since it's not entirely in our expertise, it's a big risk but I think the work she has shown proves she could oversee the opening if she hires the right contractors.

She is ecstatic and overwhelmed but I have complete confidence in her and after consulting with

Valerie she agrees and gives us the go ahead so I reach out to the board. They grant me a meeting with them and explain a few board members may not be present but they will certainly consider my idea.

The day comes and although we are both nervous, I think we smashed it. We got thrown for a loop when we showed up and a few members were joining online which isn't unusual however they were not in screen, so it was a little strange but they asked on point questions and everyone seemed intrigued by the idea.

Shelby had managed to show them a progress report on an original Louis XIV chandelier that once hung in the grand ballroom which she had researched, purchased and was currently having restored.

I worried we stumbled a little when one of the online members asked what Shelby planned to do with the chandelier if we rejected the proposal but she pulled it out of the bag when she replied that regardless of the outcome, she had every intention of donating it to the building as she believed that's where it truly belonged.

She had everyone laughing when she proclaimed however if they preferred not to accept it, she would always find space to hang it in her apartment. The thing was ginormous, so thankfully they assured her they would accept it and they would refund her the costs but she just brushed it off.

They seemed incredibly impressed by her commitment and we both came away knowing we had done everything we could, we now just had to wait.

After a few days I received an email from the chair of the board agreeing to our proposal and asking for Shelby to help oversee the night. They emailed over a list of contractors they preferred to use and she was more than happy with them, so roughly six weeks before Thanksgiving was set for the grand re-opening for The New Montgomery.

I could hardly believe it and every time I stepped foot inside the Atrium to check on the progress, I fell more and more in love with the place. It was going to be exceptional.

The only downside was how badly I wanted to share it with Sebastian. He had been scarce around the office and the site and the last I heard he was travelling back and forth to deal with the Mandarin project.

I sent him an invitation to the opening ball anyway along with the rest of his family. The boys couldn't wait to come as Kayla and Libby had both agreed to accompany them and I also extended an invite to Jackson. He had been hounding me to follow up on my discussion with Shelby but we were both so busy and she repeated she had no interest in being another '*notch*' but I sent him the invite anyway, so now he has been trying to coerce her into allowing him to escort her. He's tenacious and it looks like he may just be wearing her down.

The night before the grand opening Shelby and I take a walk through the building for a few final checks before we leave.

"Shell just think, the next time we come down this staircase the room will be full of guest looking at what we have created. Can you believe it?" I grin.

"Nope, I keep pinching myself. How on earth did we pull this off?" she laughs.

"I don't know about you but I'm thinking we crack open one of those bottles of champagne chilling in the kitchen and head over to the Atrium to check out the view."

"It's like you were reading my mind." She grins.

We head down the sweeping staircase and move through to the Atrium and I smile so wide. This place is exactly like I envisioned it. The frameless glass ceiling panels give the illusion of an open-air roof and a direct view of the twinkling sky up above. The tiny sparkling lights that have been draped everywhere reflect off the crystal marble floor which gives you the impression you are surrounded by stars. It's magnificent and I have no doubt this room will be booked out for months ahead.

"Leona this is just… Wow, it's like a dream." She smiles and hands me a glass of champagne.

"To you Leona Chalmers… for bringing this old relic of a building and me back to life. You have no idea how much joy and happiness you have brought to my life from the day we met and I cannot wait to see what the future holds for us." She smiles gently.

"Well right back at you beautiful!" I grin. "I honestly do not think I would have coped these last few months without you by my side and I am so immensely proud of all the work you have put in on this project but I am sorry to say I may have to fire you."

Her glass freezes halfway to her lips and she frowns.

"You have enhanced this old building with so much history and character that I think I would be doing you a disservice by keeping you as an assistant but I do have a proposition for you. I think you should start your own company doing …" I wave my hand around, "all of this. You took on this major renovation and have absolutely smashed it and I would like to work with you. I think we have a good thing here and I think we should give it a proper go."

She just stares at me and I begin to panic I've upset her but then I see her eyes are welling up and she is simply trying to compose herself.

"You have no idea how much I want to punch you right now; you scared the shit out of me! But what scares me so much, more is I think you may be right. I've loved every minute of this and have a million ideas running through my head. I don't want to quit though," She says sharply. "I've loved working with you on the build and I think we may be able to manage both. I never felt useful before but now I am definitely rethinking my worth, I may even ask for a raise." She says saucily and we both hug it out and just look around at what we've both achieved.

"Ok home, we have a busy day tomorrow and I for one can't wait." She sighs, dramatically.

"What's the sigh for? Could it be because you have a hot date?" I smirk.

"Piss off, that was not funny! He shows up everywhere! He has been hounding me nonstop."

"Sooooo?"

"So, I agreed he could come tomorrow." She grumbles.

"Aw honey, I'm so proud of you."

"Shut it! Have you heard anything form the Bossman about whether he's coming?"

"Nope, he has been unresponsive. I guess he's got a lot on so…" I shrug, and trail off.

"I'm sorry Hun, I really thought he would come round."

"Yeah, me too, we were getting on so well until he came back from Singapore, it's like he just flipped a switch. Anyway, let's get home for our beauty rest.

CHAPTER 25

I awake to a buzzing from my phone and check to see Shelby is calling.

"Rise and shine gorgeous. Libby and I are on our way to pick you up and head to the spa for a little pre-party pampering. See you in five."

And that's how the rest of the day goes, past in a blur. I feel like I simply blinked and I am here standing in front of the mirror looking at myself all dressed up and ready to leave for opening night. I stare at the job the girls done today fixing me up.

I've lost a little bit more weight lately with all the extra work and the punishing runs I've been keeping up to help with the missing he who won't be named.

My make-up is subtle and sophisticated which helps hide the dark circles under my eyes. I choose a simple black silk evening gown which has a rather daring dropped back and is held up by thin diamond encrusted straps. It's classy and the side split at the front makes it a little sexy too. I have a black feather and diamond eye mask, that is simple yet glamorous. My hair for once is fully down and swept to one side with a silver jeweled pin, curled in loose waves, it fits the theme perfectly, I think.

As I head downstairs, I pause to take in my two handsome men. They have both grow so much over the last few weeks and they look incredibly mature standing there in their tuxes.

"Wow, mom you look beautiful." Jacob says as they spot me on the stairs.

"Aw mom! We are not going to be able to leave you

alone for a minute tonight! You look... well too good, if you know what I mean." Noah grumbles with a huge smile on his face.

"Well, you guys are going to cause a bloody scene!" I laugh, "I hope the girls are prepared for all of that." I say as I wave a hand towards them. They both chuckle.

"Holy moly, who got you more strippers?" Shelby cries coming through the doorway.

As the boys turn around and grin, she bursts out laughing.

"Aw man the girls are gona wet themselves when they see you two!"

"Aw come on Shell don't, these guys are still my babies." I cry and Noah pouts.

"Mom, we are not babies!"

"Yeah well, you'll always be my babies." I smirk.

"Good lord mother could you have run away any quicker?" Libby moans coming in the house. "That was incredibly rude!" she says and we all turn to see what she's groaning about.

Jacob heads over and kisses her softly on the cheek, "You look beautiful Lib." he says softly.

She blushes and they move off a little to the side to let the next guest who is hovering by the door come in.

"Holy hell Jackson!" I cry.

"Yup, you see why I ran right." She glares.

Jackson comes in the door and looks at the boys tuxes and then looks at himself.

"I think I look fine. What's the problem?" he asks.

He does look fine, damn fine.

He also looks like a Hollywood heart throb from the twenties. His hair is slicked back and he is as clean shaved as I've ever saw him which also shows off his beautiful face. His tux looks an awful a lot like the boys however he has a white scarf hanging loosely around his neck and a god damn fedora on his hand, like he just took it off when he walked in.

He kind of looks like a very sexy Al Capone.

"You look more than fine Jackson that's her problem." I grin, "But maybe lose the hat, you do look a bit like a pimp." I say saving my girl a bit.

"Done." He grins. "You look hot Mrs. Chalmers." he grins.

"Hey she's spoken for." Noah shouts from the kitchen.

"Shut up, Noah." Jacob says.

"Sorry, apparently they've become unsure of the idea of me dating." I laugh. "Ok, we all set to go?"

We are meeting Tabitha, Hank and the kids at the venue so Noah of course is squirrelling away in the back seat.

As we arrive, I see the red carpet is rolled out and there are quite a few photographers on either side. It's a big night for everyone involved and the board where happy to get as much publicity as they can due to the reopening theme and its historical ties.

We exit the cars and walk the red carpet, Fortunately for me Noah escorts me in as Jacob and Libby come in behind us. I can hear Shelby groaning from here about how she did not agree to this public partnership with Jackson, but they do look great together.

Him all blonde and well hot and Shelby all dark hair and flaming temper, her deep red velvet dress shows off her figure beautifully and she looks stunning. Jackson cannot wipe the smile off his face.

As we enter the hallway, we spot Kayla and her family over to the side alcove and Noah heads straight on over. Clever boy that he is, he shakes Hanks hand first, then Tabitha's before he embraces Kayla with a light peck on the cheek.

Hank is a terrifying man and seems to like Noah fine enough but she's his baby girl, so I have no doubt he is hating every minute of it.

We head over to catch up and Andy appears through the entrance way. I feel sad that May didn't manage to come along and enjoy the night but she is doing much better lately and hopefully she will get to see it one day soon.

"Wow, girls you have done an amazing job. I think I really am going to have to remove the 'SONS' from the company name eh." Andy says.

"It's about darn time!" Valerie says sweeping in behind them escorted by non-other that Anders Van Der Bilt who doesn't seem to notice the fact that there is anyone else in the building.

His eyes are glued to Shelby and the fact that Jackson has yet to release her arm. He watches on, becoming more enraged by the second as Shelby albeit grudgingly introduces Jackson to her parents. Oh lord, there is going to be a lot of fireworks tonight and not just the planned ones, I think.

I excuse myself and head over to speak to a few of the board members and selected guests, I'm glad to see everyone is excited and has embraced the dress code.

It will make for beautiful pictures we have organized to be taken as the guests descend the new staircase in homage to the photos currently gracing the walls from the original opening.

As I take a look around, I am overwhelmed with a deep sense of achievement but also a small glimmer of sadness. I know Sebastian had a fondness for the building and he was a great supporter of my design so if feels a little bittersweet that he's not here to enjoy all the hard work we put in.

I wander around the foyer a little more alone, just taking it all in and my eyes stray to the reporters outside who are fluttering away at the newest arrival. I stop to take in the scene, when I really focus on who is working her way down the red carpet like it's a god damn runway.

Yup, none other than that superficial skanky supermodel Melania, arm in arm with some equally obnoxious looking snob beside her. The women milk the red carpet for all it's worth and I feel my temper rising. A class A bitch like her does not deserve to be in attendance of such a beautiful evening however I notice them stroll over to a few of the board members and as they thank the women for coming along, I recognize the other female.

She is a very well-respected model and a huge donator to the Arts, so I guess she may have been a publicity addition. I have no doubt she will bring a lot of attention to tonight's gathering, so I suck it up and decide to simply avoid them at all costs.

I make my way back to the group and hear the bell ring, signaling it's time for everyone to start making their way down the grand staircase and head into the ballroom.

As I stand aside and let the first of the guests take it all in, they '*ooh*' and '*ahh*' over the beautifully decorated balustrade littered with millions of tiny twinkling lights and delicate wisps of wisteria draping down the sides, It's everything I dreamed it would be and as the loud laughs and glowing smiles surround me, I smile a huge grin.

As they descend the staircase, I see the

photographers set up below taking pictures from every angle to capture this moment and I have a mild moment of panic.

Shoot! I am going to have to walk down there alone.

Noah and Jacob are escorting the girls, everyone else is partnered up and Shelby will walk with Jackson whether she likes it or not, if it's up to him.

How on earth did I not think of this? It's fine I assure myself; I will watch everyone head down then rush through the back. Normally I wouldn't even mind however the room is laid out exactly for the purpose of the whole room to watch as people descend the great stairs and I would rather simply avoid it solo.

The boys give me a huge grin and thumbs up as they escort their dates down the stairs and I cannot wait to see those pictures.

I hear Valerie exclaim a loud shocked gasp and turn to see her embrace an older gentleman with warmth.

Shelby turns to see what is going on and if I wasn't watching it with my own eyes, I would never believe it. Anders must have been waiting for just the right moment to make a move because as soon as Jackson turns to answer something Mrs. Davies says, he sweeps in, takes Shelby's arm and begins pulling her down the staircase, it doesn't look nearly as odd as it sounds.

He makes it look almost fluid but Shelby fumes and turns to bellow at him but he grins and points out the guests staring below and I watch as she reigns in her temper and plasters a fake smile over her face and begins descending the stairs and posing for a photo at the bottom.

Jackson looks to be in complete shock and I force myself not to laugh but these two are ridiculous. He keeps looking around him like she's going to reappear.

I notice Valerie does not look too amused either but her companion leans over and offers her an arm, which she takes with a small smile and follows his lead downstairs. The rest of the group begin to make their way down and poor Jackson looks to be still in shock.

"Hey handsome, it looks like you seem to have lost your date!" I smile.

"Stole Leona, Not lost, He bloody stole her right from under my nose. Who does that? Is there no honor anymore?" he looks stunned.

"Well, he has no manners that one and I'm afraid when it comes to Shell, your gona have a helluva fight on your hands."

"Yeah, I'm beginning to see that." He scratches the back of his neck and looks down at her. She is pulled over into a corner giving Anders a piece of her mind.

"You sure she's worth all this for someone who has no interest in anything long-term?" I ask and watch him closely as he keeps his eyes on her.

"Yeah, I think she may be more than worth it and if the ear bashing, she is giving that nonce is anything to go by, I don't think I'm out of the running just yet." He turns and smiles a full smile at me.

He stands up straighter, coughs a little then proceeds to make a huge performance of bowing gallantly over my hand.

"Since my date has currently been captured by an evil villain, would you do me the honor of allowing me escort you down this fine staircase and into the ball?" he smiles up at me and I mock right back, I curtsey, well as much as I can in this dress without flashing the room,

"Why I would be delighted, kind Sir." I grin and we

make our way down the stairs as our friends linger near. We both smile like loons as we have our picture taken and he kisses me warmly on the cheek.

He is such a good guy and I truly pity Shelby the idea of choosing between them both. As I remark this to Jackson, he thanks me and I decide to tease him a little.

"Well, that is if she has to choose…" I grin. He looks confused, so I enlighten him. "I mean you have been harping on and on about a threesome since we first met." I wave my hand to indicate maybe Shell doesn't have to choose.

He laughs so loud heads turn to look at us and I blush furiously.

"Definitely not the type I was thinking about sweetheart." He grins wickedly and pulls me in for a quick hug and peck on the cheek. "I am going to try and reclaim my date now, you good?"

"More than, enjoy the night and good luck." I grin.

The evening goes by swimmingly, I listen to people exclaim their delight in seeing the old place looking back to its original glory and love when they remark on the new additions. As the night draws on, I get butterflies as I think of the next part of the evening and I grab myself a glass of champagne to get ready to toast the night.

Mr McAlister from the board steps up to the podium which has been set up near the Atrium entrance which has until now been sealed off.

He takes a moment and gathers everyone's attention, beginning his speech welcoming everyone and thanking a long list of people who have all helped this vision become a reality. He holds the audience perfectly and I smile as he thanks Van Der Bilt and

Sons for all the work they have done.

"I would also like to take this moment to welcome one of our newest board members who has joined us on the road to this magnificent restoration. He joined almost at the end of the rebuild because well, quite simply folks our pockets are only so deep and as a board, we all wanted to recreate the full Montgomery project back to its rightful glory. When it looked like that was unfortunately not going to happen, he stepped right in and brought a few other investors with him. The board is entirely grateful to the Van Der Bilt family for agreeing to join us as members and they have accepted their place on the trust. On behalf of everyone I would like to thank them and personally welcome Sebastian Van Der Bilt up to say a few words."

I feel my breath catch and I freeze as I see him accept the shake of Mr. McAlister's hand, as he walks up to the podium.

He looks magnificent in his sleek black tuxedo and immaculate white shirt. His eyes are sharp as he takes in the room and my heart aches simply looking at him.

I hold my breath as he begins speaking and it feels like a lifetime since I've heard his warm smooth voice.

"Firstly, I would like to say the honor is all mine. To be asked to join such a prestigious association such as the Restoration Guild is a privilege for myself and the other investors. I would like to thank Mr. McAlister and the board for having faith in Van Der Bilt and Sons to complete such a magnificent project." He pauses, "However, On that note, I would also like to announce that moving forward personally, we have decided to update our own company name to a more befitting one, we will be now be known as Van Der

Bilt Architects. That is not just a tribute to our wonderful partner and Architect, Miss Valerie Van Der Bilt, who is very obviously not a son and reminds us of this daily." He says and everyone laughs along.

"However, this move is well long overdue and has been helped along by another member of our company we would like to take the opportunity to thank. Had it not been for her creative insight, spectacular design and dedication on this job, the room we are all about to step into would possibly never have come about." He stops and looks directly at me and I struggle to breath.

"We would like to thank Mrs. Leona Chalmers, her assistant Shelby Davies and their team for the spectacular work they have created on this project. I am honored to have had a sneak peek at what lies ahead for you all tonight and I would ask for you all to raise your glasses and make a toast to The Montgomery and her Atrium."

He holds up a glass and everyone joins in with the toast. I stand stock still as everyone turns to see the entrance to the Atrium open and they automatically flow through. The sounds of delight and awe reverberate through the room and yet I almost can't hear it. I can't take my eyes of him as he makes his way down from the podium and talks to members of the board and well-wishers.

How on earth did this happen?

"What the hell?" Shell says coming up beside me.

"I know? I don't even know what to say."

"Mom congrats the place is amazing!" Noah cries and gives me a huge hug.

"It's so beautiful Mrs. Chalmers." Kayla says beside him.

"Thank you, Kayla." I smile.

"Mom, I am so proud of you!" Jacob says giving me a hug.

"Thanks guys! You all having a good time?" I try to focus.

"Oh, it's wonderful Mrs. Chalmer's." Libby cries, "The place is too magical not to be!" she wraps Shelby up in a big squeeze. "I can't believe how much work you must have done mom to make the place look like this. I need to echo Jake; I am so proud of you." She gushes and wraps herself up in her mom.

"Thanks Lib." Shell says with a lump in her throat,

"Ok c'mon, I will take you guys through and show you a good spot, the show will be starting soon." She winks and Jackson hangs back.

He pulls me in for a big hug, "Congratulation's babe!" he grins and as he pulls back, I look up into a pair of dark eyes.

"Sorry to interrupt, Officer," he nods stiffly at Jackson, "Mr. Whitaker wanted to have a quick word with you, Mrs. Chalmers. He is one of the new members of the restoration board and was impressed with your work. Kent, this is Leona Chalmers and her… date Officer…?" he stares blandly at Jackson who looks to me in confusion.

"Eh, just Jackson is fine, I'm off duty tonight." He smiles in his easy going way. "I'm actually…"

"Ah lovely, you two finally get to meet!" Valerie says cutting Jackson off.

He looks to me and I just shake my head,

"Kent here has just arrived back in the country and has his eye set on the old Haymarket building." She grins excitedly.

Now that is a massive job! Double the size of the Montgomery. Kent is the man I saw earlier surprise

Valerie. He looks to be a little older than her but he's in great shape. His olive skin glows the same as his warm hazel eyes.

"Well, yes I am looking into it Mrs. Chalmers, you see the building holds special memories for me and I would really like to see it restored in a similar manner to here." he smiles. "That is if I can talk a few more people into investing." He grins widely.

"I think I will go find Shelby, Leona; it looks like you guys are all about to talk shop. Congrats again honey and it was nice meeting you all." He says as he wanders away.

"Lovely boy that! Especially in that uniform." Valerie remarks and Sebastian glares.

"Well, you did always like a man in uniform didn't you Val?" Kent nudges her gently and I see right there and then there is a lot more to their relationship than I first thought.

"I will leave you to it, Kent a pleasure again. Aunt, Mrs. Chalmers." he says not looking at me at all.

"Mrs.??? She's bloody married?" comes a slightly slurred voice from behind him and we all turn to see that horrible witch Melania with an appalled look on her face as she glares at me.

"I will take care of this." he says as he nods at Kent and turns and takes her by the arm and escorts her out of sight.

"Ghastly women that!" Val says and they both go on talking about the hopes for the Haymarket purchase.

I am half listening, half looking to see where Sebastian went, when I hear Kent chuckle.

"Yes, I agree Val maybe we can arrange a meeting to discuss the situation sometime in the near future, when we aren't maybe as pre-occupied?" he smiles.

Shoot!

"I am so sorry Mr. Whitaker; I am consciously aware the show is about to start next door and I am a little distracted." I apologize.

"I completely understand dear, sometimes you need to just excuse yourself and dash off and sort what needs sorting. No need to apologize at all." he smiles.

"Eh, thank you, and yes contact me anytime for that meeting."

I smile and thank them both then power walk through the room to see where the hell he went. I have no idea what I'm going to say? But still I carry on. I can't see them anywhere and the next thing Shelby is grabbing me by the arm.

"What the hell Leona! Everyone is waiting for you in the Atrium for the show."

"Shoot, sorry, let's go." I say and we hurry through the room.

I take my spot at the front of the room and tap the mike and everyone turns to look.

CHAPTER 26

"Ladies and gentleman, I'd like to thank you all again for coming along tonight," I begin,

"Many years ago, the now famous Sir Augustus Montgomery built the main house of this building for his new wife. They were both avid astronomers and they fell in love with this particular spot for the clear skyline, were they were known to lie or stroll around outdoors all year round taking in the views. A few years into the marriage Mrs. Montgomery was paralyzed in an awful horse-riding accident and confined to a wheelchair. Mr. Montgomery, undeterred set out on finding a way for him and his wife to continue their stargazing without subjecting her to the rigorous winter temperatures we are all well aware of in this part of the country."

I pause as the guests all chuckle and confirm they do indeed know how cold these parts can get during the winter months.

"He enlisted the help of an Architect to design a building that could be used from inside where it would be warm enough for them to view the stars. The Atrium at The Montgomery was the first known of its kind in a stately home. It allowed the full sky to be viewed from the room in which we stand in. In his original request he hoped for a full glass ceiling with no frames to hinder the skyline, unfortunately at that time such a thing was, well, quite impossible so they settled for a simpler frame that didn't deter from the beauty of the room. They invited friends, family and other interested astronomers and held a magnificent ball for the opening night allowing all to witness their private view of the skylight for the first time. Now thanks to new techniques, futuristic developments and a whole lot of coercing, Sir Augustus' vision has come full circle and we fortunate people here tonight get to gaze upon his dream become reality."

As I say this the lights darken, the drapes are pulled away and the night sky lights up before our very eyes. The room is still and silent for what feels like a full minute before the fireworks begin lighting up the sky above us. The guests burst out in applause and marvel over the beauty they are witnessing.

It is spectacular and I feel myself tear up.

The night has been a roaring success and I am simply exhausted. The last of the guests are clearing out and I have removed my heels and are now wearing my very stylish fluffy slipper boots under my evening gown that I hid away yesterday.

Tabitha and Hank kindly offered to drop the boy's off back home for me and Libby is staying over with them to allow Shelby and me the time to do a walk through and check everything is closed up the way we wish.

I noticed she's looking a little strained as both Jackson and Anders seem to be hanging around waiting on her finishing up.

"Shell why don't you head out, I'm just waiting on a few more people signing off before I head down to The Atrium for one last look before I head home." I say.

"Leona don't be ridiculous I will join you." She exclaims.

"Honestly Shell, I want to walk around it alone for a little bit you know, make my peace with it and move on." I sigh and she gets me.

"You sure you don't want any company?"

"I really don't and to be fair if you don't leave soon, I may have to call back some security." I say as I nod over to the men on each side of the doorway.

"What on earth am I supposed to do about them?" she groans.

"Eh pick?" I grin.

"You are no help and your smart-ass comments about a bloody threesome has not helped. Jackson has made it perfectly clear that will not be an option." She fumes at me.

"Aw, such a shame really." I grin.

"You are truly evil!" she snipes, hugs me and says her goodbyes.

I wave to both men but I barely get a second glance as they follow Shell out like a pair of pups. I laugh to myself and go chase up the venders who have yet to leave.

After another half an hour shutting everything down, I am now sitting alone in The Atrium.

I left the full fire place burning away so the room is deliciously toasty and set the alarm system so I could have just a few minutes to take it all in. I love this place so much and I give a silent toast to the Montgomery's for their beautiful vision.

"Well, so much for '*to serve and protect*', what type of man leaves his date to drink alone in an old building?"

My whole body tenses. Why is he still here?

I saw him earlier heading into one of the private rooms with Melania and almost lost my champagne.

"I don't know, what type of man dates an awful person, allows her to attend a respectable gathering such as this, make a scene, then I don't know…" I wave around to indicate she is not here, "Send her home in a cab?" I throw right back.

He simply glares at me.

"Exactly, why don't you see yourself out Sebastian, I would like to enjoy this in peace." I say tightly.

"Is your *toy boy* at least coming back to pick you up?" he growls darkly.

"Well, seeing as he is either undressing Shelby at this very moment or drowning his sorrows alone, I would say it's a safe bet to say no, he will not be coming back here!"

"What the hell is that supposed to mean?" he shouts.

"Do not shout at me! It means exactly what I said. Jackson has either convinced Shelby to date him or your creepy cousin has beat him to it, either way he is very interested in Shelby, not me, so go take your insinuations elsewhere."

"I saw you both, he is not interested in bloody Shelby!" he states firmly.

"What exactly did you see Sebastian hmm? Jackson congratulating me earlier? Am I then by default dating half of the people in attendance?"

"He escorted you here tonight, and I have saw you both together on multiple occasions, do not try play me for a fool."

"He escorted me down the staircase tonight because your idiot cousin ambushed him and stole Shelby before he could walk *his* date down the stairs. He was left with me because *I* had no date." I can't help myself mutter under my breath, *unlike some people.*

"Oh, do not be ridiculous Leona you know fine well I did not bring Melania here on a date, or frankly bring her at all."

"And yet here she was."

"Yes, because she managed to convince Maria she was interested in the Arts, not because I had in any way asked her to come. And do not change the subject. You and that police officer are more than acquaintances, so do not waste my time spewing ridiculous stories. I saw you both with my own eyes."

"You saw what? A pair of friends make the best of an embarrassing situation. Hardly a scandal Sebastian."

"I saw you bloody well kiss him on the damn street when I had just got off a fucking twenty-hour flight!" He fumes.

"What? What the hell are you talking about?"

"Never bloody mind, it's none of my business is it." He turns.

"Are you kidding me? Is this why you have been an absolute bastard these last weeks? You saw what… a friend gives me an innocent kiss and assumed I was fucking him?"

"Do not take that sanctimonious tone with me Leona. I did no such thing; I was perfectly cordial to you."

"Perfectly cordial! You went from a charming human being to a god damn robot in the space of a day! You brushed me off with no explanation and all because, what you didn't like the thought of seeing me with someone else, even though you had no interest in me yourself! If that's not being a bastard Sebastian, I don't know what is."

He pulls me up flush against him.

"That's the fucking problem, I did want you; I came all the way home from god damn Singapore, Not for a bloody meeting but for you, I walked out in the middle of an incredibly important negotiation because I couldn't stand to be away from you any longer, I wanted to be there for your pitch, only to come home and see you pull up in another man's car like you had simply moved on."

"How could you possibly think that! I was accepting a lift from a friend, who was trying to coerce me into helping convince *Shelby* to give him a shot. I was not playing house with another man whilst I was waiting on you growing a set Sebastian, for Christs sake, I thought you knew me better than that."

"But that's the thing isn't it, I don't know you, do I?"

"No-one does, you can't go into these things knowing everything, it's about trust and respect. If you didn't at least trust me Sebastian, you should have respected me enough to ask the damn question."

"Yeah, like you and your insinuations about Melania?"

"Oh, piss off! That woman is a bloody viper and you know it, what is anyone supposed to think when she shows up here at an event you are supposed to be hosting."

"Yeah, right back at you sweetheart." He grins.

"Do not bloody grin at me you…" I push at him and he just pulls me closer.

"Are you fucking that stupid looking police officer, Leona?"

"No, are you back fucking that wretched wom…"

I don't get the chance to finish my question before I am slammed against him and his mouth crashes into mine. He is like a man possessed. Forcing his tongue deep inside my mouth as I force mine right back. Everything he gives, I give back tenfold. I pull on the hair at the back of his neck to pull him closer, I nip at his lip and suck his tongue into my mouth, I can't get enough of him.

He hoists me up and I hear the split at the front of my dress tear but I am too far gone to care. We stumble around and crash into a few things but still we don't stop. He lifts my dress up further and slides his hand up my thigh, pulling my leg up, so he can push his hard erection against my core but it's not enough, I'm burning with need and I begin pulling and clawing at his clothes.

He understands my eagerness and lifts me up hard against him, my dress rips further but it gives him better access as I tear at his shirt, buttons fly off and I get my hands on those sculpted abs. I push my hand flat against his abdomen and reach down to tug at his pants, when he freezes, pulls back a fraction and holds my eye.

"Are you sure about this Leona?" he doesn't move a muscle.

"Enough messing around Sebastian you either want this or you don't but I am all in."

"Thank fuck!" he groans and pulls his erection from his pants.

It's too dark to see anything but as I feel him lift me higher and press me against the hard wall, I feel the tip of him starin at my entrance and I know I am going to be in pain tomorrow, physically but hopefully not emotionally, yet I simply can't find it in me to care.

He slows, sweeps the hair from my flushed face, and just holds us there, hovering on the edge.

"So, fucking beautiful." he says before he slams his hard cock inside and I buck firmly against him. He is definitely larger than I was expecting and he takes a minute to stay buried fully inside of me, allowing me to catch my breath.

I slowly wiggle around a little and start to rock against him. I can feel the cords tense in his back as I begin finding a rhythm, he leans down and sucks my nipple into his mouth and when he nips at it roughly, I clench my walls tightly around him and he loses it.

He takes over and forcefully changes the pace. He hammers me against the wall and we descend into a frenzy, all teeth and gasping, clawing at each other to get as close as humanly possible. He doesn't relent with the motion and continues dragging his teeth over my taut nipples, my whole body overwhelmed with sensations, I feel myself coming closer to the edge.

I tug at the hair on the back of his neck and pull his mouth up to mine, he plunges his tongue inside at a wicked pace and I feel myself cry out,

"Fuck Sebastian." as I explode around him.

It sounds breathless and throaty even to me and I hear him roar a minute later as he comes deep inside me. I rest my head on his shoulder and he continues to gently rock, still semi hard inside of me. I feel the aftershocks coursing through me as I move against him.

"You are going to be insatiable." He laughs gently and slowly begins to rub his groin up hard against me.

The feeling against my sensitive spot makes me ache all over again and I look up to see him watching me with a soft look on his face. He pulls my head forward, kisses me softly and begins to move us carefully over to the grand piano in the corner.

He sits me atop of it and it squeaks with the sound of sweaty flesh pressing against it. My dress is in scraps really and he still has all his clothes on, albeit a few missing buttons and a few tears here and there. I feel the wetness on the inside of my thighs as he grips my ass cheeks and pulls me forward to the edge of the piano.

He strokes leisurely up and down my core as I rest my head on his shoulder to take in the moment. He kisses the top of my head and sweeps my hair to one side as he presses soft tender kisses up the curve of my neck,

"All in sweetheart." he mumbles as his fingers stroke forwards and back over my highly sensitive core and I feel the heat building all over again.

I kiss at his chest and gently nip at his nipple and I feel him jerk against me, I circle it again with my tongue and then pierce a fraction harder. I feel him pulse hard against me and I reach out slowly, grasping at his thick tensing cock with my hand, I slowly work my hand up and down his length, as I circle his hard nipple and every time I nip, I give a tight squeeze at the head of his cock.

I hear him curse under his breath and I love that I am in control. I slide downwards and push him firmly onto the piano seat below us. He looks momentarily stunned and I use the moment to my advantage as I drop to my knees in front of him,

"Shit Leona you don't have to do…" he says but before he gets the chance to finish, I pull him into my mouth and slide my tongue over the salty tip.

I hear him drag in a breath and feel myself pool between my own legs. Who would have thought giving him pleasure could make me so wet! I continue to alternate from taking him as far back into my mouth as I can manage, then licking up and down his shaft and circling the tip. I feel the muscles in his thighs begin to tense and I hear his breathing become harsh. His grip straining through my hair.

"You really need to stop that sweetheart or I am going to blow my load down that pretty little throat of yours." He says as he pulls me up flush against him, kissing me deeply.

I give him a moment to compose himself but my body is aching. I slowly edge up and climb on top of his lap, placing a leg either side of him. I push high on my tiptoes and hover my core above the head of his cock, slowly and steadily sliding downwards inch by inch. I feel him forcing himself to remain still, I know it's only a matter of time before he snaps and takes over, so I begin to work my body, sliding up slowly almost to the tip then slamming hard back down, grinding a little against him with a last tight clench before I slowly slide back up. I can feel his desperation to move me quicker, can hear his breathing becoming more ragged.

"Fuck Leona! You will be the death of me."

"What a way to go but eh!"

I bite at his earlobe and run my tongue around the rim and he snaps. He flips me onto my back before I get a chance to catch my breath and crawls on top of me, he is inside me and thrusting me hard and roughly against the rug before I can even blink.

Its heaven and as I bite at his shoulder and claw at his ass he pulls back and looks me dead in the eye,

"Look up sweetheart." he says and I simply stare at him. He chuckles, "Not at me."

Then he dips his head to kiss at my neck and collar bone and I feel him smile against me as he hears my gasp.

The night sky is an inky blackness above us dotted with a scattering of diamonds and I see multiple stars as he continues to press that lean hard body of his against me. He starts to up the pace a little but continues the pressure rubbing against my core and I feel my orgasm mount so quickly that I fear it may pass me by.

It hits me so hard; I cry out in surprise and I feel him fall over with me. He continues littering my body with soft delicate kisses and I feel him in every inch of my body. We continue to lay there, before he rolls to his side and pulls me flush against him. We stare out the large glass ceiling at the changing sky.

"You doing ok down there shorty?" he laughs as I've wiggled down into the nook of his arm so I can stare up at the nights sky.

"Me? I am great. It's you I am worried about, no panic setting in yet? No getting ready to flee?" I grin.

"Well, that's not nice now is it, I told you before I was serious about giving this a shot. I have no idea if I am capable of a relationship or giving you everything you deserve but I am determined to try Leona. Is that enough for you?" he asks almost nervously.

"Shit, I thought we were just gona fool around!"

"Not a god damn chance!" he glares and I laugh softly.

"I was actually thinking more about how you would be punishing yourself for breaking your promise to the boys." I sigh.

"Well about that…" he looks a little too sheepish, so I move up slightly to get a closer look.

"Yeah, what about that?" I ask.

"Technically, I haven't broken my promise." He says with an amused smile.

"Well of course you have." I chuckle. "We both have really." I sigh.

"You have most definitely, but I have not."

I sit up straight and look him square in the eye and cross my arms. And wait.

"Now don't go getting mad…" he starts.

"That is a sure-fire way to make me mad Sebastian, spit it out."

"God, you're beautiful when you're so angry." I glare at him and he holds back his laughter well enough. "It's actually quite funny really if you think about it… So, I sort of spoke to the boys weeks ago and asked them for their permission to date you. It took a while and far too many zoom meetings, I swear Noah was just dragging it out for fun near the end but both of them eventually gave me their approval. So, as I say technically, I haven't really broken any promises." He smiles sweetly, "You on the other hand may be in big trouble." He smirks.

"And when did this conversation take place?" I huff.

"Whilst I was in Singapore, I received a very long email from the boys confirming they both had accepted my proposal to date you and would keep a copy of the said email as evidence of my promise." He grins. "I left Singapore that day and arrived home just in time for your pitch." He says softly.

"Oh Sebastian! Why did you simply not ask me? What a terrible waste of our time."

"Water under the bridge now." He says as he kisses me softly.

"But you still invested in the project, still spoke up for me even though you thought I was well… fooling around with someone else." I cry.

"Well yes apparently love makes you do ridiculous things." He smiles at me and my heart lifts.

This man. I am so madly and completely undeniably

in love with. How could he possibly think he isn't capable of a real relationship or loving someone properly, he has gone above and beyond for me time and time again and I have every faith he will be the same in a relationship as he is in every other aspect of his life, a perfect gentleman.

Well almost every part of his life, there are some parts of his devilry that I have no intentions of changing. I lean down and kiss him deeply.

"You, Sebastian Van Der Bilt, are a remarkable man. I will spend every minute you let me showing you just how capable you are at being in a real relationship and I know you will ace it but for now… well now it's my turn to let you see the stars."

I slowly slide my body on top of his and move myself over his once again hard cock. I lower myself down on top of him and proceed to make sure he sees multiple stars before the night is over.

As the night turns to morning, we lay there exhausted, half asleep in each other's arms, somewhere throughout the night Sebastian draped a warm blanket over us and we touched and kissed every inch of each other's bodies, spoke of all the crazy mishaps that landed us right where we are. As I lie here with the sun rising around us, I watch the most beautiful sight of the man I love sleeping peacefully beside me.

I lean over and kiss his closed eyes and whisper a soft, "I love you so much Sebastian Van Der Bilt."

"You bloody better or I'm telling the boys you broke their promise!" he groans.

"Sebastian! You were supposed to be asleep!"

"Hardly with you curled up naked beside me! Now stop looking at me and watch the bloody sunrise!" he smirks and kisses me gently.

"Yes, Sir!" I salute.

"Bloody death of me I tell you." He groans.

We lay there as the sun begins to climb into the sky and sunlight filters through the glass.

"Isn't it beautiful Sebastian?" I smile and look at him but he is not watching the sunrise, he's watching me.

"Spectacular." He says and I melt.

We decide to catch the sunrise some other time and proceed to show each other just how insatiable we both are.

EPILOGUE

<u>6-ish Weeks Later</u>

"Noah, get a move on! If we do not get on the road in the next five minutes we will get caught in the bloody storm and then where will we spend thanksgiving!" I yell.

"Cool it mom, I'm ready." He says as he traipses downstairs like we have all the time in the world.

"Get your ass in the car now!" I cry, I am a little tense to say the least about this weekend.

Sebastian and I have been keeping our relationship to ourselves to avoid the added pressure from his family and the boys. I just don't want to get anyone hopes up but Sebastian keeps saying I have nothing to worry about, he's not going to do a runner anytime soon.

I know, so reassuring!

"Dollar in the jar mom." Jacob says as he strolls out the door.

"Jacob! I thought you were already in the damn car." I screech.

"That's another dollar." He shouts.

I give him the finger behind his back, I know, I am a fucking child but sometimes you just want to wring one of their necks, so a little cussing or rude hand gesture is a fair alternative, I think.

I pop ten in the jar, may as well get a head start and lock up.

Shelby is waiting at the curb and as I slide in the front seat, she grins at me.

"How much is in that bloody jar already?" she grins.

"Almost enough to pay for a trip to Europe to visit Libby after the holidays." Jacob smirks. Wow, conniving little shit.

I mean it's great to see him getting back to his old self but I kind of forgot he was a smart little sucker. He and Noah high five and I growl at them both.

"God you're tenser than normal." Shell remarks. "Care to share?"

"Nope, let's just get this weekend over with." I sigh and she smirks.

"Can't be any worse than last time." She chuckles.

As we are pulling away from the curb my phone rings and look to see Jakub's name pop up on the display. I answer immediately and he informs me they are having a few issues at The Montgomery and the crew had been called back on site to check it over however no-one can reach Aleski to translate and Sebastian is on his way home from Singapore. I assure him I will be there right away and tell him to call the contractor to let him know I am on way personally to interpret for them.

"Shit, Leona! We're going to get caught in the storm if we don't get a move on, any chance this will only take a few minutes?" she asks hesitantly. She's as eager as me to avoid the storm so I sigh and give her it straight.

"Not a chance, they think there may be a burst pipe under the Atrium." I sigh.

"Fuck! Oops, sorry guys." She says and Noah starts bitching.

"Mom! Kayla and Kye are waiting for me to get there. We have that new game planned."

"I know Noah, it's not exactly my ideal start to the

holidays either." I turn to Shelby, "Look why don't you take the kids all up to the Van Der Bilt's and I will call the car service to bring me up when I'm done. Best case I'm a couple hours behind you."

"And worst case?"

"Well worst case I head up tomorrow morning, Thanksgiving isn't until Sunday anyway so I have plenty time to make it." I sigh.

"Well, we could wait about for maybe half an hour see how it goes?" she hedges.

"Moooom!" Noah cries.

"Shut it Noah, Shell just drop me off and get a head start, I don't want to be rushing then I end up having to come all the way back down tomorrow." I sigh, "It's fine, honest." I say as we start to turn into the parking lot.

I jump out and grab my messenger bag from the trunk. I lean in give both boys a quick hug and tell them I will be as quick as I can.

"Keep us posted?" Shell asks.

"Will do, now get a move on." I say and watch them pull away. The car park is surprisingly empty so I am guessing the team are parked round the back of the building already. I fire off a few texts and send Sebastian an update.

As I walk into the building it is deadly silent. It's rather unnerving and I grab my phone from my bag and call Jakub as I walk towards the Atrium. He doesn't pick up but as I get to the top of the staircase, I hear sounds coming from downstairs and I laugh at my mini freak out. I walked briskly towards the Atriums entrance when I hear quite soft music. Not what I was expecting but maybe one of the guys left on the radio.

As I push open the door, I pause a minute to adjust

my eyes. The whole room is darkened by black velvet coverings over all of the windows, there are white pillar candles everywhere in sight and large arrangements of deep red roses everywhere. There is a path leading through the room littered with scattered rose petals and I begin to realize I have walked bang into the middle of some poor saps proposal. Bloody Jakub!

"Hello, I am so sorry to interrupt…" I begin as I round the corner and freeze.

Sebastian is standing bang center of the room in the middle of a small circle surrounded by red roses in tall vases and large glass hurricane jars full of fat white candles.

He is wearing a beautiful black tailored suit with a smart shirt and tie; his dark hair is perfectly groomed and he has the softest smile on his handsome face. I have no idea what to do. Shit is this a proposal? No, it can't be, lord a few weeks ago he wasn't even sure he wanted to date!

"Hey gorgeous. You wana come join me?" he smiles.

"Eh honestly, I think I'll maybe just stay here." I say as I stare at him in confusion.

"Of course, you would." He chuckles and slowly makes his way towards me. I hold up a hand to pause him and he stops instantly. The smile doesn't drop from his face.

"I don't mean to be blunt Sebastian but what the fuck is all this?" I say.

"Well sweetheart, what does it look like to you?" he grins.

"Well, it *looks* like a very elaborate proposal but I am sure '*we*'," I motion back and forth between us,

"Are in the wrong place."

"Why would that be?" he asks.

"Well, I came to fix a burst pipe and you, well you're supposed to be on your way back from Singapore." I state.

"And yet here we are." He says talking baby steps closer with every word.

"Are we organizing a proposal for someone?" I ask.

"You could say that." He grins as he stops before me.

We both just watch each other and I feel my palms start to sweat.

"Help me out here Sebastian because I am starting to freak out a little. What is all this?"

"Well Leona some crazy person once told me that they grew pissed off waiting around for me to grow a set?" he grins.

"That wasn't exactly what I said." I frown.

"That same person told me '*they were all in*'."

"Well, I am sure when they said that, maybe they meant '*all in*' for having a sexual tryst or even simply dating. I'm pretty sure they never said at any point they wanted a full-blown fucking proposal!"

I hear the rising hysteria in my voice yet I can't help it. I mean,

WHAT THE HELL IS HE THINKING!

"Yes well, be that as it may, I am fairly sure you know me well enough by now to know that I do not go into things by half. Once I commit to something I am '*all in*' and I want to be all in with you… and those demon sons of yours." He smiles softly and I gasp as he very slowly holds my gaze and begins lowering to one knee.

"Get the hell up Sebastian! This is ridiculous, Not a

few months ago you accused me of being a philandering whore," he laughs nervously but I carry on regardless, "God you were convinced I was trying to screw your bloody grandfather into the sack and out of his money!" I cry,

"Eh sweetheart you're kind of ruining the mood here," he says trying to calm me but I have lost it.

"You cannot be serious, I never asked for all this, I am happy with us taking our time. Christ, we haven't even told the boy's yet and I am entirely sure they may try and injure you, badly, since you did promise to ask their permission first to date me never mind… whatever this is." I wave my hand.

"Well about that…" he starts rubbing the back of his neck.

"You cannot be serious?" I sigh. "Sebastian the boys are not ready for all this."

"Actually, Mom we are all more than ready for this." Comes Jacobs voice from behind me and I turn to see both my boys, Shelby, Libby and the full bloody Van Der Bilt clan all gathered at the door.

"Told ya she would be fuming." Noah grins at Sebastian. "You owe me a plane ticket." He smiles widely.

I turn my whole body away from the crowd behind me and look down at him still perched on one knee,

"You did all this, told everyone without consulting me?" I ask.

"Well, it's supposed to be a surprise, Leona." He stares.

"I have no words." I say as I just stand there frozen.

"That's a first." I hear a snigger.

"Shut up Shell, you're in my bad books too." I say without turning around.

"Well, why don't you just listen for a little bit instead then?" he says and I nod.

"You more than anyone know how much I fought this, how I never believed I was capable of being in a relationship. I had my whole life planned out in front of me, I would be the cool Uncle, perfect Grandson, work my ass off for my company's and I was happy with that. I would have been happy with that. Until I met you." He smiles softly.

"From the day I met you, you infuriated me to no end, pushed every one of my buttons and made me want to strangle you at almost every turn." I raise a brow. "But you challenged me in every single way, at work, with my family and as a bloody man. I refused to ever let any woman have a modicum of power over me, I would not be my father's son but I couldn't make even myself believe it when I looked at you. I wanted you, even when I thought you were fucking married and I apologize to you and the boys for that." He looks to them and smiles.

"But I fell in love with you anyway. I watched you stand at the edge of that ballroom looking on with so much hope and emotion in your eyes as you watched the greatest proof of love dance that night and I knew then and there I had to become a better man, for you. I just wasn't aware of how much you would test me and how much you still do but I swear to you from this day forth, No other living breathing person will ever love you as much as I do, No other person will ever want to stand by your side as much as I. I truly am sorry if you are not ready or you are not happy with how I have handled this but I will not keep my love for you a secret for another second." he smiles and takes my hand gently in his.

"I love you more than I ever thought possible Leona Chalmers," he says with a smile, "And I will not ask you anything right now if you are not ready, but know this, I will ask you. I will ask you every day for the rest of our lives until you say yes. But I am content to wait for you to *grow a set*."

"What?" comes a screech from behind us and I almost laugh as Shelby gets a rollicking from someone but I just keep looking down at this man who holds my whole heart.

"Ask?" I whisper, smiling softly.

"Yeah?" he grins and I nod.

"Leona Chalmers, would you please do me the honor of allowing me to marry you and those two conniving devils you call sons?" he grins up at me and I look over my shoulder at my sons.

Noah gives me a big goofy smile and a huge thumbs up motion and I look to Jacob. He smiles so widely at me it almost breaks my heart.

"You guy's sure? It means you're gona be stuck with that lot as well." I nod at the crazy family all watching on.

"I'm sure we will fit right in." Jacob grins and Noah smirks and nudges his brother.

I turn to look at Sebastian who he has pulled a ring box out, which is open showing me the most beautiful engagement ring I have ever seen. It is a large oval shaped midnight blue stone set on a white gold band encrusted with small diamonds all around it.

"It looks like diamonds in the night sky." I say as I feel my eyes well up.

"Well Mr. Montgomery had impeccable taste." He says softly and I recognize the ring immediately.

"Sebastian… how on earth did you get this?" I

exclaim.

"That's a rather long story sweetheart and well, I am actually kind of dying down here, any chance you might have something else to say?" he grins.

"Oh my god! Sebastian YES! A thousand times Yes!" I scream as he tries to stand up and I drop to my knees instead and grab his face and kiss him with so much force he falls over and I hear the telltale sounds of disgust.

"Aw Mom c'mon! No-one needs to see that!" Noah groans.

"Aw leave her be," Jacob says, "They're happy." he sighs.

"Yeah man I know but we're gona have to live with that!" he grumbles as laughter envelopes us.

The mad bunch all surround us with their congratulations and Sebastian eventually gets fully upright after a little light mocking from bloody Anders.

"Why are you all here?" I laugh.

"Well today was the last chance we would have the building completely to ourselves before the trust opens the doors on Monday and this room is booked out for the next ten months and quite frankly, I could not wait that long. I wanted you to be the first person to have this special moment here since Mr. and Mrs. Montgomery themselves." He grins.

"Ah, so that's the rush… I thought she was preggers." Fucking Anders!

"Piss off, Anders!" I hear Shelby say.

"What about the storm?" I cry, "Were all gona get stuck here! Shoot MAY!!! You're here! You hate the city."

I startle, as I realize she's here as well.

"Well, this isn't exactly the city dear and I wanted to

see The Atrium fully restored. It's been a while since I was last here." She grins at me knowing full well I am going to be bombarding her with a million questions later.

"Where are we all going to stay?" I say as everyone chuckles.

"Here." Sebastian says and I laugh. "We have the whole building to ourselves tonight and we will drive back home tomorrow." He grins.

"Oh my god! You lot are crazy! Are you sure you're ok to be here though, May?" I ask as we hear a loud crash.

"Yes, dear I am perfectly fine and I will be resting most of the night anyway. I plan to sit here under the stars and regale you all with some wonderful memories." She grins as Andy cuddles her up close.

"Did we miss it? God damn it Hank, I told you to just follow the damn Sat Nav!" Tabitha cries as they charge into the room.

The whole crazy dysfunctional family is here under this magnificent roof and as Sebastian pulls me close to his side and kisses me softly, I know I will always have a large ridiculous family of my own from now on.

I may tell Sebastian the possible news in a little while, I don't want to spook him too much. The boys come over for a big hug and I hold on a fraction longer and a tad tighter.

"You guys sure this is all good?" Sebastian says and they do that weird man half hug thing.

"Yeah, we're good." Jacob says.

"Good? Are you serious? You guys swore so much through that proposal I'm gona be able to fly first class to visit Kayla." Noah laughs and goes off to tell her the good news.

Sebastian pulls me into his arms and kisses me so deeply I wobble on my feet.

"Seriously, you still can't wear a sensible pair of shoes, what did we say about trips to the ER?" he grins.

Yeah, it may not be the ER we are visiting but definitely a hospital in around nine months.

Lord helps us.

Authors Note

Honestly, what a journey this has been.

Leona and Sebastian's story pushed me a little more than my first writing attempt and to be honest I'm so happy with how they turned out. This was one 'meet cute' that started with a bang.

Those Van Der Bilt's though really are something else. Who would willingly want to join that wild crazy family? Shelby?

Will Anders stop playing the fool and get his act together enough to make amends? Or will she and Officers Marks finally go on a real date?

LOOK OUT FOR BOOK TWO IN
NEXT INSTALMENT OF
THE VAN DER BILTS

Thank you for taking the time to read my book, it truly means the world x

If you would like to leave a review however large or small, I would be very grateful.

You can connect with me on Instagram for updates,
bonus content and everything in between,
@nicoleadairauthor

About The Author

About me? I am a mother of three teenage daughters and still living in sin with my very own leading man. I spend most of my time playing chauffeur from football pitch's, to Ballet classes, to nightclub pick up's at 3am in the morning, so let's just say I know my way around a map (or how to work a Satnav) and probably do more miles than the local taxi driver! I'm never far from my kindle or nowadays my laptop and find myself sneaking in a few chapters of writing at the most random of moments.

If you see me parked on the side of the road typing away furiously, just walk on past the crazy lady, don't look directly at her but in all honesty I probably wouldn't even notice.

Writing is a new addition to my crazy life… so please go easy on me.

Acknowledgments

This book would never have come to be in your hands if it wasn't for the most important people in my life, my little fam, who allow me the space and peace to type away furiously on my laptop at any given time. My poor girls put up with my constant slacking on the cooking when I'm in 'the zone' and cater for their self's. True, I normally get billed for the take-out delivery or left with the dishes but hey ho life's all about balance. With teenagers you pick your battles. Food deliveries are not a bone I want to chew on so…

But truly, they are my world. I love they're little inputs on cover ideas or blurbs, And even though they are still not allowed to read them or pass them out to their friends, no matter what books they claim to have read… they're still not getting mine until way, way, way in the future.

You mammas out there get me, I'm sure.

As always, my partner in crime, holding down the fort and giving me invaluable feedback. Listening to me rabble on about plot lines, characters, and assuring me I can in fact do this when I'm slowly losing my mind over margins and formatting that I'm still learning as I go.

Anyway, that's my thanks, I'm sure there is a lot more people you should probably thank but for me these are the people who matter most.

Well, them and all the authors of every book I've got caught up in over the years, The soppy heartfelt ones, The strictly naughty ones, even the reverse harem ones which shook up my little romantic heart. They all have a place in my kindle and my ever-turning little mind.

Printed in Dunstable, United Kingdom